kitty
STEALS THE SHOW
Carrie Vaughn

The right of Carrie Vaughn to be identified as the author of this work
has been asserted by her in accordance with the
Copyright, Designs and Patents Act 1988.

First published in Great Britain in 2012 by
Gollancz
An imprint of the Orion Publishing Group
Orion House, 5 Upper St Martin's Lane, London WC2H 9EA
An Hachette UK Company

1 3 5 7 9 10 8 6 4 2

A CIP catalogue record for this book is available
from the British Library

ISBN 978 0 575 09870 1

Printed in Great Britain by CPI Group (UK) Ltd, Croydon, CR0 4YY

The Orion Publishing Group's policy is to use papers that are natural,
renewable and recyclable products and made from wood grown in
sustainable forests. The logging and manufacturing processes are
expected to conform to the environmental regulations of the
country of origin.

www.carrievaughn.com
www.orionbooks.co.uk

The Playlist

a-Ha, "Take On Me"

Murray Head, "One Night in Bangkok"

Pet Shop Boys, "West End Girls"

Ronn McFarlane, "Greensleeves"

Janis Joplin, "Kozmic Blues"

Dexys Midnight Runners, "Come On Eileen" (BBC in Concert version)

Yoshimoto, "Du What U Du" (Trentemoller Remix)

Gary Numan, "Down in the Park"

Hüsker Dü, "It's Not Funny Anymore"

Fairport Convention, "John the Gun"

Adam and the Ants, "Stand and Deliver"

The Puppini Sisters, "Crazy in Love"

The Kronos Quartet, "Watkins..."

Chapter 1

THE PREY doesn't know it's being hunted. She stays downwind of it and steps slowly, setting each paw quietly on the forest floor, keeping her head low, ears and eyes forward. Out of her sight, more of her wolves are circling, closing in while the buck grazes, ignorant.

They've tracked several young males for an hour. Careless, this one has drifted away from the others. Soon, he'll be cut off, helpless. Its fellows will run, using its misfortune as their chance to escape. They won't even look back.

The moment of attack happens quickly. Her mate leaps from shadows. He is sleek and tawny, full of muscle and life, his gold eyes shining in the light of the fat moon. The prey bolts, spinning on its haunches to escape. But three other wolves are there to block its path. The rest of the deer run, disappearing into the woods. This one is trapped.

It spins again, toward her this time, and she snaps at its snout. Fearful eyes roll back in its head, showing *white, and its nostrils turn red, heaving desperate breaths. The pack closes in, a dozen wolves surrounding the meat. Two of the males, warriors, strike at the deer's haunches and bite, digging in with claws and teeth. Another wolf, jaw open and slavering, aims for the throat. The buck puts down its head and slashes with velvety antlers. Possessing only a couple of prongs, it's inexperienced, but manages to clout his attacker. The wolf yelps and stumbles away.*

She and her mate spring forward to take his place. She grabs hold of the prey's muzzle, closing off its nose, digging with her teeth until blood spills onto her tongue. Her mate bites into its throat and uses his weight to twist its neck and bring the meat down. Neither lets go until the convulsions, the last desperate twitching and the last hope to escape, fall still. Even then, her mate still hangs on, teeth bared, blood flowing around his snout.

The sounds of low growls and ripping flesh rise up. She bounces forward, snarling, landing on the deer's broad flank. The wolves who had been pulling at the meat's hide flee, their ears flattened and tails clamped between their legs, then circle back to linger at the edges of the kill, watching. More wolves emerge from the trees and underbrush, older and weaker pack members who had not taken part in the hunt. They would have their chance; they'd feed, too, in their time. Her pack forms a circle around her, waiting for permission. One of them limps—the one the deer struck—and she flickers her ears at him, smelling. He licks his lips, bows his head. Bruised, he'll heal. She turns her attention to the task at hand.

Her mate is chewing at the deer's underbelly, the softest part of its gut, breaking through to offal and treasure.

They feed. They all feed.

I AWOKE to birdsong.

The sun hadn't yet risen, but the sky was pale, waiting for the first touch of gold. The air smelled fresh, wet, woody. Overhead, the branches of conifers reached. If I lay still I could see the critters flitting among them, cheeping and trilling, full of themselves. Way too manic. I stretched, straightening legs and arms, pulling at too-tight muscles, reminding myself of the shape of my human body after a full-moon night of running as a wolf. My furless skin tingled against the morning air.

The birds weren't the only ones having fun this morning. My movement woke Ben, who stretched beside me and groaned. Then his arms circled me, his skin warm, flush in contrast to the chill. One hand traveled down my hip, the other reached to tangle in my hair, and he pinned me to the ground, pressing against me with his lean body as my arms pulled him closer and I wrapped my legs around his.

Instead of sleeping with the pack, Ben and I had gone off by ourselves, as we did sometimes, to make love, naked in the wild, and keep the world to ourselves for a little while.

Eventually, the cool morning burned away and the air grew warm. Ben lay pillowed on my chest, arms wrapped around me. I'd been tracing his ear and winding my fingers in his hair. Finally, as much as I hated to do it, I patted his shoulder.

"I think it's time to get moving."

"Hmm, do we have to?" His eyes were still closed, his voice muffled.

"Theoretically, no," I said. "But I think I'd like to go home and take a shower."

"Maybe next time we can bring the shower out here," he mumbled.

I furrowed my brow. "Like a camp shower? I think that'd be more trouble than it's worth." When I said shower I meant lots of hot water and a pressure nozzle, not just anything that happened to drip water.

He propped himself upright on one arm, keeping the other on my belly, idly tracing my rib cage, his fingertips leaving a flush behind them. "I'm thinking bigger. We could move out of Denver, get a house out here. Go out on the full moon and end up on our doorstep. I think I'm getting a little tired of that condo."

Stalked by an unbidden memory, I froze. A house in the foothills, where the pack could gather—the idea brought back old, reflexive trauma.

"That's what Carl and Meg did," I said. When I took over the pack I promised I would never be like them.

Ben tilted his head to look at me. "We're not them." He said it with such simple, declarative finality.

If I separated myself from the memories, could I

imagine walking out of my own front porch to a view like this every day? Yeah, maybe. "You sure you want to take the step away from civilization?"

"Ask yourself this: If you weren't a werewolf, what would you want? Where would you want to live?"

I couldn't trust my answer, because Wolf was always on the edges, nudging, pointing to certain preferences over others. I'd never eaten rare steak before becoming a werewolf; now, it was my dinner of choice.

"I used to want a nice house somewhere," I said. "Probably in the suburbs. Big yard. Good shopping. But now? A house out of the city sounds awfully nice."

"Yeah," he said. "I grew up in the middle of nowhere, that's half the reason I moved to Denver in the first place. But I don't think I want to live in the city forever."

"So you can see us living in a house out of town? Even without our wolves talking?"

"Yeah, I can," he said. His smile was thin and wistful. I brushed his hair back from his face, an excuse to touch that expression, that little bit of his soul. He caught my hand and kissed the inside of my wrist.

"Hey, you guys fall into a ditch or something?" Shaun's voice carried from the next cluster of trees.

"If I say yes will he go away?" Ben said.

We could only avoid the inevitable for so long. I held Ben's face and kissed him, lips firmly planted against lips that melted against mine.

"Time to go?" he asked when we finally parted. I nodded.

Hand in hand we made our way to the den where the rest of the pack bedded down. Human shapes stretched in strangely canine manners, backs arched and limbs straight, or scratched heads of tangled hair. Some were far enough along to be pulling on shirts and jeans that had been stashed under trees and shrubs the night before. Already dressed and keeping watch toward the road, where our half dozen cars were parked, Shaun waved at me.

"Tom, you okay?" Ben asked. "You took a pretty good hit there."

Tom was in his early thirties, with dark hair that reached his shoulders and a shadowed expression. He seemed to be moving a little slower than the others, sitting up and catching his breath.

"Yeah, I'll be feeling that for a little while." Wincing, he rolled his shoulder, where a bruise, splotching purple and gray, colored the skin. It was mostly healed. If he'd been a wild wolf, that hit might have killed him, or at least broken bone, which would have been the same thing in the wild.

"That'll teach you to look before leaping," Shaun said, laughing. Some of the others joined in, chuckling and teasing him. Tom blushed and gritted his teeth.

"Hey, it could have happened to anyone," I said, and they quieted. Tom ducked his gaze when I glanced at him.

One big happy wolf family, that was us. And I was Mom. It still weirded me out sometimes.

The sun was up and the spring chill starting to fade

when we divided ourselves among the cars to head back to Denver and its suburbs. A couple members of the pack had to rush home to showers and clean clothes before going to jobs and pretending to be human for another day. I thought again about what Ben had said about a shower, a home base—maybe it would make things easier for everyone.

Shaun called out a question before climbing into his car, "Hey—when are you leaving for London again?"

"Two weeks," I said. "They were kind enough to schedule the conference over the new moon 'to make our lycanthrope guests more comfortable.'"

"Nice of them," he said. "You know what you're going to say in your speech yet?"

I was giving the keynote address for the First International Conference on Paranatural Studies. I figured if I didn't think about it too much I wouldn't get nervous. "That would be no," I said, with more of a wince than a smile. Shaun just laughed.

Ben and I were the last to leave. We made sure everyone else was safe and happy, keeping it together, before we took one last look around our wild refuge, gave each other another kiss, got in the car, and headed out to the rest of our day.

There it was. Full moon over for another month. We traveled back to reality, such as it was.

A FEW days later found me deeply embroiled in the act of making my living.

I was trying to do meaty on the show tonight. Meaty was good. And not just rare steaks or fresh kill for the Wolf. Meat—real topical substance—gave me credibility. Sometimes, it even gave me answers.

"All right, we're back from the break and station ID. This is Kitty Norville and *The Midnight Hour* coming to you from KNOB in Denver, Colorado. Unlike next week when I'll be prerecording a show for you in London, England, where I'll be attending the First International Conference on Paranatural Studies. This will be the first time that scientists, academics, policy makers, and pundits like me from all over the world will gather to discuss the topics that are so near and dear to my heart: vampires, werewolves, magic, what science has to say about it, what's their place in the world. As you know I'm a werewolf and have a vested interest in some of those answers. I'm hoping to line up some really slam-bang interviews, because when else am I going to have this many victims all in one place? In case you haven't figured it out, I'm very excited about the trip.

"Now I want to hear from you—once I get these scientists and diplomats where I want them, what questions should I ask? What would you want to learn at the conference? The lines are open." I checked the monitor and hit a line at random. "Hello, you're on the air."

"I want to know if it's true that vampires are going to lobby for a seat at the United Nations." The caller was male and enthusiastic, a fast talker.

"Where did you hear that?" I asked.

"On the Internet," he said, with a tone of *duh*.

"I'll certainly keep my highly sensitive ears open for rumors on that topic, but I don't think it's a real possibility, because I don't think vampires have any interest in deferring to human authority on anything. They've got their own systems of organization and haven't felt much of a need to take part in ours over the centuries. At least that's my impression. Next call, please. Hello, talk to me."

"Hi, Kitty, thanks for taking my call!" The woman sounded bubbly and nice. Maybe she wouldn't be crazy. "I was wondering, do you think you could give us a sneak preview of your keynote address for the conference?"

Well, no, because I hadn't written it yet, but I wasn't going to admit that. "I'm afraid I'm keeping that firmly under wraps until I actually give the speech. More fun that way, don't you think?"

"Well, I can't wait to hear it!"

Neither could I . . . "Thank you. I'm going to take another call now." I punched another line, glancing at the screener info on the monitor. "Jane from Houston, what's your question?"

"Hi, Kitty, big fan here, thanks for taking my call. I've been listening to you for years and you've been talking around these questions that whole time. For all the so-called scientists you've interviewed and research you've talked about, nobody seems to have any answers. I have to tell you, I'm shocked there's even anything like a conference happening. Does that mean there are finally going to be some answers?

Have scientists finally been able to figure out where vampires and lycanthropes came from? Are they actually going to tell us it's a mutation or a disease?" She sounded genuinely frustrated.

I said, "Science isn't like an Internet search. You don't just stick a question in one end of a machine and have the answer pop out the other side. I don't see the conference as a sign that scientists have finally found answers so much as it's proof that there's now a critical mass of researchers even asking these questions, that they can benefit from this kind of gathering."

"Or maybe the conference is so they can get their stories straight about the cover-up."

"Excuse me?" I said. I heard a new one every show, it seemed like.

"You don't really think anybody actually wants answers, do you?" my caller said brusquely. Here was someone so wrapped up in her conspiracy-laden worldview that the truth was obvious to her. "These 'researchers' are only pretending to be researching anything. They can keep putting out half-baked theories forever. In the meantime, anything they discover they can keep to themselves and use against the rest of us."

"Anything like what?" I said, truly curious.

"The secrets of mind control, of immortality. The rest is a smoke screen. That's what they're looking for, and they're not going to tell the rest of us when they find it. They don't even care about the real questions, like where we came from."

We—she was some brand of lycanthrope, I guessed. Vampires didn't tend to get this intense about anything—they were used to sitting back and watching events take their course. Whatever she was, she was feeling lost and helpless in a world gone out of control. I could understand her position.

"I know some of these scientists personally," I said in what I hoped was a soothing voice. "Most of them are more worried about their funding than about taking part in any kind of cover-up. But I'll tell you what—I'll ask as many people as many questions as I can about the origins of vampires and lycanthropes. I'll bring the answers back to the show. How does that sound?"

"You say that now, but they'll rope you in," she said, as if I'd already personally betrayed her. "They'll get to you, threaten you or bribe you, and then you'll be in on it, too. Just watch."

"So little faith," I said, put out. If she could act like she'd been betrayed, I could act offended. "You said it yourself, I've been doing this for years, and no one's stopped me yet. I don't see this conference changing that, no matter how weird things get. Moving on."

I clicked off Jane's call and punched up the next. The caller didn't waste time with so much as a hello.

"There's no mystery where you all come from," said a flat male voice. "It's not even a question."

"Oh? And where do we come from?"

"The devil! You're all from the devil!"

I fielded one of these calls about every fourth show. The fanatics had learned to say what they needed to say to scam the screening process, and when they finally got on the air they'd give The Speech—the supernatural was the spawn of Satan and the world was racing toward Armageddon on our backs. Blah blah blah. Sometimes, we'd let the calls through on purpose, because the best way to counter these jokers was to let them keep talking.

"You can dress it up in all that science double-talk, but science is the devil's tool! This conference is another sign of the End Times, the new world order. There's a reason it's called the number of the beast. That's the best thing about this, once you're there you'll all be stamped with the number, so the rest of us can see you, and you won't be able to hide anymore."

I leaned into the microphone and used my sultry voice. "I wasn't aware I'd been hiding."

"There's a war coming, a real war! You may sound all nice and sweet, you may have brainwashed thousands of people, but it's a disguise, a deception, and when the trumpet sounds, Lucifer will call his own to him, even you."

"I like to think I'll be judged by my deeds rather than what some crazy person says about me."

"All your good deeds are a trick to hide your true nature. I've listened to you, I know!"

"So what does that make you? A media consumer of the beast?"

The caller hung up before I did, which was a pretty good trick. The game of "who gets the last word" meant that no matter how badly I mocked them, no matter how agitated they got, they kept on the line, thinking I'd somehow, eventually, admit that they were right. They always seemed to think that they were different than the last guy I hung up on. Suckers.

"I've said it before and I'll say it again: if I'm the spawn of Satan someone sure forgot to tell me about it. And I believe we have time for one more call. Hello, you're on."

"Uh, hi, Kitty. Thanks." He was male, laid back. He sounded kind of stoned, actually.

"You have a question or comment?"

"Yeah. So, this thing's in London, right? You're going to London?"

"I think that's what I've said about a dozen times over the last hour in a shameless bid for self-promotion."

"Right." He sniggered, like he was suppressing giggles. "So, that'll make you"—more sniggering—"an American werewolf in—"

I cut him off. "I'm sorry, I seem to have lost that call. And I'd better not hear any Warren Zevon references, either. Sheesh, people. Let's break for station ID."

I had a feeling I was going to be hearing a lot of cracks like that over the next few weeks, I didn't need to start now.

THE BIGGEST issue about me attending the conference wasn't time, expense, or inclination. It certainly wasn't whether or not the conference wanted me there—they'd invited me, after all. The problem was whether or not Ben and I, as werewolves prone to a bit of claustrophobia, could reasonably survive the flight to London, sealed in a metal tube with a few hundred people our lupine selves classified as prey, and no escape route. My longest flight since becoming a werewolf had been to Montana, an hour or so away. Ben hadn't been on an airplane at all since becoming a werewolf.

I called a friend for advice.

The last time I'd talked with Joseph Tyler, formerly of the U.S. Army, he'd become part of the Seattle werewolf pack and was rooming with a couple of the other bachelor werewolves. I liked the idea of him having people to look after him—he suffered from post-traumatic stress related to his service in Afghanistan in addition to being a relatively new werewolf.

So I was a little surprised when a woman answered his phone. "Hello?"

"Um, hi. May I speak to Joseph Tyler?"

"Yeah, just a minute," she said, and a rustling signaled her handing over the phone.

"Yeah?" came Tyler's familiar, curt voice.

"Hey, it's Kitty." His enthusiastic greeting followed. "So who's the girl?" I asked.

I could almost see him blushing over the phone line. "Um, yeah . . . that's Susan. She's . . . I guess she's my girlfriend." He said it wonderingly, like he was amazed by the situation.

"Is she a werewolf?"

"Yeah—I met her just a little while after I moved here. And, well, we hit it off. She . . . she's been really good for me."

I grinned like a mad thing. "That's so cool. I'm really happy for you—and her."

"Thanks."

"Not to distract from the much more interesting topic of your relationship status, but I have a question for you. Really long trans-Atlantic flights—how do you do it without going crazy?"

He chuckled. "I'm about to find out—I'm headed to London for the Paranatural Conference, too. Dr. Shumacher asked me to be there for her presentation on werewolves in the military."

The conference was sounding better and better. "Oh, that's great! But wait a minute, you flew to Afghanistan—"

"On military transports, with no civilians around."

"I don't think I can get a military transport to London," I said, frowning. "I don't suppose it's realistic for us to see about chartering a private jet, just for werewolves?"

"Shumacher's springing for first-class tickets," he said. "That and a sleeping pill to take the edge off should do it."

First-class tickets—what an elegant solution. More space and free cocktails. I wondered who I could convince to spring for first-class tickets of my very own. "You're sure it'll work? It'd suck getting a couple of hours into the flight and finding out the sleeping pills don't work."

"I don't expect them to work—it takes a lot of drugs to knock one of us out. But it should help. It's like you're always saying—you just work on keeping it together. I really want to go to London. This'll work."

If Tyler could do it, we had to try. I thanked him for the advice and congratulated him again on Susan. I wanted pictures. I wanted to fawn over them. It was adorable.

Then I called my producer, Ozzie, to ask how we could foot the bill for a first-class upgrade.

Chapter 2

I DIDN'T KNOW that some organizations offered grants for people like me to travel to scientific conferences. On the other hand, Ozzie did, and as a result we—Ben, Cormac, and I were all going—got first-class tickets to London. Ozzie sold me as "a socially conscious journalist breaking new ground in the emergent arena of paranatural research." He made me sound *good*. I told him this, and he grumbled, "That's my job. *Somebody* has to do it."

We had a week of hectic preparation getting ready for the trip—checking passports, reassuring Shaun and the pack, squaring away Ben's law practice, packing, and wrapping up my own work. I still hadn't written my keynote speech for the conference. I could get a start on it on the flight. Maybe it would distract me. Ben kept having to reassure me, tell me that everything would be fine, that we weren't going to have any trouble. Cormac looked at us like we were crazy.

Then I had to deal with my mother. My endearing,

chatty, cancer survivor mother was incredibly hard to say no to. She was just so darned enthusiastic. She called me every day of the week leading up to the trip. She usually only called on Sunday.

"Take lots of pictures. You got that link I sent you about the walking tours, right? They're supposed to be really good—"

"Mom, I'm just not sure how much time I'm going to have for sightseeing."

"I looked at the map and you'll practically be right in the middle of London, surely you could pop out and see *something*."

"I'll try. You've done all this planning on my behalf—when are you and Dad going to London?"

"Oh, we're talking about it . . . You'll have such an amazing time, Kitty. And *be careful*."

Yeah, that was Mom.

FINALLY, THE day of the trip arrived.

We solved part of the problem of the long flight by stopping for a night-long layover in Washington, D.C. I wanted to visit with Alette, the vampire Mistress of the city.

The living room—parlor, rather—in her Georgetown town house was filled with Victorian elegance. Lush carpets, perfectly kept antique furniture, curio cabinets, shelves full of books, polished silver tea service on display on the mantel. Heavy velvet drapes were drawn over the windows overlooking the street.

Alette herself waited in a wingback chair by the

fireplace. She wore a tailored suit jacket with a calf-length skirt, a cream-colored blouse, and ankle boots, an outfit that recalled a bygone style without seeming old fashioned. An ebony clasp held back her chestnut hair, and a single pearl on a chain around her neck was her only decoration.

When we arrived, she rose and reached for my hand, clasping it. Her skin was cool. She spoke in a crisp British accent. "Kitty, it's very good to see you."

"How are you, Alette?"

"Enduring," she said with more than a little pride. I wondered if that was a vampire inside joke. Her apparent age was around thirty—no longer girlish, her beauty came from her dignity, her haughtiness. She stood with her chin up, gazing at us appraisingly.

"I know you met them briefly before. But, well—this is my husband, Ben O'Farrell, and our friend Cormac Bennett." Ben came forward to shake her offered hand; Cormac did not, moving instead to the back of the room, away from us. In fact, he was wearing his sunglasses, at night and indoors. Not like that was real obvious. But Cormac was Cormac. Alette only glanced at him, her smile wry.

She had tea brought for us, and gestured for us to sit on the sofa across from her. Tom, who'd driven us from the airport, stood at attention at the doorway. Smartly turned out in a tailored suit and tie, he might have served the role of butler, waiting for a command from Alette. But he was more than that—he kept most of his attention turned toward Cormac rather than Alette. Tom was as much bodyguard as butler.

Alette kept above it all and said conversationally, "You weren't a lycanthrope the last time you visited my city, Mr. O'Farrell. I don't suppose you had anything to do with that, Kitty—"

"God, no!" I said.

"It was an attack," Ben added, more sedately. "By someone else."

"Ah, I see. So much for my romantic notions, then. If you don't mind my asking, how are you managing?"

"I have a lot of help," he said.

"I have no doubt on that score," she said, giving us both a sly, knowing look. She glanced to the back of the room. "Mr. Bennett, are you all right?"

Cormac was pacing along the front of the room, like a wolf looking for an exit from a cage. On each pass, he twitched the curtains back an inch and peered out.

He paused. "Fine," he said flatly. He eyed Tom, whose gaze remained blank, disinterested.

"I remember you're not particularly comfortable around vampires," she said.

"It's fine," he muttered again. Cormac was a bounty hunter specializing in supernatural targets—including vampires. At least he had been before serving a prison sentence for manslaughter. He was still adjusting to his changed circumstances—but vampires would always make him nervous.

I wondered what Tom would do if Cormac drew one of the stakes he no doubt had stashed in a jacket pocket.

"He's quite the friend, to follow you into this," Alette said.

"Yes, he is."

"Now, what did you want to discuss?"

"I'm hoping for your opinion. How much do you know about Dux Bellorum? Roman?"

Her gaze narrowed. "You've been turning over all kinds of stones, haven't you? I can't say I know very much at all. He's a vampire, quite old by most accounts. He's also a shadow. A myth, even. The Master of masters, all knowing, all seeing, all powerful. I've heard enough about him to believe that he's real. He's manipulative, driven, obsessed with some arcane plan of his own. But I know little else. I've never met him myself. Tell me, Kitty—what do you know of Dux Bellorum?"

"He's the chief player in the Long Game," I said, as if I knew what I was talking about, as if the very concept didn't terrify me. "He's collecting allies, and I—I have a grudge against him." From my pocket I drew a pendant on a leather cord. It had once been a bronze Roman coin, but the image on it had been smashed, so that the blackened layer of verdigris was flattened and mangled beyond definition. "Have you ever seen one of these?"

I lay the coin across her hand and she studied it, rubbing a thumb across it. "I haven't. What is it?"

"Roman gives these to his followers," I said. "Maybe you haven't met him, but I'm betting you know a few vampires who have one of these."

"They have some kind of magic attached to them," Cormac said from his place by the window. "Binding, identification."

She frowned at the coin before giving it back to me. "Extraordinary. I had no idea. Roman—Dux Bellorum—has always kept his cards so close, revealing so little. But now he's letting spells get away from him."

"He's showing his hand," I said. "I think he's getting ready to make a move."

She leaned back against the chair, her gaze pursed, studious. "And the world gathers in London. The vampires are gathering in London as well, you know. This conference of yours will be a tempting target for him."

"I'm afraid so," I said. "I can't say I'm looking forward to it."

"Then it's good you're staying with Ned. He'll do well by you. You can depend upon him and Emma to protect you."

Ned was the Master vampire of London and an old friend of Alette's. Very old, I imagined, though she wouldn't give me details. Emma was her own protégé, a young vampire as well as a biological great—lots of greats—granddaughter. They'd offered me and mine a place to stay in London. It was Emma who convinced me to accept that offer.

"We don't need that kind of protection," Cormac said curtly. Tom actually took a step forward at that, and he and Cormac finally met gazes. Tom stepped back and stood at ease quickly enough that I wondered if he'd even moved. They both had too much self-control to want to be the one to start something. Alette's lips pressed together, as if she was hiding a smile, amused at their behavior.

"Can we trust them? Really?" Ben said. He'd gone tense, and I rested a calming hand on his knee.

"You're right not to trust vampires," Alette said, not appearing the least bit offended. "Especially in the Old World. I had many reasons for leaving Europe—the Masters there are a big one. I find them . . . frustrating."

"But Ned's not like that?" I asked.

"Ned is, as you like to say, one of the good guys. But he's a character—don't let him charm you."

Ben's expression had turned sour—he generally had the same attitude about vampires that Cormac did. And yet, they kept listening to me when I insisted on calling them my friends.

"We'll be careful," I said. I always said that, and yet, I could only keep an eye out for the dangers I knew about. What would the conference throw at me that I couldn't possibly expect?

Alette asked, "Do you know, will Dr. Flemming be at the conference? This seems exactly his milieu."

"He wouldn't dare show his face," I said. "He's notorious." Dr. Paul Flemming had once headed up the Center for the Study of Paranatural Biology. If this conference had happened a few years ago, he would have been one of the people running it. Then his predilection for experimenting on unwilling human subjects came to light. The last time I saw him was the night he locked me in a cell during the full moon and trained a camera on me to broadcast my transformation live to the world. The video had five million views on YouTube, baby. He'd skipped town rather than face kidnapping charges. If the two of us ever ended up in a room together, I might get violent.

She said, "But it wouldn't surprise you if he did make an appearance, would it?"

"No. I'm afraid not."

The night and conversation wore on after midnight, until Alette agreed that we ought to sleep, in preparation for the flight tomorrow. I took her up on her offer of guest rooms, and a ride to the airport bright and early.

Before we went upstairs, she took hold of both my hands and beamed. "Kitty, you've come so far since I first met you. I thought then that you might do well, but you have exceeded my expectations."

"Thanks, I think. I just hope . . ." I thought a moment, then shook my head. "I just hope it all works out."

"Oh, my dear, you live as long as I have you realize it never *all* works out. You're giving the keynote address at the conference, aren't you? Do you know what you'll be speaking about?"

I wasn't able to suppress a groan. "I wish people would stop asking me that. I'm going to work on it on the flight over." I had to change the subject before she offered me suggestions. "How is Emma?"

"You'll hardly recognize her. Give her a kiss for me, won't you?"

"I will. Thanks, for everything."

Chapter 3

IN THE end, the trans-Atlantic flight wasn't nearly as bad as I was expecting. We just had to grit our teeth and settle in for a few hours. Like Tyler said, you had to not concentrate on being locked in a metal tube flying at an insane height and speed—you focused on going to London. I ate, slept, watched movies, slept some more.

Then night fell, and I was in London. We gathered our things and stumbled off the plane.

I hardly knew what to think. I was euphoric, exhausted, glassy-eyed all at the same time. I'd never been out of the U.S. before. I'd just flown across the Atlantic. I was in *England*. I'd just spent eight hours surrounded by people in a little metal box and wanted to run as far and fast as I could. I wanted to see a castle. I wanted to sleep.

Once off the plane, a wide corridor filtered us toward immigration. The crowd filed along like cows being herded to the slaughterhouse, making me twitch. Heathrow's international terminal, a modernist structure of glass and girders, gave a deceptive impression of space, light, and freedom, until we reached the side room with a maze of barriers separating the lines of people into different areas, signage directing the lines, and a general air of resignation. The place smelled antiseptic and tired, wholly unnatural. Wolf tensed.

My new goal in life was to become wealthy enough to own a private jet and never have to travel like this again. What were the odds? Just another hour and maybe I could have a nice soft bed. A hot meal and a bed. A hot meal, shower, and bed. No, a drive around Trafalgar Square first, then a hot meal, shower, a cuddle with Ben—I'd never had sex in a foreign country before—and bed . . .

Ben was actually paying attention and directed us to the sign labeled NON EU COUNTRIES, but before we could join the line, a uniformed official, a stout man in his late thirties, round face and serious expression, approached. Shaking myself awake, I tried to seem calm and collected rather than defensive.

He glanced at a sheet of paper before addressing me. "Are you Katherine Norville?"

But we hadn't done anything wrong, we had all our ducks in a row, we'd worked so hard making sure we had the paperwork, that Cormac wouldn't be held at the border for his felony conviction—and how did they know, we hadn't even had our passports checked yet.

I wet my mouth and tried to think through the fog

of jet lag that said it was seven in the morning rather than seven in the evening. "Yes. Is there a problem?"

"And Benjamin O'Farrell? Cormac Bennett?" He looked at each of us.

He could see we were, he had our pictures on the page in front of him. I caught Ben's gaze, trying to ask him what this was about. *Hold on, wait and see,* he seemed to reassure me.

The official gestured toward a closed door labeled RESTRICTED at the back of the room. "If you'd come with me, please? Right this way."

He was so agonizingly polite, and yet his manner invited no argument. My stomach flipped; I didn't want to have to deal with this, not now.

"I'm sorry, but what's this about? Is something wrong?"

"Just step along, please. It will only take a moment." His expression hardly changed—just a guy doing his job.

"Ben—" I murmured.

"Wait," he said. "If we were in trouble there'd be more than one of them."

Him and his logic. Sullen, I followed the immigration officer. Rumpled and glassy-eyed people in line stared after us, radiating curiosity and schadenfreude. This trip couldn't have gone completely smoothly, could it? But for heaven's sake I'd hoped to at least get out of the airport without any trouble.

The officer held the door open for us and we filed inside. The tile-floored room held a table and chairs, for interviews. None of us sat. I turned on the officer, questions ready to burst, when the door on the opposite side of the room opened and Emma stepped in.

We'd taken a flight that arrived after dark; of course she'd come to the airport to meet us.

The last time I'd seen Emma she'd been cute—a ponytailed college student in jeans and a sweatshirt, her whole life ahead of her. She'd worked as a part-time housekeeper for Alette to pay tuition. Then Emma had been turned, and it had been the end of that world. She hadn't wanted it, had even considered opening the curtains at dawn on herself. But that would have been an even bigger tragedy. Instead, she learned how to be a vampire, and she seemed to have developed a talent for it. She wore a flowing skirt in a trendy print, a gray shirt, purple high-heeled shoes, and a black silk wrap draped around her shoulders, too fine to be anything but decorative. She didn't need shielding from the cold. Her brown hair was swept back and held by a sparkling clip. Her makeup was subtle and perfect. She was gorgeous.

She saw me and grinned. "Kitty!"

I grinned back, and we came together in a girly hug. "You look amazing," I said.

Pulling apart, we regarded each other. "I'm so glad you're here, I've been looking forward to this for weeks," she said.

"Yeah, me, too. What's with this?" I tipped my head to the immigration officer, standing politely out of the way.

"Ned has connections," she said. "He thought you'd appreciate not having to stand with the crowds. So—shortcut."

"This is the power that comes with being Master of London?" I said.

Her eyes—her whole face, really—sparkled with glee. "Neat, huh? He can't wait to meet you."

Yeah, I could just bet. What kind of vampire was he, then? Haughty and arrogant? Permanently amused and detached? Something else entirely? At least Emma seemed happy here, which was a point in his favor. He couldn't be all bad if she liked him.

I pulled Ben and Cormac into our circle and introduced them. They'd actually seen her before, in Washington, D.C. She'd been technically dead at the time, though, attacked by Alette's traitorous lieutenant and still three days from rising again.

Ben smiled and shook her hand, and Cormac did likewise, grudgingly.

"Welcome to London. You ready to see the sights?"

My energy roared back, the travel fog slipping away. I could have bounded.

The officer stepped forward. "If I could just check your passports, then?"

We weren't completely getting out of procedure—it was, as Emma had said, a shortcut. He looked at our passports, glanced at our immigration forms, and produced a visa stamp, which he punched into our passports.

My passport was no longer virginal.

"Welcome to Britain," he said when he'd finished.
Indeed.

EMMA LED us through another restricted door to
an exit, which opened to a curb outside the airport,
where a black cab was waiting for us. A real honest-
to-God London black cab. Mom would want me to
take a picture, so I pulled out my camera and did. Ben
looked at me. "Really?" I just grinned.

Our luggage had been fetched for us. The driver was
loading it into the trunk. Boot, rather. I'd been studying. He wore a smart black suit with a conservative
striped tie. Young, dark-haired, and clean-shaven, he
stood at attention and nodded smartly to Emma. He
was human—one of the Master's human servants. Not
a cab driver, of course, and the car wasn't marked TAXI.
We were getting chauffeured.

When he'd finished with the luggage, he opened
the back door for us.

"Thanks, Andy," Emma said, smiling, and he tipped
his head.

Emma sat in front with Andy, and we climbed into
the spacious back of the car, which had wide seats
and lots of legroom. Our wolves would have been
happy in here, even. Ben and Cormac put me between them—I'd meant to get a window seat. I gave
up arguing about it.

"You really do look great," I said to Emma.

Leaning on the back of the seat to talk to us, she
bit her lip and ducked her gaze. "Thanks. It's been a
pretty wild ride these last few years."

No doubt. I thought back to my own first couple of years as a werewolf and the way the world turned upside down. I couldn't imagine what becoming a vampire would be like.

"And now you're in London living the high life," I said.

"I'm thinking of it as grad school," she said. "Alette wanted me to get out and see the world, or at least see how a different Family works, and Ned was happy to take me in."

"What's Ned like?" Ben asked.

Emma's expression melted and turned downright dreamy, her eyes going wide and her smile going soft. "He's amazing. You'll just have to meet him—I don't want to give anything away."

"Hmm, just like a vampire to keep secrets," I said, then wished I hadn't because her smile fell. I'd meant it as a joke, but I could have kicked myself. Emma hadn't asked for this; she was making the best of a bad situation—the only thing she could do.

"Good God," Cormac murmured, leaning forward to press himself to the window. "This is London?"

"We're in the suburbs," Emma said. "It's still about fifteen miles or so to the city center."

"But it's *all* city," he said.

That wasn't Cormac speaking, I realized. During his time in prison, he'd acquired a ghost: Amelia, the Victorian wizard woman living in his head. He insisted it was a partnership, not a possession. Sometimes, though, she was in control. It was weird, hearing another person's words spoken in Cormac's voice.

A big reason he'd wanted to come along was so Amelia could see home again, after more than a hundred years as a ghost trapped in a prison's stone walls. She'd probably been at the front, the driver's seat so to speak, since we landed, ready for a glimpse.

Emma looked to me for a cue, and I didn't know how to explain.

To Cormac/Amelia I said, "It's changed a lot, I imagine."

He/she glanced at me, lips pursed. "It's just a bit of a shock to see it for myself."

He sat back and stayed quiet the rest of the trip, watching out the window. I put my hand on Ben's knee, and he squeezed it.

"You guys must be wiped out," Emma said, regaining her previous cheerfulness. "Maybe we should go straight home and save the sightseeing for later? Ned's main house is in Dulwich, south of London. We'll be in Mayfair for the conference but I really want to show you the Dulwich house, if that's all right."

The car turned south before heading into London proper. We passed over a bridge, and Emma confirmed that the river below us was the Thames. Orange lights flickered on the surface of rippling black water, and the shores were an almost solid wall of buildings. We never did encounter anything like the rolling green hills and meadows of a stereotypical English countryside, not that we could see any of it at night. I wondered if that was what Amelia was looking for.

Eventually, we passed a sweeping, well-groomed park bounded by reaching, gnarled trees, then approached a brick wall supporting a tall iron gate. Beyond that lay a magnificent manor house—colossal, redbrick, with filigree accents carved in white granite, neo-Gothic towers and cupolas, and ornate windows opening into what seemed to be a vast main hall. How could I expect anything else from the Master of London?

"Pretty swanky," I said.

"This isn't Ned's house," Emma said. "Not directly, anyway. This is actually a boys' school, Dulwich College. We'll end up a little farther on."

The cab passed the impressive school and a minute later turned up the drive of a much more modest, but even more venerable and beautiful house, with a brick façade, painted accents, and warm light showing through the mullioned windows.

"Here we are," she said. "Fortune House."

The car pulled into a gated yard, letting us out before continuing on to a building that might have been a small stable in another age. Now it was the garage—same purpose, different context. Emma took us through a mudroom that was nicer than Ben's and my whole condo, with slate tile on the floor in a checkered pattern, shelves made of some expensive polished wood, and brass fixtures. This opened into a hardwood foyer. A kitchen lay through a doorway, and a maid came toward us—an honest-to-goodness maid in a black uniform dress and apron.

"He's in the library waiting for you, miss," the young woman said to Emma.

The house must have been bigger on the inside than it looked on the outside. We went from the foyer through a long hallway with a fancy carpet runner, antique sideboards and accent tables that held stunning porcelain vases, a row of paintings on the wall showing everything from hunting dogs to light-suffused cityscapes. The hallway let out into a parlor with a big fireplace, marble mantelpiece above it, more antique furniture, more paintings. Tall windows had heavy drapes drawn over them. Over the fireplace was what seemed to be a life-sized portrait of a man in late-Renaissance attire: a starched white ruff, long black coat lined with fur, a glimpse of doublet and knee-length trousers, shoes with buckles. He was tall and stately, brown hair going to gray, a full beard hiding his expression, and he looked down on us with some amount of pride. The Master, maybe? Next, Emma opened a set of heavy double doors, polished wood, simply carved, and ushered us into the library.

I could have sat on the lush antique Persian rug and stared at the room for hours. Floor-to-ceiling shelves occupied all four walls, with scant allowance made for the door and a set of tall windows opposite. Some of the shelves appeared to slide back to reveal even more shelves. And they were all filled with books. All of them. A myriad of comfy chairs and sofas—the arms scuffed, the seats lumpy and soft—

had been well used by people lounging in them, reading all those books.

In addition, the room held display cases and curio cabinets—and yes, they contained even more books. Special books, no doubt, hermetically sealed and brought out for holidays. Many of them lay open on stands for admiring. The cases did hold a few other items—ornate daggers, a thin sword, jewelry, pocket watches, miniature portraits. That was just what I could see from the doorway. I might have squeaked in awe.

"You seem impressed," the man standing by the curtained window said in a rich voice, an orator's voice.

He wasn't young like most vampires I'd met. His brown hair, tied back in a shoulder-length ponytail, was streaked with gray, and his beard was salt and pepper. He might have been in his sixties—he'd lived a whole life already before he'd been turned. He wore a long smoking jacket, pushed back. His cream-colored shirt was open rakishly at the throat, his dark trousers were plain, and he went stocking-footed. The ensemble managed to give off an air of casual elegance. All this wealth and centuries' worth of collected riches were his and he was quite comfortable with it. He stood hand on hip, shoulders back, posing like the man in the portrait over the fireplace—maybe because he was the man in the portrait.

"This is Ned," Emma said proudly. "Ned, may I present Kitty Norville, Ben O'Farrell, and Cormac Bennett."

"Excellent work, Emma," he said. "Any trouble at Heathrow?"

"None at all," she answered.

"Hi," I said, waving, feeling a bit inadequate for the surroundings. "It's quite a place you have here."

He smiled broadly at us, like we were new acquisitions for his collection. "I bet you say that to everyone."

"Oh no," I said, shaking my head quickly. "Not everyone."

"Please, look around if you like. Ask questions. I rarely have a chance to show off for visitors."

"Questions, huh? Anything?" I said.

"Here it comes . . ." Ben murmured.

"How old are you?" I asked.

His gaze went soft, as if he was doing math in his head. "Four hundred forty-three years old."

Ben laughed. "Wow, he actually answered!"

I gaped. "I have never, ever, *ever* gotten that specific an answer from any vampire *ever*," I said. I might have fallen in love with the man in that instant. I did a bit of my own math—it took a couple of tries. "Fifteen sixty—"

"Fifteen sixty-six," Cormac said, and Ned nodded.

"And you were born in London," I said.

"Born, bred, proud to be so."

"Wow," I said. "We have to talk, you have to tell me everything, what was it like, what did you do, who did you know—Queen Elizabeth, did you ever see her? Meet her?"

"You were right," Ned said to Emma. "She doesn't stop, does she?"

"Most vampires are so secretive, they won't say anything about how old they are, where they came from. Like that life is dead to them and they'll be damned if they talk about it. Why aren't you like that? Why just let it all out there?"

"Of all the secrets I could keep, the ones about myself are the least useful."

A vampire not interested in keeping secrets. Oh, the things I could ask . . . "Next question. Why Ned? Most vampires I've met are a little more fancy-pants with their names. Not Rick, it's Ricardo, that sort of thing. But it's Ned, not Edward?"

"My friends call me Ned. I've been known by both names all my life. Why do you prefer Kitty instead of Katherine?"

"Fair enough." I looked around, taking in the thousands of rich leather spines, smelling the vast collection of paper, parchment, and ink, and guessing that every item was here because Ned wanted it to be. This wasn't a museum, these were his *things*. "You've been building your library for over four hundred years, then. You want to point out the highlights?"

"Look around and tell me what catches your eye."

I did, my gaze skimming over shelves and glass cases, having trouble stopping on any one thing because there was too much to focus on. Start with the books or the artifacts? Try to read one of the rare editions? But which one?

One of the cases held sheets of papers, letters maybe, some drawings, individual pages with short pieces of writing. The old-fashioned handwriting was hard to make out, but I spotted a phrase that repeated: Edward Alleyn. Or Alleyne, or Allan, and a few other variations of spellings. At the tops of letters, on lists of names, and in the title of what seemed to be an admiring poem.

"Edward Alleyn, that's you, yes?" I said to him.

"It is."

I continued to the next case, which held only one large book, as big as an old picture atlas, open on its stand. The object had been well cared for; its pages were only just aging to yellow. The text was typeset rather than written, but it was still antique, hard to read. Even so, I only needed a few lines to understand what it was—one of Hamlet's soliloquies.

"This is a First Folio," I said to Ned.

"Are you a scholar of the Bard, then?" he asked.

"More like a fan. I majored in English lit, if that means anything. It looks like it's in really good condition."

"Hot off the presses you might say," he said. "It isn't even listed in the official census of how many First Folios still exist."

"That's so cool! You must have seen the plays when they were first being performed—oh my God, I can't even imagine."

"I saw most of them, I think. You might say the theater was my life, back then."

At that, a synapse in my brain clicked into place—the English major coming back online and earning its keep. "Edward Alleyn," I murmured. "I've heard that name before."

Ned quoted: " 'Stand still, you ever-moving spheres of heaven, that time may cease, and midnight never come.' "

It was obviously supposed to mean something. I stared, blank.

He tried again: " 'What are kings, when regiment is gone, but perfect shadows in a sunshine day?' "

Still nothing. "Is it Shakespeare?" I ventured.

He rolled his eyes. One more time . . . " 'Was this the face that launched a thousand ships?' "

"Oh, that's Marlowe," I said. "Wait a minute. Edward Alleyn—the actor?"

"I told you she'd get it," he said to a beaming Emma.

"You knew Christopher Marlowe. And Shakespeare, you knew Shakespeare—" I put my hand on my mouth. I was now two degrees of separation from William Shakespeare. Back home, Rick gave me such a hard time because I was always bugging him for stories about the famous people he'd met in his over five hundred years of life, how I constantly assumed that vampires must have some kind of insider information, when really, why would they be any more likely to know famous people than the rest of us? But here it was, the reason I asked all these questions in the first place, because sometimes, *sometimes,* I got the answers I was looking for. What secret corners of history could vampires illuminate, if I could figure out what to ask?

At this point, though, all the questions seemed moot. This man had known Shakespeare. He was a window into an amazing time and place—and I didn't know where to start. So I teared up and tried to wave away the burst of emotion. Everyone was staring at me and all I really wanted to do was cry from the wonder of it all.

"Is she okay?" Emma asked Ben.

"I don't know," he said. "I've never seen her like this."

"I get this reaction quite a lot," Ned said cheerfully. I imagined it was one of the reasons he didn't bother keeping his identity secret—he'd been a celebrity his whole life, why stop just because he'd become a vampire?

"How?" I managed to stammer. "How did you go from . . . from there to *this*? What happened?"

"That's a much longer story, Ms. Norville. May I get you a drink?" Ned asked.

"I would very much like a drink, yes."

Ned rang and an attendant—the young woman who'd greeted us when we arrived—brought in a tray with a couple of decanters and several glasses, and we gathered on the chairs and sofas around one of the small tables in the library. Emma poured scotch for Ben, Cormac, and I, and she and Ned sat back to watch us sip. It was probably excessively expensive and luxurious, but all I tasted was the burn. I was still staring at Ned in bewilderment, imagining some scene in an Elizabethan tavern, the actors and playwrights of the day, Shakespeare and Marlowe and so on, gathered around, laughing and drinking, the music of lutes and pipes in the background . . .

Ben grinned at me. "Hey Kitty, now you're supposed to ask if Shakespeare really wrote Shakespeare's plays."

That broke the spell. "Oh, don't even start with that. It's not even up for debate." But I looked at Ned sidelong. "Is it?"

"No," he said, shaking his head.

"Good. You know, you could end a lot of epic academic debates if you'd just come out and say that."

"And ruin all the fun? Not me."

I sighed. "What was it like? All of it—I mean, did he have any idea? Did Shakespeare have a clue that people would be performing his plays four hundred years later, that they'd be held up as the pinnacle not just of theater but of *literature*?"

Ned shook his head. "You must understand, we weren't trying to create fine art. We were trying to tell stories. All of us, we loved to tell stories. Well, and we loved the attention. For those who were successful at it, the theater was a very good way to make money. Several of us, including Will, made our fortunes at it, but not from writing or acting—it was from investing in the theaters themselves. We worked for shares and retired when we had enough cash to do so. Of course, most of us didn't mind a little fame in the meantime. I admit, it's been an odd experience watching what's happened to Will's work over the years."

"Oh my God. You're on a first-name basis with William Shakespeare." My vision went a bit hazy.

"Perhaps a little more scotch, there," he said, and poured another finger into my tumbler.

My companions hadn't taken more than the tiniest sips of their own drinks. Ben sat next to me on a sofa, but Cormac had taken a seat apart, in his own chair, and had been studying the room around us, maintaining a bodyguard's stance.

Now, he leaned forward, setting his glass back on the tray. "I imagine a lot of folks are coming in from out of town for this conference. You probably know just about all of them."

"You want to know if there's anyone you need to worry about? Anyone with designs on our Kitty?" Ned said, and Cormac gave an offhand shrug in agreement. "I imagine there are. Many of the Master vampires of Europe or their representatives are here, as well as some from farther afield, along with their entourages. Lycanthropes are attending the conference in some official human capacity or another. Others are here simply because they're curious. Many vampires and lycanthropes are unhappy with the light that Kitty and others have been shining on our activities, and are here to add their opinions to the conversation. Those are just the ones I know about—there are shadow realms that I know little about and have no control over that surely have a presence here. It's as if everyone wants to see what's going to happen next. In the meantime, I've declared London neutral territory for the duration of the conference. No battles, figurative or literal, will be fought here. No one will act against you, or they'll face me. I so will it."

Cormac turned away to hide a wry grin, which gave us all an idea of what he thought of Ned's will. "You aren't worried? All those rivals, right in your backyard."

"No," Ned said evenly, a smile curling. "I'm not. If they make a move against me or mine, they lose any protection they had here and their existences are forfeit."

"We'll be fine," I said to Cormac, more for something to say than trying to be reassuring. I wasn't sure I could be reassuring—the assembled vampire aristocracy of Europe? Not at all intimidating . . . I asked Ned, "You'll be there, right? At the conference. There's a whole track on vampirism."

"We'll be keeping an eye on things from a distance," Ned said.

"If that many vampire Masters are going to be there, don't you think you'd better be there, too?"

"You're assuming they're going to be at the hotel with all the hoi polloi. May I make a suggestion?" Ned asked.

"Sure."

"A convocation assembles Monday night. Come and meet them."

"Convocation?"

"A gathering of the vampires who've come to London. A little conference of our own," he said. "You'll get a good look at them all, they'll get a look at you. No surprises on either side. What do you think?"

I looked at Ben for his opinion.

"Walking into a room full of Master vampires?" he said with a huff. "You'd either be a rock star or completely screwed."

"You'd have my protection," Ned said.

"Until you leave the room," Cormac added.

The vampire turned to me, chuckling. "You have staunch defenders."

"Yeah, I do," I said. "I think I'd rather face them all at once. Get a good look at them. Besides, it'll be interesting."

"You always say that just before we get into the weirdest shit," Ben said.

No doubt. One of these days I'd have to go for uninteresting. Spend the weekend in front of the TV eating popcorn. What were the odds?

Chapter 4

WE SPENT the night at Fortune House, in rooms that would have outdone the most spectacular five-star hotel: antique furniture, silk sheets, attentive room service bringing eggs and toast and fresh-squeezed juice for breakfast, and views of a quiet suburb out the window. In the morning, a horde of teenage boys decked in blue jerseys flooded one of the pristine grassy lawns outside the school to play soccer. Football, rather. It was a scene from a movie.

We got more of Ned's story. He'd founded Dulwich College, at least its earliest incarnation as a charity hospital, back in his previous life, at the start of the seventeenth century. He'd had no children of his own so he funneled his fortune into various charities. He'd been watching over them ever since. I still didn't know how a man who'd lived a full life, been famous and successful, became a vampire at the age of sixty. I'd looked up the official date of his death. There was some debate about the exact day—with a three day difference, which suddenly made sense, if you knew about the vampirism. An infected person lay effectively dead for three days before rising again. I wondered if Ned had been attacked and turned against his will, and I wondered if he'd ever tell me how it had happened.

Emma and Ned had made plans to send us on ahead to Ned's Mayfair town house, where he stayed when he wanted to be in London proper. It was near the conference, and we'd have a day to get settled, sleep off more of the jet lag, and take a look around before the conference started. Andy the driver took us north in the sleek black cab, and I got my first look of Britain in daylight.

The city was a mix of ancient, modern, and everything in between. Nineteenth-century brick row houses mingled with 1960's concrete office blocks, then suddenly the gray stone spire of an old church would rise in the distance, past supermarkets and sub-divisions. Springtime made everything green—green lawns in parks, a bright green fuzz on trees, carpets of daffodils blooming on roundabouts. I had to quell an instinctive panic from being on the wrong side of the road.

London proper was a big city, with countless traffic-filled streets, tall buildings occupying entire blocks, and the sense that I had seen all this before in a movie. I imagined people felt the same thing when they visited New York City or Los Angeles.

Ben nudged me. "Kitty, look." He pointed out the window to an iconic red double-decker bus. I started to "ooh" in admiration, when I realized he was actually pointing to the ad on the side of the bus: MERCEDES COOK IN CONCERT, THIS WEEK ONLY! The vampire's gorgeous, smiling picture showed her in a spectacular black sequined gown, arms flung out to take in the audience she was singing to.

Oh, just great. Just *horrible*.

If I was the world's first celebrity werewolf, Mercedes Cook was its first celebrity vampire. She'd been a star on Broadway since the sixties, and people had started to notice that she was looking remarkably well-preserved for her age. She hadn't graduated to crazy mother and grandmother roles like most of the actresses of her generation. Turned out she was well preserved because she was undead. A vampire. She broke the story on *The Midnight Hour,* and I'd thought we were friends. Right up until she plotted to get my friend Rick killed, to prevent him from taking over as Master of Denver. She failed, he took over, and sent Mercedes packing.

So, at some point this week I was probably going to have to face the vampire who tried to take over Denver, probably on behalf of my archnemesis.

"That's so not cool," I stated.

"Ned called a truce, right?" Ben said. "What can she do?"

"I hesitate to even imagine," I said.

"What you're saying is I ought to keep a couple of stakes handy," Cormac said.

"You mean you don't anyway?" I said.

He shrugged. "There's handy, then there's handy."

We rounded a corner and passed a stretch of sloping lawn lined with trees that were brilliant with new
foliage. Andy identified it as Hyde Park. Wolf perked
up her ears at the wide open space in the middle of the
city—would it be useful in a pinch? I didn't particularly want to find out. But as urban pastoral spaces
went, the place was gorgeous.

I'd asked Ned and Emma about the local werewolves, and he'd said he'd be sure to introduce me
to the alpha at the earliest opportunity. *When,* I'd
whined, and he'd promised it'd be soon. Would the
alpha be at the conference? At the vampire convocation? If I'd had the time, I'd have gone looking for
werewolves myself. I'd heard that London was a good
city for lycanthropes: tolerant, serving as it had as a
crossroads for the world since the days of the British
Empire, Indian were-tigers rubbing elbows with
were-lions from Africa, and so on. I wanted to see it
for myself.

There'd be time.

The neighborhood where Ned's place was located
looked like it had traveled through time: blocks full
of stately façades, rows of windows, decorated molding, wrought-iron accents, elegant in the midday light.
I flashed on any number of Jane Austen films or Sher-
lock Holmes reruns on PBS. There should have been
fancy horse-drawn carriages clopping past.

The car turned onto an impossibly narrow lane
packed with town houses, and through a gateway into

a small, cobbled yard with a lovely, reaching tree in the corner. The building overlooking the yard was four stories of pale brick. The windows had white frames and stone balconies to lean on, and the roof was made of sloped gray slate.

Andy let us in through the front door. The interior was as much a time capsule as the neighborhood. A vestibule let out into a parlor with brocade wallpaper, age-darkened paintings decorating the walls, a carved mahogany mantelpiece over a marble fireplace, and so on.

"He did say make ourselves at home, right?" Ben said. "I feel like I'm going to break something."

"It does feel a little like a museum, doesn't it?" I said.

Cormac gave a shrug and slumped into a velvet-upholstered wingback chair, sprawling out and propping his booted feet on what must have been an extraordinarily valuable lacquered circular coffee table. "It's a little much," he said.

I had to admit, the right kind of vampire hospitality was impressive.

We were directed to bedrooms upstairs. There were six, and we got to pick. I pounced on the one in the corner, with a view down the street which gave me the feeling of falling back through time. I could imagine the horse-drawn carriages, the women in huge bell skirts and men in frock coats, walking on the cobbled streets, the glow of gaslights and smoke curling from clay chimneys.

We battled jet lag by taking a walk. Found Hyde Park, then Green Park, and explored all the way to Buckingham Palace, which seemed even more excessive with all its gilt, statuary, and unflinching guards. Thinking of someone living there was a little like thinking of someone being a billionaire. I had no frame of reference.

"What do you think of Ned?" Ben asked us both.

"He's a vampire," Cormac said. "Talks a lot. Who knows what he really wants."

"I'm still getting over him knowing Shakespeare," I said, sighing.

"Don't get too starry-eyed," Cormac warned.

"I know," I said. "I don't know what to think. Alette trusts him or she wouldn't have put me in touch with him. He seems to be taking good care of Emma."

"They're all vampires," Cormac said. Which meant that we ought to be careful about trusting any of them, including Emma.

"We don't have to stay at Ned's place," I said. "It's not too late to find a hotel."

We walked several steps before Ben said, "It'll be fine. This way we can keep an eye on him, right?"

Cormac made a noise that was almost a laugh.

AFTER A good night's sleep, Ben and I went downstairs in the morning to find breakfast—and Cormac—waiting in the dining room. We learned that Ned and Emma had arrived before sunrise, after we'd gone to bed, and that we would see them this evening.

Eggs, tea, toast, slices of thick bacon, stewed tomatoes, and beans—which had never even occurred to me to eat for breakfast—waited on expensive-looking china, dense with a blue floral pattern around the edges. One of the staff stood by and seemed pleased at my gaping reaction. Cormac was cleaning up the last bit of egg yolk with a piece of toast.

"Don't wait for us or anything," Ben said.

"You're not going to need me the next couple of days, are you?"

"Why?" I said.

"It's Amelia," he said. "She wants to check some things out."

"What, like her old haunts? No pun intended."

"Her older brother had kids. Assuming they had kids . . . she may still have family."

"That's so weird," I said absently. He was talking about kids who were born over a hundred years ago—tracking a family tree for real. "What happens if you do find these great-grandnieces or nephews?"

"Cross that bridge when we get to it," he said, spreading butter on a second slice of toast, not looking at us.

"You okay with this?" Ben said. "Is she making you do this?"

"I want to do this. Why do you follow Kitty around on her crazy expeditions?"

"Hey," I said, and Ben snorted a chuckle. I considered what Ben's answer to that question might be, and what that said about Cormac's answer. I didn't know why I was worried—he could take care of himself. Rather than dig, I said, "You're sure we'll be okay without you standing guard?"

"Keep your eyes open. Don't do anything stupid," he said. "If you need me, call."

I looked at Ben for backup, but he just shrugged. Cormac left on his mysterious errand.

Ben and I walked to the conference hotel, which was only a mile and a half away. The housekeeper, manager, whatever she was at Ned's Mayfair house offered to loan us the use of a car and chauffer, but I declined. I wanted to get a sense of the place. An idea of where the escape routes were.

We were still a block away from the hotel when I heard what sounded like a lot of people shouting, more people than should have been at what was billed as a scientific conference. A rumbling of conversation was punctuated with shouting. Someone hollered through a bullhorn.

Then we saw the signs. People held up poster board on sticks, others strung banners between them.

GOD HATES VAMPIRES!

WOULD YOU TRUST YOUR CHILD WITH THIS? Along with a picture of a snarling rabid wolf.

NO NEW WORLD ORDER!

and

V.L.A.D.: VAMPIRE LEAGUE AGAINST DISCRIMINATION.

EQUAL RIGHTS FOR ALL!

NO MORE BURNING TIMES!

A police barricade separated what turned out to be two different crowds, whose members were screaming at each other. Two sides of the debate, hurling slogans. For the moment, it was just slogans, but the anger simmered. At opposite poles of the debate, they were never going to convince the other of their stance. News crews, vans, and cameras were on hand to cover the chaos. It seemed a perfect display of entropy.

"I suppose it would have been too much to ask, hoping these guys wouldn't show up," I said, nodding to a sloppily written sign, red paint on yellow poster board, reading REPENT, WEREWOLVES! If only I could.

"Is there a back door to this place?" Ben asked, searching.

"Don't want to run the gauntlet?" I joked.

"I just don't want to see what happens when one of the holy righteous over there recognizes you."

Well, that was enough to freeze my spine. If this much mayhem was happening the first day, it seemed inevitable that the protests would devolve into riots at some point. I didn't want to be the one to start said riots.

Turning the corner, we went down the block and found an unlocked side door that led into the convention area of the hotel. We weren't the only ones who'd come this way to avoid the chaos outside. Others arrived in pairs and small groups; official-looking people in suits carried briefcases; others dressed in business casual, talking with hand gestures and lights in their eyes. They carried with them an air of anticipation that buoyed my own. I couldn't wait to start talking to people. Breathing deep, I caught the scent of werewolves, plus other brands of lycanthrope I didn't recognize. I studied the people around me, but couldn't sort out what scent went with whom.

The hallway wound around to the main lobby, where the noise from the protestors carried through the glass doors. Barricades kept them from blocking the entrance entirely.

Check-in tables stood in the back of the lobby, and people were lining up before them and talking to the half-dozen young-looking volunteers planted there. Grad students, wanna bet?

"Kitty?" a male voice behind me said. I turned to look. "Kitty? It is you!" He was about my height, athletic, with handsome Latin features. He had a smell of feline about him—lycanthrope. That big sexy smile of his hadn't changed at all.

"Luis!"

I opened my arms for a hug, but he came right up to me, trapping my face with one hand, planting the other hand on my hip to lock me against him, and he kissed me, long and leisurely, on my lips. My hands clenched on his shoulders, but it happened so fast I didn't have a chance to push him away. He'd pounced on me like the cat he was. My knees went weak and my body flushed before my brain could respond.

"No," I said, peeling myself away from him. Bracing my arms, I kept a space between us. "I cannot do this."

Ben stood at my shoulder, staring a challenge at Luis. "So. You two know each other," he said, dead-pan.

Luis stared right back, and I tried to interpose myself between them. Ben got in my way.

This probably looked terrible on the outside. "Um. Luis. This is my husband, Ben."

Luis looked him up and down and pursed his lips, skeptical. "Husband, huh?"

"Yeah," I said, trying to cool the blush in my cheeks by force of will. It wasn't working.

"But you're not wearing a ring," he said, taking hold of my left hand, bringing it to his chest, rubbing his thumb over the knuckles.

"I keep it on a chain," I said, peeling out of his grip again. "Rings tend to get lost during shape-shifting."

"Ah," Luis said with a sigh. "Well, congratulations, I suppose. You're a very lucky man." He winked at Ben, who managed to stay bland.

"I think so. Most of the time," he said, glancing at me out of the corner of his eye. Oh, I was never going to live this down.

"And you're happy?" Luis said, in a tone that indicated he didn't think I possibly could be.

"I am," I said. "And you?" Deflection was always a good strategy.

He shrugged dramatically. "At the moment, I'm suffering a terrible disappointment."

I rolled my eyes, trying to project annoyance. I was still blushing. Ben was still glaring.

"So . . . what brings you to the conference?" I asked.

"I'm here with my sister, representing Brazil."

That put me on firmer territory. "That's great. I hope I get to meet her. Is she around?"

"I think she's outside heckling the opposition. She's as much an activist as ever." He glanced at the front doors to the protests outside, then noticed my frown and lined brow. "You think this is going to turn serious?"

I shook away the concerned expression. "I don't know. I hope not. If it does, it's been coming for a long time."

"I wouldn't worry," he said. "These days, you can't have an international anything without someone protesting it. It'll blow over." His smile was probably meant to be blasé and comforting.

"Yeah," I said, unconvinced.

"As happy as I am to have run into you, I'm on my way to a meeting with some of the other delegates." He touched my arm and looked deep into my eyes, totally ignoring Ben.

"I'm sure I'll see you around," I said, waving a little.

"I very much look forward to that," he said, running his gaze up and down my body before turning to saunter to the hallway and meeting rooms.

Oh, dear . . .

"Okay," Ben said. He was still glaring, at me this time. "You want to explain that?"

Um, yeah . . . "You remember the Senate hearings in D.C.? You remember a couple of mornings when I showed up looking sleep-deprived and pleased with myself?" This had happened before Ben and I were married, before we'd hooked up. Before he'd been infected with lycanthropy, even. I had nothing to be guilty about.

"Yeah, I think I do," he said.

I pointed the direction Luis had gone. "That was him."

"Oh. I see. He smelled weird—what is he?"

"Jaguar."

"Really? You've seen him? His jaguar, I mean."

"Yup."

"Sexy jaguar?"

"If you like that sort of thing," I said.

"I think I want to kill him," Ben said.

I furrowed my brow at him. "That's your wolf talking."

"No, it isn't."

"You can't kill Luis. Your *wolf* can't kill Luis."

"Oh, I think we could. But we won't. At least not right now." His smile was a tad feral.

"Ben—"

"I'm just saying," he said.

This was going to be a long week.

Chapter 5

WE ARRIVED in time for opening remarks by the director of the British Alternative Biologies Laboratory, the British version of the NIH's Center for the Study of Paranatural Biology and co-sponsor of the conference. The main auditorium had room to seat over a thousand and was currently half filled. A few of the people scattered around were lycanthropes—I could almost spot them without smelling them, seated in the back and along the edges, near the doors and away from other groups of people. Close to escape routes, away from crowds. Ben and I did the same, sitting in back. Oddly enough, Wolf had reconciled to the situation. The smell of strange werewolves in someone else's territory should have set me on edge, but there was so *much* strangeness here, so much sensory overload, getting worked up about it seemed pointless. We'd keep our eyes open, sure, but we weren't going to panic. I settled into my seat a little more firmly and started to enjoy myself.

The sleekly modern room had reasonably comfortable padded folding seats that sloped downward to the stage, holding a podium where spotlights focused. A large screen toward the back of the stage meant we would probably be subjected to PowerPoint presentations. At the end of the week, I'd be giving my speech from this stage. I still didn't know what I was going to talk about. I had some ideas. Maybe I could get the audience to ask me questions for an hour . . .

While waiting for opening remarks to start, we studied the schedule of events for the week. Within moments, my eyes blurred. I wanted to see it all, every single panel and lecture. I was pretty sure I'd done a show on every single panel and lecture topic at some point. This was going to give me enough material for the next six months.

"There's too much," I said. "I don't even know where to start."

"We could tag team it. Cover twice as much ground," Ben said, looking much less awestruck.

"What are you interested in?"

He pointed to one of the evening's lectures: "Case Law and Paranatural Citizens: A Survey."

"Huh. Better you than me," I said.

"Forewarned is forearmed," he said.

"Then you'd darned well better sit through that. I'm trying to decide between 'In Plain Sight: Did Hammer Film Studios Know Something We Didn't?' and 'Theoretical Notions of Space and Time as Applied to Vampire Physiology.'"

"What does that even mean?" Ben said.

"I don't know, but I'd like to find out."

Conferencegoers filed in, the auditorium filled with the white noise of dozens of murmured conversations. Only five minutes after the scheduled time, a middle-aged man in a smart gray suit and wire-rimmed glasses came onstage with a set of note cards. Our presenter, obviously. Polite applause greeted him.

"Since the National Institutes of Health in the United States made the announcement four years ago, a vast new field of study has opened to us, encompassing not only biology but sociology, anthropology, and even folklore . . ."

His perfunctory account of the controversial field of paranatural studies made no mention of my own contribution in mainstreaming the topic, my role in prompting Dr. Paul Flemming of the NIH to make his announcement proclaiming the existence of vampires and lycanthropes to the world, *his* role in trapping me in order to broadcast me shape-shifting on live TV, which meant that no one could really ignore us anymore. Probably just as well.

The PowerPoint slides, which he did in fact include in his presentation, *did* reference Flemming's work. Footnotes mentioned his name, papers he'd written, research he'd sponsored. I tensed, wanting to stand and declare—Flemming had been thoroughly discredited, how could anyone possibly even mention his name? Surely his research had to be discredited right along with him? The presenter may not have actually spoken the name, but it was there, clearly written,

blazing across the room. Because even after everything that had happened, Flemming had helped establish the paranatural as a legitimate field of study. He'd
be here in spirit, if not in flesh, all week.

The slides were mostly pie charts that had dis-
claimers about how no one could really be sure of the
number of vampires and lycanthropes in a given pop-
ulation, these were estimates, and so on. Nothing ne-
farious, nothing earth-shattering. At least the guy's
British accent was fun to listen to.

The whole conference was going to be very staid, I
gathered, which was probably a good thing. The subject was so sensationalist on its own we hardly needed
to be adding to the hype. If we were all calm and bor-
ing about it maybe we could counteract the proto-riot
going on outside.

Maybe I could work some of this into my speech—
why the supernatural evoked so much emotion in
people, why establishing much less maintaining ob-
jectivity was so difficult, and what that meant for all
of us here. And whether maybe the topic deserved a
little sensationalism.

"THEORETICAL NOTIONS of Space and Time as
Applied to Vampire Physiology" turned out to in-
volve a dark room and another PowerPoint presentation describing obscure bits of quantum physics
and string theory. Not good in combination with
lingering jet lag. I sat in the back of the room, notepad and pen in hand, trying to make sense of what

the lecturer, a physics professor from the University of California at Berkeley was saying. Dr. Shumacher had worked with the guy on some of his research and recommended the talk. When the lecture opened with a physics joke—"Vampires: alive or dead? Does Schrödinger's cat walk among us?"—I knew I was in trouble.

He went on to describe his hypothesis that vampirism was characterized by anomalies at the atomic level in the bodies of those affected by it. I hoped he had a question-and-answer period, because I really wanted to know if—and how—he intended on testing his ideas on actual vampires. Had he ever looked at a vampire tissue sample under, say, an electron microscope? If you did, what would you expect to find? Surely a vampire somewhere would donate a sample for such an experiment, since vampire blood contained the contagion that caused the disease. Maybe I could talk Rick into it.

I had to keep bringing my focus back to the slides that flipped past on the screen in the front of the room. Diagrams with arrows and squiggly lines kept showing up, and I kept not understanding. I wrote down the lecturer's name and e-mail address so I could grill him later, when I was more conscious.

My attention drifted away again to study the rest of the audience. My werewolf eyes saw just fine in the dark. The room was about two-thirds filled, mostly with the academic types I'd seen throughout the conference so far. Many leaned forward, listening studiously. A pair of men in back stood together, whispering, pointing to the slides. A few journalists might have been here. Someone with a netbook on her lap seemed to be taking notes.

There weren't any vampires here.

I straightened, breathing more calmly and deeply to make sure I was right. Vampires smelled cold, lifeless. They didn't have heartbeats, and I could usually spot one across the room, even in a crowd. I searched for the familiar chilled eddies, the hair pricking along my neck and shoulders, and sensed nothing. Everyone in the lecture hall was alive, with steady heartbeats and fresh flowing blood. Well, that was interesting. I found it hard to believe that not a single vampire would be interested in a topic like this. Apparently not. All the vampire-specific lectures had been scheduled after dark specifically so that vampires could attend. So much for that idea.

Many vampires I'd talked to insisted on telling me how they moved outside of human interests and didn't concern themselves with such pedestrian matters. But . . . really? Not to mention the fact that this stuff was cool?

I'd ask Emma. She wouldn't give me the runaround.

On my way out of the room, I caught the scent of a werewolf nearby. The conference had so many werewolf delegates the distinctive fur/skin smell had become almost invisible, part of the background. But this one, a middle-aged, brusque-looking man at the back of the room, looked out of place. He had a conference badge on a lanyard around his neck, but instead of a professional-looking suit, or even the geeky business-casual most of the delegates managed, he wore jeans, a rough corduroy coat, and had a scruffy, unkempt appearance. I hated to think it, but he looked too blue-collar for the conference. I thought I remembered him from earlier—also standing in the back of the main auditorium after the opening speeches. I only noticed him now because his gaze flickered my way, and he seemed to smile.

I kept my pace steady, not revealing discomfort as I walked away.

WE PLANNED to meet Emma in the front lobby of the convention center after the evening's events. Ned's vampire convocation was tonight, and she was our ride.

Ben approached me from the other end of the hallway. "How was your shindig?" I asked.

"Leave it to a roomful of attorneys to pioneer a whole new branch of law they can specialize in and charge extra for. I think I may have a new line to add to my letterhead."

"Specializing in supernatural law? Really?"

"Yup. Did you know I'm not the only werewolf lawyer in the world? I'm not even the first. Or second." He seemed pleased at the prospect, and I wanted to give him an encouraging hug.

"So you had a good time?"

"It was just like law school graduation, we were all

passing around business cards and sizing each other up." His wry smile fell, and he put his arm around my shoulders when I sidled up to him. "Some of them are worried about where we could be headed, with legislatures taking up the status of supernaturals. Maybe even criminalizing it."

"What? Making it illegal to be a werewolf?" Like we could even help it. Some people chose this life, but Ben and I had both been attacked.

"Yeah. It turned into an argument, the human lawyers saying it'll never get that bad, the lycanthrope lawyers arguing that it already has in some places. Most of the lycanthropes think we need to do what we can to bring cases and establish precedents that make our status a civil rights issue rather than a criminal one. Make sure it gets decided in courts first."

"What do you think?"

"That they may have a point? I don't know. It's surreal to be talking about it in the open. I know this stuff has been public knowledge for years, but it seems like such a no-brainer. I'm still a person, still a U.S. citizen, why are we even arguing about this?"

I squeezed him. "The way I understand the argument is that we regulate guns because they're dangerous weapons, and werewolves are dangerous, therefore . . ." I waved my hand, leaving the rest of the statement open.

"It's enough to make you want to run off into the woods and never come back," he said.

The police had cleared out the protests after

dark—we could safely leave through the front doors, now. Waiting for us on the front sidewalk, Emma looked as enthusiastic and hip as she had at the airport, in a silky blue dress with a hem that danced at her knees and a sweater over her shoulders. Her hair hung loose, shining.

"Ready to go?" she asked.

"Sure," I said. "Are we dressed for it?" I was business-casual, in khakis and a blouse, and Ben wasn't wearing a tie with his suit jacket. I expected vampires would treat this kind of event like dressing for prom: a celebration of fashion, excess, and an exercise in one-upping each other. How did a couple of werewolves fit into that?

"You're fine," she said, smiling.

The car drove what felt like the long way around, but I was beginning to wonder if London had a direct route between any two points.

"I wanted to ask you—I went to a lecture on vampire physiology, and there were no vampires in the audience. Aren't you guys interested in that sort of thing? I figured one of you was sponsoring a research lab somewhere."

"There isn't really a tradition of funding scientific research among vampires," she said. "Was it interesting?"

"It was a little over my head. A sufficiently advanced technology is indistinguishable from magic kind of thing. I took notes."

"I think it may come down to vampires not really

being interested in what mortals have to say about them."

"Yeah, so I've gathered," I said.

She fidgeted with the edge of her sweater. "It doesn't even seem real sometimes. Some days I feel like I ought to be getting up in the morning and going to class. I'm still young by human standards, never mind vampire. It's like I don't know what I am."

"But is it getting any . . . I don't know. Easier doesn't seem like the right word."

"Alette says that in another ten years, when I stop relating to people who look my age, and the people my age start looking older, I'll feel less torn. The old life slips away, and it really does feel like you've died. You move on. Ned says the same thing. So I guess I just have to wait a few more years before it starts to feel normal."

Normal. How could we even use that word to describe our lives? Because normal was what you lived with every day, no matter what it was. Nobody had the same normal when you put it like that; normal didn't exist.

"You look really good," I said. "Have I mentioned that?"

She shrugged, but her expression brightened. "I'll never have to worry about wrinkles, will I?"

We drove on.

Chapter 6

THE CAR turned a corner and maneuvered between buildings that must have been a couple of hundred years old—tall, looming, neoclassical. A cobbled space had been reclaimed into a small, exclusive parking lot, lit by muted orange streetlights. Expensive luxury cars, big sedans, a few elegant limos, all polished to a shine, were lined up. Uniformed drivers lingered nearby, vigilant. A couple of them were werewolves, who straightened when they saw Ben and me. I kept my chin up, my gaze steady, prepared for posturing. But they only watched.

There were a couple of makes of sports cars I didn't even recognize. I had the sudden feeling I was on the set for the latest James Bond movie. This obviously had to be a meeting of mobsters, trust fund babies, or vampires.

"Holy shit, is that a Bugatti?" Ben said.

"What's a Bugatti?" I said, thinking it was some kind of local wildlife.

"Two million dollar sports car," he said.

"Yeah?" I looked to where he was staring, like a kid with his face pressed to the window of a candy shop.

Colored a shade of blue that verged on black, the thing was shaped like a teardrop and didn't seem to have any hard edges. Even knowing nothing about cars I could tell it was impressive.

"Maybe you could ask Antony to let you drive it around the block," Emma said.

"Antony?" he said.

"Yeah. He's pretty laid back, for a vampire."

Ned's driver, Andy, guided us to the front door. The building standing before us was a neoclassical marvel, with wide columns of pale granite holding up a peaked roof that showed friezes of toga-draped figures reclining and dancing in various states of merriment. Many wore or carried masks, smiling and frowning. This was a theater, I realized. I shouldn't have been surprised.

Arms spread wide, Ned was waiting for us at the top of the wide steps that led to the theater's ornate, brass-decked front doors. "Welcome! Thank you for joining us!"

"Wouldn't miss it," I said wryly, bracing for more vampire bullshit than I'd ever encountered in my entire life. Somehow, I had to make it through the rest of the evening without saying anything snarky. *Too* snarky, at least.

"It's too late to back out, isn't it?" Ben said.

"Never too late," I said. "Just as long as we know where the exits are."

He offered me the crook of his elbow, and I put my hand in it. Together, we climbed the stairs and met Ned. Emma followed.

"Any trouble?" Ned asked her.

"No," she answered.

"Expecting any?" I said.

"Oh no, nothing apart from the usual."

"What's the usual?" I said, and he just smiled.

We passed through the doors into a gorgeous carpeted lobby, where crystal chandeliers hung from ceilings painted with lush baroque murals, chubby rosy cupids pulling goddesses of love in golden chariots, that sort of thing. The box office windows had gilt bars over them, and the walls had mahogany wainscoting and elegant antique chairs with embroidered seats.

Ned admired me admiring the scene. "The Restoration of the English theater took place in palaces like this."

"It's amazing," I agreed.

"You seem less impressed, Mr. O'Farrell."

"It's a little busy for my tastes," he said.

"Ah, you're minimalist, then. A Beckett man."

"I don't know that I'm an anything man."

"That just means you haven't had a chance to develop a taste for anything yet," he said.

We crossed the lobby and Ned put his hand on the painted door that presumably led to the main part of the theater. Ben's hand moved to mine, pressing it where it rested on his arm, just as my nose flared, taking in a thick, coppery smell that reached through the cracks around the door.

"I smell blood," I said, hesitating. It was lots of blood, for me to scent it through the door like this.

Ned nodded. "Before we enter, you need to understand that there hasn't been a meeting like this, a gathering of the Masters of Europe, in over a century. We've never had one that included so many from abroad. What you're about to see . . . it's a rare thing, and I must remind you that you are guests here."

"Great. Warning taken," I said, and Ned looked at me sidelong.

The Master of London opened the doors and led us down the central aisle of the theater.

The rows of seats, red plush and marked with brass number plates, were empty, and the house was dark. All the action was happening on the brightly lit stage, and I might have thought we were here to watch a play. There was a dinner party in progress, a dozen or so people sitting at long tables covered with brocade cloth, set in a horseshoe that faced the audience. The diners were looking out, and at each other. Gold candelabras held burgundy candles, dripping wax. The only silverware or place settings on the ornate tables were knives—slim, wickedly sharp steak knives, most of which were bloody.

A dozen bodies lay piled in the middle of the stage. Male and female, many of them were naked, arms and legs splayed, long hair tangled, heads thrown back, mouths hanging open. All had wounds clotting at their necks and wrists. The scene displayed baroque decadence taken to the ninth level of hell.

My stomach flipped and my throat closed on bile. Ned watched calmly, studying my reactions as he had since I'd met him, so I turned to Emma, my friend, reaching for her in despair and disbelief. "Emma?"

She stood back, just out of reach, and her expression seemed indifferent. The stink of blood stuck in the back of my throat, and it didn't taste like food, like the feast and frenzy with which Wolf would normally react. It tasted like danger—we were in terrible danger. All those bodies, at the center of a vampire orgy. I looked at Ben, my eyes wide.

"Wait a minute," Ben said close to my ear, keeping a tight grip on my arm. "They're not dead."

Letting my nose work, I searched past the bloody reek for other signs. Settling, tamping down the panic and rage, I could sense beyond the initial shock: all the blood in the air was still warm—still alive. The bodies were flush and breathing, just unconscious. This was an orgy, but not at the ninth level. Maybe the seventh.

This was like something out of an overwrought opera or a story of Caligula. I needed a long, disbelieving minute to take it all in, and even then my mind shied away from the scene, and Wolf rattled the bars of her cage, fighting to break loose and flee. And still, there was more to see.

I breathed the room's air until I could start to differentiate scents, between the antique furnishings, chill vampires, warm bodies, and spilled blood. The wild fur-and-skin scent was subtle under the on-slaught of the rest of it. Those at the tables were all vampires. Two dozen or so more figures—vampires, lycanthropes, and mortal humans—stood in the positions of bodyguards and retainers behind the tables where the gathered Masters and Mistresses of Europe and beyond sat. They wore all manner of clothing—costumes—from loincloths and lingerie to ornate historical gowns and frock coats. Some were obviously bodyguards, fit men and women in suits who gazed watchfully, suspiciously. I smelled wolf, tiger, and another beast I couldn't identify. A couple of them were ornaments, sleek women in skintight gowns and gold jewelry. There was a dark-haired, cinnamon-skinned woman whom I thought must have been a fox. Literally. But then . . . something else entirely.

One of the vampires seated at the end of a table held a pair of chains that led to collars, thick bands of steel secured around the necks of a man and a woman kneeling at his side. They were both naked, physically fit, muscular, well-tanned. They crouched like pets, and they were werewolves, chained and submissive.

"I'm not okay with this," I said, feeling ill, panicked, furious. This wasn't my world, and I didn't want to be here.

"Ned says it's so much better than it used to be," Emma said softly. "Imagine what this must have been like in a culture where bearbaiting was like prime-time TV."

"I'd rather not, thanks. You can't defend this, Emma."

"I'm not . . . it's just—it's the way things are."

This was her world now, I reminded myself.

"I thought this was a meeting, not a horror show," I snapped at Ned.

One of the vampires on stage, at the middle table, the place of power, stood and leaned forward. She had brick-red hair, curled and flowing down her back and over her shoulders. Her skin was fine china, her smile practiced, her gaze fierce. She wore a gown of midnight blue silk that molded to her figure, and my hackles rose at the sight of her: Mercedes Cook.

"I think we've damaged the girl's modern sensibilities," she said to her colleagues in her honeyed, purring voice. She actually winked at me, and I buried a growl.

Some of them chuckled in appreciation; others stayed quiet. All those gazes looked down on me, trapping me. I might have been the one on stage.

A few seats down, another of the vampires played with his knife, running the handle between his hands, spinning it. Wearing a suit with a brocade waistcoat and jacket with tails, he was polished and gorgeous, sharp features framed by slick black hair and a trimmed goatee, like a nineteenth-century villain, but he made the look work. He probably invented it. "Modern sensibilities? We are ancient creatures. What do *human* mores have to do with us?" His accent wasn't British but rounder, lilting.

"It's not like we kill anyone—civilized vampires don't," said a third, a man with long brown hair, Mediterranean features, a floofy poet's shirt, loose tan pants, and knee-high boots. "Why kill mortals for their blood when they so obligingly make more?"

"Humans—a renewable resource."

"We recycle! We're green!"

Much laughter. Ha.

One of them didn't laugh. He sat at the far end of the table from Mercedes and her cohort. He wore a simple suit jacket with a band collar shirt. On the stout side, he seemed careworn, his gaze tired, as if he'd seen it all.

"A werewolf with morals," he said. "I never thought to see such a thing." His voice was kind, his accent flat American. Him—I wanted to talk to him. I wondered if that was a trick he'd developed.

"Maybe it's because I come from a country that fought a war to put an end to this sort of thing." I pointed at the werewolves in chains and fumed. "God, what is this, the Dark Ages?"

Some of them laughed. Some of them looked at me as if I had asked a very silly question. The *well, duh* look. The last vampire who'd spoken, the careworn one, didn't react at all.

"Mistress Norville, please settle. You're under my protection here," Ned Alleyn said.

"I didn't ask for your protection," I said.

How the hell were Ben and I going to hold our own against this? This whole setup—them on the stage, looking down on us, with no way for us to move to a dominant position—was contrived.

"We can always leave," Ben said calmly. He stood straight and tall, chin up, not cringing a millimeter. It made me stretch a little taller, and I imagined my tail and ears standing up, superior.

We could leave. But as Ned said, this was supposed to be neutral ground, an opportunity to meet with each other without fear. When was I going to get another chance to size up the gathered vampire might of Europe?

"No," I said, taking a breath, forcing myself to at least pretend that they hadn't gotten my hackles up. "I haven't asked any of them how old they are."

He chuckled. "They never answer that."

"Ned did. Can't stop trying now."

"Good luck with that."

"Thanks. So, how about it? Any of you up to telling me how old you are? How about if I promise not to tell anyone else?" I raised my voice and scanned the table, looking at every one of them—not meeting their gazes, but making it clear I had noted them, and remembered. Seated at the table were three women and eleven men, plus retainers, servants, and pets. Plus the victims of the dinner. I pointed at the guy in the poet shirt. "You—I bet you're going to try to tell me you knew Lord Byron, right?"

He laughed, a point in his favor. Guy with a sense of humor couldn't be all bad. The rest of them regarded me with expressions ranging from amusement to disbelief. Even Ned stood aside, hand to his chin, intrigued. I had a sudden feeling they were feeding me rope, waiting for me to hang myself with it.

"Nobody? Aw, come on, I thought you were all supposed to be badass. What're you afraid of?" Ben, bless him, smirked at them all right along with me, though I imagined he was mentally slapping his forehead. Did I have to poke quite so much? Yeah, I did.

It kept my gaze from falling to the stack of bodies in the middle of the stage.

The impeccable anachronistic guy with the goatee made an obvious sniff, nostrils flaring, and wrinkled his nose. "The bitch is in heat."

Ben stepped forward, putting himself in front of me, and bared his teeth in challenge. I put a calming hand on his arm and moved back into view. "Well, that's a little personal. Ned, if we're going to be sharing like this do you want to at least introduce everyone to me? I thought you guys were into all that formality and crap."

Ned started to speak, but the goateed vampire sneered and said, "Too much barking. It's obscene." He turned away from us as if disgusted.

"You hear that, honey? I'm obscene," I said to Ben. "I think that means we win."

"High five," he said, holding up his hand. I slapped it and held it.

"High paw."

Yeah, they were definitely looking at us like we were the ones on stage, now. The figures on the fringes, the bodyguards and such, had pressed forward to watch, even. I didn't know how much longer we could keep up the banter and hold their attention.

"I don't think you understand your position here, young lady," said another of them, a man with dark skin and an Arabic-looking robe of white linen tied with an embroidered sash. "You are here at our pleasure. Our sufferance."

"See, what does that even mean?" I said, my arms out. "You think I'm going to go along with that, just because you expect it?"

"Has no one taught you manners?" he said in a disappointed tone, as if he was lamenting the fallen state of the world, where a lowly werewolf could talk smack to a vampire.

"Yeah, you should ask the vampires back home about that. I'm real popular."

"She is," Ben said. "That eye rolling thing you're doing? She gets that all the time."

I looked at him. "Really?"

"Just trying to help."

Man, the two of us should go on the road. Some of the retainers standing in the wings had begun to fidget. I hoped I was making them nervous.

Ned stepped forward. "If I could make those introductions now—"

The goateed vampire slapped the table, causing knives to rattle and candle flames to flicker. "Edward, you are a terrible host for allowing one of the wolves to speak so out of turn."

Ned smiled. "She's not mine to command, Jan. You know that."

"It's the principle—"

Ned countered, "If you're offended—"

"Oh, I'm not offended," one of the other women said. She had black hair and wore a rhinestone-studded ball gown that glittered like shattered glass. "I thought this was the evening's entertainment." That got a few more laughs. Several of them started talking and laughing over each other, leaving Ned cut off in the middle of his intervention.

Enough of this. I looked at Mercedes and raised my voice.

"How many of you are carrying the coins of Dux Bellorum?" I said, loud and sure to carry.

The room fell still, quiet, and every vampiric gaze, thick with power, turned on me. Mercedes actually took a step back. Well, hallelujah.

"What did you say?" The flip guy in the poet's shirt asked this softly.

"You heard me," I said.

Again, the long silence and studious gazes dominated. I kept still, chin up, eyes steady. I did not slouch. Neither did Ben. We weren't the strongest ones here; it was us against all of them, the whole room. But we had startled them. We had an advantage.

"Well," Ned said wonderingly to the assemblage. "You wanted to know if she had any real power. Now you do."

Every one of those gazes had become appraising.

Calculating. Then—they turned those gazes on each other. Because they didn't know who among them belonged to Dux Bellorum, and who didn't. Oh, this had gotten very interesting.

Mercedes pointed at me and smiled. "She has no power. She hides her weakness with words. I want to see her fight. Wolves are nothing without their teeth and claws."

"Yes, a fight," said her goateed colleague—Jan. "That will settle this. Clear out the middle here." He pointed at several of the retainers, both vampire and lycanthrope, nodding with distaste at the discarded blood donors. The retainers began picking up the unconscious bodies and hauling them away. Some of the victims twitched muscles as if coming to wakefulness, their heads lolling and expressions wincing. No one paid them any mind as they were carried off, through the doors to another room. I hoped one with beds and food and lots of juice and water.

"I'm not going to fight," I said.

"I'll get in there before you," Ben said.

"Neither of us is going to fight."

Jan called, "Which one should she fight? One of them, the female—" He pointed at the pair of werewolves wearing the steel collars and chains.

"No," their Master said. He had short cropped hair and wore a tuxedo with white leather gloves. He had some kind of accent, Scandinavian maybe. "She's submissive, it wouldn't be proper." He actually stroked the woman's hair, leaning over her, protective. In turn, the woman pressed into his touch, turning her face to his thigh as if to hide. She was scared. The other prisoner, the man, put his arms around her, a heartbreaking move to shelter her. He stole glances at me, but his gaze was more often on the floor—he was submissive, too, and terrified of me. Of *me*.

The vampire put his hands on both of them and looked at me, beseeching. As if I could better protect them from this horror show. I almost could think they were beloved pets and not prisoners. If not for the horrid chains.

"I'm not going to fight anybody," I said, and the vampire slumped, relieved.

"I think you will," Mercedes said, thinning her smile and waving fingers at the very burly man behind her—a werewolf, one of the bodyguard types in a suit, who started loosening his tie.

They really expected us to strip down, Change, and go at it right here. Ben had tensed, his fingers curling into a shadow of claws. My own jaw was stiff—I'd been baring my teeth unconsciously.

Ned waited, as always, watching to see what I would do. Maybe if it really did turn into a fight, he'd step in to stop it. Emma was looking scared. I wasn't going to leave it to either of them to decide.

"You people really need to get over yourselves," I muttered, shaking my head. "I'm not fighting anyone. I'm not your monkey, I'm not putting on a show for you, I don't *really* care how old any of you are, and we're leaving."

Turning around, I marched out, past Emma, up that long aisle, past all those empty seats. Ben was right with me—in fact, he reached out to open the door and gestured me through, making the move seem suave and planned. It must have looked great from the outside. I walked through the doorway without breaking stride; he followed, and gave the door a nice little slam behind him.

I went another twenty feet into the lobby before I collected myself enough to stop, covering my face with my hands and groaning. "God almighty you've got to be kidding me. It's like they've been playing orgy in Rome for the last thousand years."

Ben was grinning. "That was awesome. The looks on their faces."

"How long do you think until they burst through the doors and drag us back in there to teach us a lesson?" I said, thinking not just of the couple of dozen vampires, but the lycanthropes and anyone who happened to have a gun with silver bullets. Anyone whose sensibilities we'd damaged.

He regarded the door. "You know? I don't think they're coming." Head cocked, listening, he waited another moment. "They're talking."

When the blood stopped rushing in my ears and I managed to calm my breathing, I could hear the voices, muted but angry. People were talking fast, speaking over each other, accusing, pleading, soothing.

Ben added, "I think they're arguing with each

other to figure out who belongs to Roman and who doesn't."

"The ones who called for the fight, Mercedes and the guy with the goatee. They wanted a distraction."

"They're Roman's," Ben said. "They don't want anyone to know."

We'd pretty much known about Mercedes already, but even the faintest scrap of information about her or any of the others made the whole confrontation worthwhile.

We stepped aside just as the door swung open and Emma came through, harried, lips pursed and upset.

"I'm sorry," she said. "I'm sorry, I know that was awful, it was . . ." She put her hand on her forehead and looked downright human. "I'm sorry. I don't have any influence here or I'd have tried to do . . . I don't know. Something."

"Just tell me the blood donors were volunteers. That it was consensual," I said.

She didn't answer, and I rolled my eyes. I wondered where the nearest Underground station was and if the trains were still running so we could get back to Mayfair without getting a ride from Ned and Emma. I wanted to move out of the town house and check into a hotel. I wanted to get out of here.

The door opened again, and the stout, careworn vampire came through. He carried a polished, carved cane, surely an affectation. A vampire wouldn't need a cane. He was short, which surprised me—he'd given the impression of filling more space.

Emma made room for him, stepping aside and bowing her head deferentially. Ben and I stood side by side, braced, waiting. The man studied us as we studied him.

"You've broken up the party," he said finally. "They're all leaving through the stage door."

"Can't say I'm at all sorry," I said. "I was having a terrible time."

He curled the tiniest smile. "The party wasn't for you. Ned invited you because the others wanted to have a look at you. None of them really believed your reputation could be at all deserved."

"What reputation? The one where I'm an antiestablishment loudmouth, or the one where I can't seem to keep out of trouble?"

"Yes," he said, and I sagged. "It's a very great pleasure to meet you, Ms. Norville. It's been a long time since I've encountered a Regina Luporum."

"A what?"

"Queen of the wolves," Ben said.

"I'm not the queen of anything," I muttered.

"You stand up for your kind when few do," he said. He bowed slightly, bending forward at the shoulders, a gesture that managed to confer respect without detracting from his own dignity. "I am Marid, I was born in the city of Babylon, and I am two thousand, eight hundred years old. More or less."

I could have been forgiven for falling on the floor with hysterical laughter right then. But I was stuck. "I didn't think I could be surprised anymore."

"Neither did I," he said.

"It's not that I'm skeptical or anything, but you sound so . . . so . . ." I could have said any number of words—modern, ordinary, *American*. But that wasn't right. "You don't sound like you're over two thousand years old."

Ned came through the front doors, looking pleased with himself. "That's because you have to change your accent if you want to blend in, but no one ever mentions that, do they? You think actors on the stage of the Globe sounded anything like the fellows on the BBC? God, no. We've all adapted. Most of us, anyway."

"Well, Ned," Marid said amiably. "Did you get what you wanted out of this?"

The Master of London was rubbing his hands together, gleeful. "This turned out to be far more interesting than I was expecting."

"What were you expecting?" I said, horrified.

He shrugged. "A bit of banter, a bit of posturing. Not the threat of a werewolf pit fight there on the stage."

I turned to Ben. "Can we call a cab or something?"

Emma said, "No, we can take you back—"

Sighing, I said, "No offense, but I think I've had enough vampire hospitality for a while."

Ned raised placating hands. "Please, Kitty, peace. You can't afford to throw away allies."

"Is that what you all are?"

"Kitty. Please stay," Ned said. "You'll break Emma's heart if you go elsewhere."

I would, too. Damn. She actually had her hands clasped together, pleading. Heaving a sigh, I turned away and paced, wolflike. I didn't say yes, but I didn't say no.

Marid—the man who had just told me he was alive when Babylon was the height of modern civilization—interrupted with a calm statement. "You know of Roman. You know of the Long Game."

"Yes. I've faced him down twice," I said.

He raised a brow. "And lived?"

"I had help," I said.

"No doubt."

"So you know about him, too," I said.

"I've known about him from the beginning. There was no Long Game before Roman."

Another piece of information landed with a thud. "Then you must know who his allies are, where he has power, how to stop him—"

"I didn't say that," Marid said, tilting another inscrutable smile.

I looked back and forth between the two Masters. "Do either of you know who's with Roman and who isn't?"

"Not all of them," Ned said. "Some have been playing both sides against the middle for centuries. They'll have to choose allegiances soon. Many of them don't believe that time has come."

"I think many of those will not take Roman's coins in the end," Marid said. "They've known their own power too long."

"I hope you're right, of course," Ned said. "I'm not sure I'll depend on that hope, however."

They were like generals forming a battle plan. "Where do we fit into this?" I asked.

Ned said, "We, meaning you and your mate? Or all the werewolves?"

Taken aback, I had to think a moment. "I don't know," I said simply. Queen of the werewolves, huh? Was it too late to go home? "You were the only Master in there who didn't have werewolf bodyguards. Why not? Do you have a relationship with the local wolves, or are you just not as cool as the other vampires?"

"Please," he said, an attempt to brush me off. But there was a status thing involved. He hadn't tried to present Ben and me as belonging to him.

"Does London even have an alpha wolf?"

"Yes. I'll introduce you to him soon."

"I may just go looking for him myself."

"Kitty," Ned said, hands flattened in a placating gesture. "Don't interfere in situations you don't fully understand—"

"Did you even *try* to stop that bloodbath in there?" I pointed at the door. "Or did you join in? And you want me to *trust* you?"

He opened his mouth to answer, but Marid got there first. "You should understand, this—this is play-acting. Harmless, in our eyes. In the old days—" He smiled wistfully, shaking his head. "We built temples to ourselves, bought slaves by the wagonload—don't look at me like that, Ms. Norville. Don't judge. If you'd lived in those times you'd have felt the same. We slaughtered them in worship to our gods. We never worried about how we would feed ourselves, or how we would dispose of the bodies. Some of my colleagues would go back to those days, if they could. I think those are the ones most likely to follow Roman."

"Do you know—is Roman here, in London, for the conference?" I asked.

"No, I don't believe he is. Only his servants."

"No chance to go after him directly then."

"Only his servants," Marid repeated.

Ned said, "I should remind you that I've declared London neutral territory for the duration of the conference. For either side to make an offensive would invite retribution."

"We'll see how long your truce lasts, Ned. We'll talk further on this." Marid tipped an invisible hat to the London Master and went to the front door, and out.

Ned drew a breath and sighed.

"If I get a chance to hurt Roman, I'll take it," I said.

"I suppose you will. Marid's right, I suppose hoping a truce will last is wishful thinking. But I have to admit, I rather like wishful thinking. It doesn't do to let the imagination stagnate."

TOGETHER, EMMA and Ned talked me off the ceiling and convinced us to stay at the town house. They persuaded me we'd be safer there, especially now that Mercedes and her allies had seen me. I thought I'd been coming to London for a conference. I had hoped all my battles this week would be verbal and academic. Wishful thinking, indeed.

In our luxurious borrowed room, Ben and I curled up in bed, naked, holding each other. I pulled all the covers up to cocoon us, making us too warm, but the heat was comforting, and Ben didn't complain. Just played with my hair and breathed against my scalp. I rambled.

"I just keep thinking of how much worse it could have been," I said. "They had slaves, bodies, and blood, like it was all a big party, like it was *normal*. Like I shouldn't complain because it used to be so much worse. Like I'm supposed to be happy that they didn't go so far as to kill anyone. Am I deluded? Is this the way the world really is and I shouldn't even fight it?"

Ben said, "You're an idealist. And that's okay. The world needs idealists to keep the rest of us out of the gutter."

I tilted my head to look up at him in the darkness, the slope of his cheek and flop of brown hair over his ear. "Really? Or are you just trying to make me feel better?"

"Of course I'm trying to make you feel better." He squeezed, settling me more firmly in his arms. "Is it working?"

"Hmm."

"Was that yes?"

I had to think about it for a minute. If I focused on

the moment, yes, it was working. But my mind kept drifting back to images I would never be able to erase from my memory. Right, then, time to stop that. At the moment, in the whole world, there was only me and Ben.

"Yes," I said finally, and kissed him.

Chapter 7

CORMAC GOT back to the town house even later than we did and was gone in the morning before I had a chance to ask him if he'd had any luck finding Amelia's family. I hoped he was all right.

For my part, no matter what the vampires had said, or the implications of last night's macabre presentation, the conference was important, did mean something, and I was going to treat it as such.

Dr. Elizabeth Shumacher and Joseph Tyler's presentation on lycanthropes in the modern military focused on the case study of a group of werewolves who formed an Army Special Forces unit that had served in Afghanistan. The unit had been entirely unofficial—a captain and lone wolf took it upon himself to create other werewolves in order to form a squad uniquely suited to the challenges of battling extremists in the mountainous wilderness of Afghanistan. The experiment had started well—the unit had an impressive record of accomplishing its objectives—and ended disastrously. When the captain, the alpha of the pack, was killed in an explosion, the rest of the pack lost its moral compass and all control. They began fighting each other for dominance until only three remained. Those three returned to the U.S. damaged by post-traumatic stress and trapped by their wolf sides. It was assumed they'd never be able to leave their cages, much less rejoin human society. Shumacher called me in to help. I did what I could to teach them how to live with lycanthropy, the monster inside. Mostly, I failed, and two more died in a violent escape attempt. Sergeant Joseph Tyler was the only survivor of the original unit.

They'd gotten permission from the army to tell their story. Tyler was no longer active duty, and Shumacher's scientific sensibilities wanted the information made public, so no one else would make the same mistakes. She felt that Captain Gordon couldn't have been the first person who ever thought of using werewolves for combat.

I sat in back and listened to the story, told clinically and professionally, which made it seemed detached from my experience of it—it had all happened to someone else, and I'd never seen those men whose faces appeared in the photographs on the slide show.

The conclusion she left the audience with had been my own—taking soldiers and making them werewolves was ill-advised. They had training that made them excellent warriors, but none of the skills they needed to control the terrors that came with lycanthropy. A more successful project was taking werewolves, people who had already successfully adjusted to lycanthropy and had learned to deal with the drawbacks as well as the abilities, and training them to be soldiers.

Even that left something to be desired, I thought. Probably because I wished we didn't need soldiers at all.

Tyler answered questions at the end.

Joseph Tyler was a solid black man, tall and broad, with a stern expression and distant gaze. He held himself apart, and his quiet strength was intimidating. At first, the questions came slowly, as people hesitated, unsure of him. He loomed over the podium. But he was articulate, and met the gazes of everyone who spoke to him. People were able to talk to Tyler the person and not Tyler the big scary werewolf. They asked personal questions about his choices, his emotions, the fallout, his recovery. He answered calmly—or politely declined to—and even said "yes, sir" or "no, ma'am." I wondered how much of his military training was keeping him upright.

At the end of the session, I hung back to watch as people mobbed Tyler. Some asked questions, some tearfully thanked him and expressed sympathy— pity—for his predicament. They seemed to be thanking him for his simple existence. A few handed him business cards. Tyler handled it all with grace, though he kept glancing at the exits as if looking for escape. As she put away her presentation, Shumacher looked on like a proud teacher.

Finally, my turn came. Tyler saw me and smiled wide. "Kitty! Good to see you."

"You look great!" I said, opening my arms and feeling gratified when he stepped forward into a hug, which wasn't at all a wolfish gesture, but he was special. One of my extended pack members—family, practically. "You're pretty popular, I see."

He winced at the handful of business cards people had given him and drew more from his suit pocket. People must have been mobbing him all day.

"Recruiters, can you believe it?" He handed the cards to me, and I read them: private security firms, foreign militaries, government offices. "Mostly consulting jobs. At least that's what they say now."

"You think you'd ever go back to that? Take up one of these offers?"

"I'll tell you, I'd never go back, and I wouldn't even be here, except I'm pretty sure some of these outfits have already tried recruiting werewolf soldiers, who may be sitting in a cage somewhere, out of control and miserable like we were, with nobody there to help them."

"And you want to help them."

"Not even because they're werewolves, but because they're soldiers."

I squeezed his arm, a gesture of solidarity. Tyler was one of the good guys.

As I shuffled through the last of the cards before handing them back to him, a name caught my eye. The card itself was simple, just words on white stock, no logo, no affiliation, no business name or government listed. But the name blazed forth: DR. PAUL FLEMMING.

I held the card up. "Where did this come from?" The edge to my voice was sharp.

"Same as the others, some guy wanting to recruit."

"Describe him."

"Kind of mousy, bookish. Didn't wear his suit well. He smelled like he doesn't get out much. Kitty, what's wrong?" His brow furrowed with worry.

"He's here? At the conference?" I looked around, scanning the few faces remaining in the lecture hall.

"Yeah—"

"Dr. Shumacher?" I called over his shoulder.

She'd put away her laptop, collected her things, and brought them over to join us. She was a contrast to Tyler: a prim white woman with short dark hair, glasses, and a focused expression. She wore a cardigan over a blouse and skirt. "Yes?"

"Flemming's here." I showed her the card.

"He wouldn't dare," she muttered, but she looked at the printed name and her eyes widened.

"Who is he?" Tyler asked.

"He ran the center before I took over," Shumacher said. "He wasn't entirely ethical."

"Yeah," I grumbled. "I recommend not taking a job from him."

"What are we going to do?" he said. The card had a phone number and e-mail address, but not a physical address. And want to bet the number went to a pay-as-you-go untraceable cell phone?

Shumacher shook her head. "I'm not sure there's anything we can do. I think there's still a warrant for his arrest outstanding in the U.S., but I'm not sure what good that does here."

Tyler took back the card. "I'll drop this off at the embassy. Let them know he's here."

Maybe they could track him down and at least let us know where he was staying, so we could avoid him. And here I'd thought the conference was going to be the safest place this week.

". . . AS THE work of my colleagues has shown. Dr. Brandon demonstrates here that the cellular stasis present in vampire physiology prevents the mitosis necessary for embryonic development. On the male side, the motility of sperm appears to be zero in every case. Male vampires simply do not produce sperm and female ova appear to be entirely inactive.

"Moving on to the lycanthropes involved in our study . . ."

I perked up and readied my pen to take notes.

"Unlike the victims of vampirism, both male and female lycanthropes appear to have entirely normal, viable sperm and ova . . ."

I knew I had viable ova. That wasn't the issue.

"In fact, we have evidence that male lycanthropes have fathered normal, healthy children with uninfected women."

I had evidence of that myself. I was reasonably sure that General William T. Sherman had been a werewolf, and had been one during the Civil War. One of his sons had been born after the Civil War. Too bad I'd decided to keep the evidence I had of Sherman's lycanthropy secret.

"The obstacle in sexual reproduction among lycanthropes is not fertilization or embryonic viability, but gestation. Implanted embryos do not survive the physical trauma of shape-shifting."

Again, this wasn't anything I didn't already know.

"A few obvious solutions present themselves—in vitro fertilization and surrogacy could allow the offspring of two lycanthropes to be carried to term. However, on review, such procedures may not be advisable. A lycanthrope's preternatural healing ability makes many surgical procedures—such as the retrieval of ova—problematic. But another issue may be biological—an as-yet-undiscovered reason why lycanthropes cannot sexually reproduce, and the trauma of shape-shifting on lycanthropic reproductive capabilities is, in effect, a fail-safe to ensure that such reproduction is impossible. More experimental data is required to confirm some of these speculations."

I needed a few minutes to parse what the lecturer was saying. Oh, I understood it well enough, my brain processed it, but the lump in my gut rose to my throat and I had to squeeze my eyes shut for a moment, fighting tears of disappointment. I had been looking for a revelation, a solution, a bit of magic. For hope. That I didn't find it shouldn't have come as a surprise. But that hope had been stronger than I thought. I had let myself hope more than I'd intended.

The lecture was done, the projector shut off, and everyone had filed out of the room. There didn't seem to be another presentation after because the room stayed empty, and I remained sitting in the middle of the back row, my blank notepad resting on my lap, staring and thinking.

It was just a thing. A branch on the road, one of the ones you didn't get to pick, like getting infected with lycanthropy or losing your best friend. You just dealt with it. We could adopt. Once our lives settled down a little, we could adopt.

I lurched out of the seat and stomped off to find Ben and someplace to get a drink.

BEN MUST not have been out of his latest session. I called him—we'd all gotten quad band, internationally capable phones—but he must have had the thing switched off, because it rolled to voice mail.

"Hi. I'm ready for a drink and food that bleeds. I'll meet you in the hotel lobby." I switched the phone off and tried to calm down. I wanted to *run*.

Through the wide glass doors at the front of the lobby, I could see the protesters were back, rowdy as ever. Police barricades and supervision kept them away from the doors and mostly off the street. I'd made a habit of ducking out the side doors in and out of the hotel; I wanted to avoid the gauntlet if I could help it. On the street, one of the red double-decker buses made its way slowly past the crowd, changing lanes in preparation for turning. It had one of the Mercedes Cook ads on its side. My gut sank, and not just because Mercedes was on my shit list and after last night the very sight of her made me ill. The ad had been vandalized, spray painted over in sloppy, drippy black: STAKE THE DEMONS, with the vampire's face crossed out by an angry scribble. I could hate Mercedes on principle, but this was a bigger issue. Maybe I had another topic for my keynote speech.

I caught his scent just before he pounced and turned to face him.

Luis had been stalking, his arms raised for grabbing, a mischievous glint in his eyes. He was within reach, but I crossed my arms and glared. "Hello, Luis."

"Aw, I was moving from downwind so you wouldn't smell me."

"Luis, we're inside, there is no downwind!"

He grinned like he knew that fact very well and didn't care. "You look like you're just waiting for someone to sweep you away to dinner and dancing."

Hmm, dinner and dancing, escaping the cares of the world with a big bottle of wine . . . "I am. Ben's meeting me here and we're going for lunch and drinks." Any minute now . . .

"Ah. Right. He seems very nice."

"He is."

"I have to admit, Kitty, I just never pictured you as the marrying type."

"Why not?" I said, pouting. "Just because I happened to jump into bed with you within hours of meeting you?"

His smile went vague and he gave a heartfelt sigh. "That was a very good night, wasn't it?"

And why on earth had I brought it up? My skin shouldn't have been tingling like that at the memory. "Yeah, it was. It was also years ago and I met the right guy in the meantime."

"Yes, and so much has happened we clearly have a lot of catching up to do. I read your book—it was really good. Really thoughtful. I very much enjoyed it."

My expression melted into a smile. "Oh, you did? It was? Thank you! I'm thinking it's time to do another."

"That's great. Seriously, I'd love to take you to dinner and we can talk about what we've been up to. Maybe tomorrow?"

"Yeah. Okay. I think we can manage that. Maybe your sister can come along?" Sister, chaperone . . .

He reached out and caught my hand, cradling it gently in his as he brought it to his lips and gave the knuckles a light kiss. Truly a lost art, the kissing of hands.

Of course that was when Ben walked up.

I pulled my hand away, and Luis hung onto it for just that extra moment before I could take a step back. I didn't know why I was blushing, I didn't have anything to be embarrassed about. Ben had his hands in his trouser pockets as he strolled up to me, but kept a hard gaze on Luis.

"How's it going?" he asked.

"Just fine," I said. "Ready to head out?" I hooked my arm around his and steered him toward the lobby's side exit.

"I very much look forward to dinner tomorrow night," Luis said, waving after us.

Ben and I had gone ten or so strides when I looked at him and said, "What?"

"I didn't say anything," he said.

"You were thinking it."

"You want to have dinner with an old friend. Nothing wrong with that."

"Except . . ."

"The guy gives me the creeps, that's all."

"Because he's a were-jaguar?"

He glanced at me. "He's a little slimy, don't you think? That whole hand-kissing thing?"

"Maybe you ought to try it sometime."

"Me? The guy who can't remember to bring home flowers on our anniversary?" He actually sounded a little sad.

I hugged his arm. "You cook. That's better."

We made it outside and down the street, took our life in our hands by crossing the street, which was helpfully marked with arrows pointing the direction we needed to look to keep from being plowed into by oncoming cabs in bizarro traffic land. I'd get used to looking right first just when it was time to go home.

The pub was called the St. George, and was exactly what I imagined an English pub should be: a mock-Tudor building with a painted sign hanging over the door showing a mounted knight fighting a lizard-like dragon; gas lamps mounted over the windows and flower boxes housing ivy and pansies under them. I was pretty sure it was all built this way for the American tourists.

The English pub theme-park décor continued inside, with wood paneling, boxy booths, brass fixtures on the bar, and darkened paintings of hunting dogs and dead pheasants. I recognized people from the conference among the customers—doctors, scientists, journalists. A couple waved at me, and the place began to feel a little more friendly. Ben ordered lagers for us at the bar, and I found us a small, round table and chairs in the corner. We sat with our backs to the wall and looked out. The alcohol warmed me, and I began to relax.

I noticed the burly man who smelled like werewolf sitting at the bar, but didn't worry about him until he stood and looked over at Ben and me—and I recognized him as the man I kept seeing in the back of conference rooms, watching me.

My hand closed on Ben's leg, and I was on the verge of standing to face the wolf who was staring a challenge at us, but Ben said, "Wait." So I waited.

After giving us a moment to look him over—as he looked us over—he approached and gestured at a third chair. "Mind if I join you?"

"Go ahead," I said, guarded. He pulled over the chair and sat, sprawling, knees and elbows out, and regarded me like I was a problem.

He wasn't a large man but he gave the impression of bulk—broad shoulders, stout through the middle, a jowly face. He must have been in his fifties. He had thick, working-class hands that looked like they could punch through walls. He wore comfortable trousers, a white shirt untucked, and a plain vest.

More gazes in the pub turned to us, watching. They seemed casual enough, sitting in pairs or small groups. No one else would have noticed them, but they carried themselves like sentries, like they were on watch for something. The way they seemed aware of each other and their surroundings made me think they were part of a pack. My gaze darkened, less friendly by the moment.

"I'm Caleb," the stranger said in what might have been a permanently annoyed tone of voice. His brow was furrowed, his gaze hooded. "And you're Kitty Norville."

"Nice to meet you," I said, trying to figure out what was going on.

Caleb didn't smile, didn't move. His expression remained hard. The longer we sat looking at each other, the more Wolf wanted to tuck her tail and grovel. But I couldn't look away—I stayed straight and kept my gaze steady. Next to me, Ben sat just as still, like a statue. I prompted, "And you're here be-cause . . ."

"I'm the alpha of Britain." He just kept staring, like he expected me to do something.

I blinked. I didn't doubt what he'd said, but I sure wasn't expecting it. One man declaring himself the werewolf leader of the entire country? It seemed a little . . . much.

"You're pretty unassuming about it," I said.

"Don't particularly see a need for posturing. We're all friends here, aren't we?"

I had a feeling that was what he was here to find out.

"I've been asking about you. Ned said he'd introduce us," I said.

The werewolf snorted a chuckle, brief and full of commentary. "Of course he did. Are you that much under his thumb, then?"

"Is that what it looks like?"

"You're in awfully tight with the Master of London."

"You've been watching me. A lot."

"There's a whole lot of people watching you. The foreign vampires, their wolves, those protestors, a gaggle of scientists. You really put yourself out there."

"Yeah." I couldn't tell if he was judging me or admiring me. We were circling, snapping at each other to no purpose. "So, alpha of Britain?" I said, to distract myself as much as to gather information. "I didn't know there could be such a thing. All the packs I've known have been local, maybe regional. But you have a whole country?"

"Two," he said. "Ireland reports to me as well. I've got all the bloody islands."

My professional instincts overcame my wolfish ones, and I leaned forward. He didn't even flinch at what most other wolves would have taken as an aggressive stance. "How does that even work?"

Caleb looked at my husband. "You're Benjamin, correct? You ever think about putting a muzzle on her?"

"Nope," Ben said. "Things wouldn't be nearly as much fun if I did that."

"Like you could," I said to him.

He shrugged. "What can I say, I'm a sensitive New Age werewolf."

Caleb didn't even flicker a smile. Did he ever?

"To answer your question," he said, leaning back and tucking his hands in his pockets. "It's safer this way. We have a network, havens, rules. These islands have been through a lot of turmoil the last hundred years or so, and our forefathers decided we'd get a lot further working together than not. This way we don't have to depend on the vampires for protection, the way the wolves in Europe do. London stays an open city, with no one scrabbling for territory around it."

"Did you have to fight for the spot, or did you draw straws?" Ben asked.

He chuckled. "The way I see it, if you have to fight to be alpha, you're doing it wrong. Better if you can scare the piss out of the buggers without layin' a hand on 'em."

It was all I could do not to roll over and show him my belly. An alpha after my own heart.

I glanced at Ben. "Can you imagine if we tried to do some kind of United Packs of America thing back home? We'd get laughed at."

"At best," he said.

"You lot don't need it," Caleb explained. "You have lots of wide-open spaces and no history of entrenched feudalism. You don't like the locals you just go somewhere else. Am I right?"

I remembered my own flight from my first pack. I'd had the freedom to be a lone wolf with relative ease. "You don't get too many lone wolves here, then?"

"Oh, occasionally. As long as they keep the peace, I leave 'em be."

"If I'd known who to contact, I'd have asked permission to enter your territory, if that's what you're here to talk to me about."

"If I'd said no, would you have stayed out?"

"I'd already bought the plane tickets."

He smiled like he'd won a point. "Lucky for you that's not what I'm here about."

"Oh?"

"Where do you stand?" he said. His tone made the question very large indeed.

"On my own two feet?" I suggested. Ben snorted a laugh.

"Regarding the vampires," Caleb answered, not missing a beat. "The vampires here, in Europe, in your own country. Do you serve them?"

People kept asking me that. Kept making assumptions. "No," I said. "I'm friends with some of them. But I protect my pack. That's all."

"You sure about that? It's rare, for a territory's wolves to be so . . . independent."

"I think I know what you're really asking," I said. "I met some of the vampires of Europe last night. And some of their wolves. I didn't like what I saw."

"You've never seen wolves as slaves, you mean."

"No," I said. "Not like that."

"It's been that way for centuries on the Continent," Caleb said. "It's different, here. The arrangement Ned and I have is unusual."

"What arrangement is that?"

"We leave each other alone."

"The European vampires don't like either one of you because of that."

"They'd take Ned out, if they could."

"And if they took him out, the wolves here could lose their autonomy."

"It won't come to that," he said, but it sounded like bluster. His gaze fell, the tiniest sign of a loss of confidence. "There are rumors that a war is coming. Between those who want us in the open and those who don't. Between us and regular people. What do you think? Is war brewing?"

War was such a big word. I wanted to deny it. "I think so, yes," I said.

"This conference of yours has brought the likely

instigators to my doorstep. What am I supposed to do with that?"

He said it like it was my fault. Like the conference was even my idea. Or maybe that the war was. "I suppose that depends on which side you're on."

"I'm on the side of angels, love."

I liked him. That didn't mean I could trust him. I looked to Ben for his opinion. He kept a neutral expression; his hackles were down, though, his shoulders and back relaxed.

I turned back to Caleb. "Does the name Roman mean anything to you? Or Dux Bellorum?"

"No, but if I run into these fellows what should I do?"

"Stake the hell out of him," Ben said.

Caleb smiled. "That bad, eh?"

"If there is a war coming," I said. "It's because of him." In a hushed voice I explained what I knew of the Long Game, that two-thousand-year-old Roman had been gathering allies and taking control of territory, for the purpose—near as anyone could figure—of having the most power. Of ensuring that the supernatural world, controlled by him, had supremacy over humanity in whatever conflict, instigated by him, ensued.

"Not even the vampires know which of them's aligned with Roman and who isn't," I said. "I think it's on purpose. Keeps them at each other's throats. At least that's what happened last night."

"Better each other's than ours. They're nervous,"

Caleb said, thoughtfully scratching the stubble on his chin. "Things are changing too fast for 'em—they're used to watching the world move slowly around them, manipulating events behind the scenes. They can't do that so much now."

"If Roman can gather allies, then so can we. The more people know about him, the less power he has. So now you know."

The alpha werewolf leaned back in his chair. "You're all right, Kitty Norville. Unfortunate name, there."

"Don't start," I muttered.

He chuckled. "One more question for you. There's another American werewolf here for the conference, a Joseph Tyler. What do you know about him?"

I straightened, hackles stiffening again. "What about him?" I said, my voice low.

"Steady there," he said. "Friend of yours, I take it?"

"If you hurt him—"

He huffed. "What makes you think anyone can hurt him? He's a tank. That's what I want to ask—is he going to be trouble while he's here?"

I was shaking my head before he'd finished talking. "No, not at all. He's had enough trouble. He was Special Forces in Afghanistan, he's worked really hard to adjust to civilian life. To werewolf civilian life. He's a really good guy." I could defend Tyler for hours.

Caleb nodded. "All right. I trust you." He pushed his chair away from the table. "I don't know if you'll still be here for full moon, but if you need a place to run, to let off steam or whatnot, I can show you territory where you won't be bothered."

"Thanks," I said. "I appreciate that."

"Can we get you a drink? You and your friends?" Ben asked, gesturing to the handful of other wolves in the place obviously keeping watch.

"Maybe next time," he said. "I should be going."

We exchanged phone numbers before Caleb and his pack left, and I felt like I had another ally.

Ben and I finished our drinks, ate some food, and were on our way out when my phone rang, making me jump. Just when I felt like I was able to let my guard down . . . caller ID said Cormac.

"Yeah?" I said in greeting.

"I need to talk to you. Is Ben there?"

"Yeah, what's wrong?"

"Where are you?"

"That pub a couple of blocks from the hotel."

"Right. I'll be there in a couple of minutes."

"Cormac, wait—" But he'd already hung up. I looked at Ben. "Cormac's on the way."

"What's wrong?" Ben asked, concerned. I had to shrug.

We went back inside and ordered another round of drinks while we waited.

Chapter 8

CORMAC APPEARED at the door and took off his sunglasses before looking around. He brought his fingerprint-unique scent with him—the aged leather of his coat, soap on male skin. Ben waved, and he took the seat Caleb had been using.

"I need help," he said, before hello even.

Ben and I both straightened. "What's wrong?" I asked.

He scratched the corner of his mustache, an uncharacteristic nervous gesture. "Really it's Amelia who needs help. Or thinks she does. *We* do, I mean." He winced, and I gaped. Cormac, tongue-tied and awkward? Something really was wrong. "Amelia thinks you can help," he said finally.

I raised my brow and waited some more. Scowling, he ducked his gaze, and if he looked like he was having an argument with himself, he probably was. My curiosity boiled.

"You want to explain?" I asked.

He shook his head. "*I* say we just break into the place—"

"Maybe from the beginning?"

"You want something to drink first?" Ben said.

"Yeah, I think I do."

Ben went to get him a beer, and by the time he got back, he'd figured out how to tell the story.

"I spent most of yesterday in libraries," he said. "Looking up genealogies, family histories. Amelia tracked down her family—her brother and his descendants. They've still got land and money, her couple of greats grand-nephew owns the house where she grew up, the one she was living in before she left." Before she set out on the travels and adventures that took her around the world and eventually to Colorado, where she'd been wrongfully executed for murder.

He continued, "She hid some things in the house. Journals, odds and ends. She wants to try to get them back."

"You can't exactly walk up to some guy's door, knock, and ask to go searching for his dead great-aunt's lost journals," I said.

"*I* can't." He pointed at his scowling face and rough appearance, then pointed at me. "*You* might be able to."

I huffed. "Oh, come on! You can't expect me to try to sell that story to a total stranger."

"That's what I think—but for some reason she doesn't want me breaking in and grabbing the stuff."

"No breaking and entering," Ben said. "Especially not in a foreign country, not while you're still on parole. Not *ever*." Ben glared, and Cormac actually lowered his gaze, chagrined.

I started to ask why they didn't just write a letter or make a phone call explaining the situation, then realized—who would believe that? The nephew might not believe someone telling him this in person, but he wouldn't be able to ignore the plea, like tossing a letter in the trash.

The story was far-fetched, unlikely. I sympathized.

"Are you sure she isn't trying to get part of her old life back?" I said.

Cormac pursed his lips, engaging in another of their silent, internal discussions. He tilted his head and said, "Wouldn't you?"

I glared across the table at him. At them. I was going to get roped into this, wasn't I? They weren't just playing on my sympathy, they were playing on my curiosity. I'd chase the story. It might have been crazy and misguided. It might even have been sad, another reason to pity the tragic woman who'd attached herself to Cormac. But it also couldn't hurt to try. What was the worst that could happen? The British equivalent of a restraining order? I knew better than to ask that question.

"Ben?" I said, glancing over.

He shrugged. "It never hurts to ask. But if he says no and kicks us out, are you going to be okay with that?"

"We just have to make sure he doesn't say no."

Cormac slid over a piece of paper with a name and phone number written on it. What could I do but pick it up? He watched, his hunter's gaze cool and steady, as I pulled out my phone and dialed the number, writing a quick script in my head.

After only a couple of rings, the other end of the line picked up and a female voice answered. "Nicholas Parker's office."

I glanced at Cormac, thinking I maybe should have gotten a little more information about Nicholas Parker, apart from the belief that he was Amelia's great-great-grandnephew, before calling. Oh well. "Hi, may I speak to Mr. Parker, please?"

"May I tell him who's calling?"

"My name's Kitty Norville, I have some information for him." Maybe that would be enough. I didn't even know what kind of office Parker had. Doctor? Lawyer? Stockbroker? Hairdresser? Lawyer, I bet.

"One moment, please."

Waiting, I imagined what kind of indignant conversation Nicholas Parker and his secretary were having. *Kitty who?*

Then a male voice came on. "This is Nicholas Parker." Tenor, BBC British, the kind of voice that narrated nature documentaries, that automatically inspired confidence in a backwoods American. Surely I'd be able to explain the situation to him.

My script kicked in. "Hi, I'm Kitty Norville, I host a radio show and I'm tracking down a story you might be able to help me with."

"Yes, I've heard of you. You've been in the news recently, I think."

Right. Now, was that a good thing or a bad thing? "I have some information about a distant relative of yours, a great-aunt, I think. Amelia Parker?"

"Yes. She's a bit of a family legend, came to an awful end in America if I remember right. Something of a scandal. I only know the family stories. I don't even know if any of them are true."

I took a deep breath. "What would you say if I told you I have a message for you from her?"

I expected the long pause. The question was, would there be a click of him hanging up at the end of it. But no, he answered. "I'd say I thought it was a bit odd."

British understatement, gotta love it.

"She died, but that wasn't the end of it. If you've heard of me then you know I deal with some pretty crazy stories, and this one's a doozy. Can we meet in person?"

"I'm really not sure what to say, Ms. Norville. If you have some artifact that belonged to her, surely you can send it—"

"I said I have a message from her. I'd really like to talk to you about it. I can come to your office." A nice, familiar, public place. That should have been comforting.

He sounded subdued, nervous. Of course he did. "I suppose I have a few minutes to spare this afternoon."

"That's all I need," I said, trying to sound reassuring. He gave me the address and a time, and I promised to be there before hanging up.

I grinned at Cormac. "What do you know? Diplomacy beats breaking and entering."

He sighed, relief softening his features. "Thank you."

Chapter 9

THE THREE of us took a cab to Nicholas Parker's office, which was a couple of neighborhoods over in Bloomsbury. The address was in a row of picturesque town houses, painted white with geraniums in flower boxes and with wrought-iron fencing in front. A short set of steps led to a red front door. Next to it, a brass plate announced PARKER, ALDRITCH, SOLICITORS.

"You ready for this?" I asked Cormac. He was searching the windows, as if he could see past the gauzy curtains to the shadows within. As for Amelia, I couldn't imagine what she was thinking. You leave the world for a hundred years, then return, incorporeal, in search of an object you lost, or descendants, or some scrap of connection. Filtered through Cormac, a century dead, I didn't know her well enough to be able to guess. I hoped this was worth it.

I opened the door; Cormac followed me inside, and Ben followed him, hands shoved in the pockets of his jacket.

Ahead of us a set of stairs was blocked by a gate

that said NO ADMITTANCE. To the right was a doorway that led to what was probably a parlor or sitting room in the house's earlier days. It had been converted to a reception area, with several nicely upholstered chairs and a small coffee table of antique mahogany holding copies of high-end architectural and travel magazines. Decoration included bookshelves, tasteful knickknacks, and copies of Impressionist paintings that might have been hanging here for a century. A desk and a young, polished receptionist sat as guardians to a far doorway.

All three of us were out of place here.

"Hi," I said, moving forward to the desk, letting momentum carry me. "I'm Kitty Norville, I have an appointment with Mr. Parker."

The prim woman flashed a brief glance at us before looking over her shoulder at the door. "Yes, he's expecting you."

"Thanks." We went to the second door, and I wondered if I should have come alone. We looked like a pack moving in, intimidating. But Cormac needed to be here, to plead our case, and we weren't going to leave Ben behind.

Nicholas Parker might have been pacing, waiting for us. We caught him stopped by the window, looking out at the street, hands clasped behind his back, fingers twined anxiously. He glanced over his shoulder and sighed. He was in his thirties, clean-cut with upper-class polish, perfect shirt and tie, and neat hair. The jacket to the suit, charcoal gray, hung over the back of the chair. He had meat on his bones and probably spent time at a gym. A gold wedding band glinted on his finger.

"I'll try to make this painless," I said, with what I hoped was a friendly smile. "I'm Kitty." I approached with an offered hand, and he took the cue automatically and shook it. "This is Ben O'Farrell, and this is Cormac Bennett. He's the one who actually discovered the information about Amelia." Parker shook their hands, too. Both Parker and Cormac fidgeted, and I had a feeling Parker wasn't any more used to feeling this uncomfortable than Cormac was. Ben, bless him, stayed quiet and watched.

"I'm afraid I still don't understand what this is about," Parker said. "Shall we sit? Would you like tea, coffee?" He gestured us to chairs across from the wide antique desk occupying the center of the room, off center from the window. We took the chairs; Parker remained standing, which was okay. He needed to feel safe.

"How much do you know about what happened to Amelia Parker?" I asked.

Parker shrugged. "She was a bit of an eccentric and died rather violently in America. I can't say I know much else about her. The family gets requests every now and then from scholars wanting to look at her papers, but she didn't leave much behind. I thought everything that was possible to know about her had already come to light. We have a few photographs, a painting, a childhood diary, the few letters she wrote home. That's all."

"Did you know she was researching the occult?"

He chuckled nervously. "She caused quite a scandal with her interests. I can show you the letter her brother—my great-great-grandfather—wrote to their parents, lamenting her fallen state. Too many gothic stories as a child, he said."

"Actually, all her research had a purpose. She became a fairly accomplished magician."

His polite smile turned stricken. "You don't mean the kind that pulls rabbits out of hats, do you?"

"No," I said. "I can't claim to understand exactly what happened or how, but she cast a spell. Part of her survived her execution in Colorado. She's here, right now."

The smile fell, and he stared. "If you want money, if you think you can claim some sort of inheritance, I'm afraid you're sorely misguided and I will call the police—"

"Not money," Cormac said. His voice stabbed, sudden and out of place in the antique office. "A box. She just wants some of her things back. She hid them in the house in Sevenoaks."

"You've done your research," Parker said.

"I didn't have to. Amelia told me."

"I don't know what kind of charlatans—"

"There's a second stairway into the attic, a servant's passage from the kitchen up the back of the house. In the attic, she rigged up a secret compartment under the floor. The box should still be there."

"That stairway was boarded up years ago—"

"You don't have to believe me. Go and look for yourself, see if it's there. If it is, Amelia wants it back. That's all. We'll leave you alone after that."

Parker maintained a rigid dignity, despite the anger in his gaze. "If this is a publicity stunt—"

"It's not," I said. "I'd have brought cameras if it were."

Cormac said, "The house has three stories, a cellar under the pantry, and the attic. The nursery has always been on the second floor on the south side of the house, and has two sashed windows and a fireplace. The kitchen is on the north side of the house, on the ground floor, and Mother always complained that it was too small for the entertaining she wanted to do. There are five bedrooms, two sitting rooms, a music room, and a dining room. I doubt the bust of Admiral Nelson still sits on the mantel in the larger sitting room, but perhaps the painting of Sir Richard Parker, my own great-grandfather, who knew him, still hangs over the fireplace."

Parker stared. "No, that painting was taken down in the forties, replaced by one of my grandparents. But the bust is still there. Mostly as a conversation piece."

"Ah," sighed Amelia, using Cormac's voice.

"How could you possibly know—"

"It's Amelia," I said. "She's here, and she knows."

The anger fell away, his expression falling slack—as if he'd seen a ghost. "You're serious, aren't you?"

Cormac regarded him with a flat expression— Parker had stated the obvious.

"We need a favor, Mr. Parker," I said. "Let us look for the hidden door in the attic of the house. If it's not there, if we don't find the box, we'll leave you alone and you'll never hear from us again. If it is—then you know we're right."

Ben leaned forward. "I'm an attorney in the U.S., and while I'm not at all qualified to discuss British law, I'd be happy to look over any kind of waiver or document you'd want us to sign, protecting your rights."

"Except Amelia's box," Cormac said.

Parker said, "Assuming you are right—what am I supposed to do with this information? You tell me a long-dead ancestor isn't really dead—am I expected to welcome her back to the family? What do I tell my wife? My father?"

"You don't have to do anything," Cormac said, brusque, steady. "She's the one who left the family, she doesn't expect anything now."

"But—but what if I *want* . . . Mr. Bennett, not many people have the opportunity to speak to an ancestor. Perhaps she knows about some other treasures buried about the estate."

Cormac paused, the sign of an internal conversation. "If there are, she doesn't know about them."

"All right, then," he said. "You've got me. It may be a joke, but I'm willing to see it through. A contract won't be necessary, Mr. O'Farrell, but you'll understand if I leave a detailed account of this meeting behind with my associate. I assume you want to search for this hidden treasure as soon as possible?"

"As soon as it's convenient for you," I said, trying to be reassuring.

Parker said that the village was about a half hour by train from Charing Cross Station, and that he could meet us there in the morning to drive us to the house. We'd have an hour or so to look.

"There's always a chance someone found it and got rid of it," Cormac said.

"Got rid of something? From that house?" Parker said. "I don't know what it was like a hundred years ago, but since then everything's just gone into the attic. You may have to dig to find your compartment."

"That's fine."

We finalized our plans, and the receptionist on the intercom announced that Parker's next appointment had arrived, so we made our way to the door.

"Thank you for your time," I said, shaking his hand again. "It really does mean a lot."

Parker remained thoughtful. "You hear about things like this in the news, but you don't think of it because it doesn't impact you. Then something like this happens. I have to confess, Ms. Norville, I'm not sure I know what to believe."

"It's like that for a lot of us," I said.

Then we were back on the street, in the middle of the afternoon, among the streets and town houses that were simultaneously familiar and otherworldly.

"That went a hell of a lot better than I was expecting," Cormac said.

"What were you expecting?" Ben asked.

"That he'd say we were crazy and call the police."

"It's a brave new world," I said. "Werewolves are real. So are ghost whisperers, apparently."

THAT EVENING, Emma and I sat in the lobby of the hotel's convention center and people-watched.

"There, that one." She nodded at one of the few vampires who'd finally shown up at the conference. He was male, wearing a conservative suit and tie, and had a suave demeanor. "He's one of Njal's lieutenants. Njal was the one with the wolves in chains."

"So they're bad guys."

"Not necessarily. Njal has a reputation for taking very good care of his people, including the werewolves. Not all vampires are like that."

"It just never occurs to him *not* to keep werewolves as pets on chains?" I said.

"Yeah," she said, wincing. "They do because they can."

"Doesn't make it right," I said.

"Ned says Njal's been playing both sides. There's no telling where he stands—or if he'll even stick with a side once he finally decides."

Cormac said he had more exploring in London to do. No doubt Amelia was fascinated with the changes the city had undergone in the last century. Ben and I returned to the conference and another round of lectures and presentations. Emma had arrived after dark to take a look around—to scout on Ned's orders, I was pretty sure.

I debated telling her about meeting Caleb. Her, and by extension Ned. The two camps in London, vampire and werewolf, seemed autonomous and separate. Which shouldn't have surprised me—that was how it seemed to work most places the werewolves weren't overtly under the vampire Master's control. Maybe I had hoped that the situation Rick and I had in Denver—independent but allied—was more common. If other places worked that way, we wouldn't be such an anomaly.

A few minutes later Emma pointed out another one—a thirtysomething woman whom I recognized as one of the underlings from the convocation last night arriving to talk to Njal's lieutenant. They left together a moment later.

"She's with Petra, the dark-haired woman with the flashy gown," Emma said.

"So Njal and Petra are on the same side, whichever side they're on."

"Again, not necessarily. They could be feeling each other out, trying to cut a deal, or trying to spy on each other."

"Can't we make any assumptions with you people?" I said.

She shrugged. "Not beyond the obvious. We drink blood and sleep at dawn."

"I can point out a dozen lycanthropes here, and they may or may not have a pack back home. Some species don't even have packs, and even if they do most of them probably haven't checked in with the local pack alpha. Are there any unallied vampires? Any of them here on their own and not affiliated with a Master?"

"You do occasionally get lone vampires, but it's rare," she said. "Being part of a Family makes things so much easier."

"I've had people call into the show—new vampires who say they'd never even heard of Families. They were victims of random attacks, and they have no choice but to take care of themselves. What about them?"

"They usually don't last very long," she said, frowning. "Denver's Master, Rick—Alette says he was unaffiliated for centuries."

"Yeah. I'm guessing he was always a bit of a black sheep." It wasn't my story to tell. But it was a good story.

"I'd like to meet him. He sounds interesting."

"He is. He's a really good guy. You should come visit." I spotted a familiar face across the room and nudged Emma. "There, that guy? Were-jaguar."

"Really?"

Luis had spotted me by that time and strolled over, arms spread wide in greeting. "Kitty, my love!"

I blushed. Why did I always blush? I smiled at him and tried to cover it up. "You know it's true, you sit here long enough you'll see absolutely everyone at the conference walk past."

"So you're saying you were waiting for me?" he said, and winked.

He looked at Emma, and his smile fell a milli-meter—only a bit of chill. His nose flared, taking in her vampiric scent. He seemed uncertain, though his tone was bright as ever. "Who is this very lovely person?"

"This is Emma, a friend of mine," I said. "Emma, Luis."

"Hi," she said, offering her hand.

He tucked it in both of his, bowed over it, but didn't kiss it. "Lovely to meet you." She nodded graciously in turn.

"Any plans this evening?" he said, straight to me.

"Conference, work, hanging out with my husband."

"I still suspect that you're pulling one over on me with that."

"It's not a joke," I said.

He sighed in mock despair, hand over his chest. "Well then, I'll have to leave you to it. We're still having dinner tomorrow tonight, yes? You *and* your husband."

"And your sister," I added.

"Until then." He prowled away, throwing a last half-lidded, cat-like look over his shoulder.

"Wow," Emma said. "He's *nice*."

"Hmm, he can be. I actually met him in D.C. when I was there for the hearings."

Her smile seemed wistful. "I get the feeling he doesn't like vampires too much."

I shifted my seat so I looked at her instead of out. She didn't seem at all insecure or self-conscious. She sat tall, chin up, gaze out, at ease. She had all the elegance and poise I attributed to vampires.

"Is it getting any better?" I asked. "Or easier, at least?"

She continued gazing over the lobby as if she commanded the space. "I've stopped gasping for air when I think I've forgotten to breathe. It's . . . it's hard to describe. The rules all changed. And the new ones make perfect sense."

Emma was the only vampire I'd known before she'd been turned. I hadn't known her long, then, but I remembered. She'd changed, since then. Still, people were always changed by crises, by the trauma in their lives. I'd certainly changed. I hardly recognized the naïve kid I'd been before I was attacked, or even the super scared one I'd been right after. That was years ago. How could we not change?

If what I'd told Luis—that if you sat here long enough you'd see everyone associated with the conference walk by sooner or later—was true, I figured I'd eventually spot Paul Flemming, and I could . . . confront him. Not tackle and maul him, alas. Find out what he'd been doing for the last four years, besides dodging criminal charges in the U.S. But he hadn't made an appearance.

"Oh! You're Kitty Norville aren't you? *Really?*"

Emma and I both jumped, startled.

Two young-looking women, holding onto each other's arms, came up to us, eyes wide, biting their lips, giggling. They wore skirts and T-shirts, hip scarves and jewelry, and had their pale hair bundled up in scrunchies. They were so thin they might fall over in a slight breeze. I pegged them as grad students or lab assistants of one of the attending scientists— old enough to be here, young enough to not care if they had any dignity about it. They carried on like groupies, and I felt that little flush of celebrity. Getting recognized in public was simultaneously weird and flattering. The human side of me never got tired of the feelings of validation and accomplishment. Wolf thought it felt a little like being hunted.

"Yeah," I said. "Hi."

"We are *huge* fans," one of them said. Might have been the one who spoke before, might not have. "We'd heard you were going to be here, but we didn't really believe it, but here you *are*!"

Emma looked like she was clenching her jaw to keep from laughing.

"I'm glad I could be here," I said. "I hope you'll be able to come to my talk on Saturday."

"Oh, we wouldn't miss it! Um, I know you probably get this all the time, but we were wondering— can I get your autograph? I have a pen around here somewhere, and some paper—"

A scramble in handbags for pen and paper ensued, and they found a little hotel notepad and a slightly fancier fountain pen soon enough. I gave them both autographs made out to them: Daisy and Rose. If the pair of them got any cuter I might have gagged. I put smiley faces under my signatures, and they squealed.

How could I not smile back? They wandered away tittering, evidently happy.

I beamed after them until they turned a corner and were out of sight. Then I frowned.

"Is that weird to you, that neither of us sensed them coming?" I said. I couldn't for the life of me remember what either of them smelled like. They should have smelled like *something,* even if it was over-scented shampoo or soap.

Emma pursed her lips, worried. Because yeah, that was weird.

"Were they even human?" she asked.

We looked at each other, blinking in the same confusion. If they weren't human, what were they?

Chapter 10

I WANTED TO enjoy the trip to Sevenoaks more than I did. Under the arcing glass and steel roof of Charing Cross Station, I once again had this bubbling wonderment of being caught in a movie. I got to ride on a *train,* into that green English countryside. I'd only ever been on a real cross-country train once, visiting my grandmother when I was a kid. But this trip was weighted by a lingering sense of anxiety. Amelia was returning home, and none of us knew what to expect.

"I'm still worried he's going to have the cops waiting for us," Cormac said.

"Even if they are, we haven't done anything wrong," I said.

"Attempted fraud?" Ben said.

"So not helpful," I muttered.

We occupied a booth, four seats around a plastic table by a large window, and watched the scenery pass by as the train clacked smoothly on its rails. I could have let the movement rock me to sleep.

"It's all changed and yet it's all the same," Cormac

observed softly. He leaned close to the window and stared out, studying the world.

The city gave way to suburbs, with bits of country-side scattered between them, distant green hills and stands of old trees, villages with square brick houses, tiny train stations with only a small length of platform. The stop Parker directed us to was one of these.

Parker was waiting for us by a nondescript sedan, a blue Renault. No police in sight.

"Thanks for doing this, Mr. Parker," I said.

"Call me Nick, please. Are we ready?"

Nick drove us away from the village along a curving road lined with hedgerows. Several side roads took us past shops, gas stations, then farmhouses, then nothing but open pastures. Here was the postcard landscape I'd been looking for. Finally, we turned onto a drive marked by tall brick pillars that must have once held up gates, but the gates were gone. Past the pillars, we continued on a gravel drive for another quarter of a mile until we approached an honest-to-goodness manor house, three stories of pale stone, rows of sashed windows, peaked roofs and narrow clay chimneys reaching up, and wide steps leading to a porch with a pair of columns marking the front door. The car stopped at the base of the steps.

"It's not Pemberley, but it serves," Nick said, regarding the edifice with obvious fondness. We all climbed out, us three Americans gaping and Nick watching us gape.

"Amelia says that there used to be hedges and flower

beds on that side of the house." Cormac pointed to a stretch of pasture-like lawn that sloped to a border of thick trees.

"The grounds suffered some neglect between the wars. My great-great-grandfather—Amelia's brother, I think—lost his eldest son in the First World War and never really recovered. It's a common story, I think. In his case, he turned his attention from the property and put his time and money toward charities, causes and memorials and the like."

"His eldest son—James? He was just an infant when I left," Cormac murmured, then shook the spell away.

Nick pursed his lips, bemused, then continued. "We've kept up the tradition rather than reestablish the gardens. Especially since the boys in the family have taken to playing cricket on the lawn."

Cormac turned a smile that wasn't his. "The house looks just the same," he said, studying the façade with a narrowed gaze.

"Shall we go inside?" Nick led us up the stairs and drew a ring of keys from his pocket.

This place had some similarities with Ned's two houses. There were bookshelves; old-fashioned wallpaper, textured and covered with flowers; collections of antiques that looked rich to my eyes. The windows had long drapes on brass rings, and carved wood trim surrounded the doorways. Where Ned's houses were opulent, this was homey, lived in. It didn't feel like a museum, and no servants lurked nearby. A box of plastic toys, trucks and balls and things, sat in a corner of the foyer.

"The house is shut up most of the time," Nick said, opening drapes in the front sitting room to let in light. "We spend most of the year in London. We come here on weekends and holidays."

Cormac moved around Parker and headed unerringly to the back of the house; he didn't have to ask or be shown where he was going. We followed, but couldn't match his urgency.

The kitchen was a blend of antique and modern. A brick fireplace stood against one wall, but it seemed decorative, with copper pots and wrought-iron tools hanging around it. A gas stove had replaced the open flame. Cormac—Amelia—looked around for a moment, then went to a whitewashed closet, moved a wooden table, and forced open a door that had been painted over. He revealed a narrow staircase, which he climbed, again without hesitation.

I ducked in behind him. He'd taken his mini-Maglite out of his pocket and shined it ahead, to the darkness. The staircase went up two stories, the height of the house, curving around narrow landings, but the other doorways had been sealed off with squares of plywood. By the time we got to the top, this felt like a cave, smelling of dust and old wood.

The staircase ended in a smallish trapdoor set into the ceiling. Cormac shoved at this a couple of times, but it didn't move.

"You'll need a key," Nick called up. Cormac

flashed the light down past me; Ben and Nick had followed us up the stairs. The latter held his hand out, offering a small, ancient iron key, which I took from him and handed to Cormac. Light in one hand to guide him, he fitted the key into the lock and jiggled it. The mechanism must have been stiff beyond reason—he wrapped his whole hand around the key to get enough leverage to turn it. Finally, though, it clicked, and the attic door popped with a puff of dust.

He swung it open and went inside.

The attic was exactly how I imagined the attic in an old English manor house to be like. The slanted ceiling, bare wooden framework exposed and decorated with dust and cobwebs, forced us to stoop. All along the short walls, and in islands throughout the space, stood wooden crates, antique leather traveling trunks, abandoned pieces of furniture—small tables, worn-out chairs, cabinets, more trunks, some draped with graying, dust-covered drop cloths, some not. Also stored here were odds and ends—coat trees, some with coats on them; a stack of round hatboxes; a pair of saddles set one on top of the other; a weathered sign with a boar painted on it that might have come from a pub. Hazy light seeped in through a ventilation grating and gave off a ghostly, otherworldly gleam.

Nick was right, the family seemed to have kept everything. Surely we should have expected the house and anything inside it Amelia was looking for to be destroyed—nothing survived that long, did it? But here we were, in a country where a two-hundred-year-old building was on the young side.

We crowded into the attic, lingering by the door while Cormac went to one end and counted off boards in the framework, then stopped and counted again. Giving a curt nod, he hauled a large travel trunk, almost as big as he was, away from the wall. The thing must have been full of more artifacts, and my hands itched, wanting to dig through it. But he ignored it. Kneeling, he felt around the floorboards, searching by touch.

The heat closed in; the air was thick, ripe, and didn't move at all. I wanted to pace, but there was no room. Claustrophobia threatened; Ben and Nick blocked the stairs. Nick was fidgeting, tapping fingers on the edge of the open trapdoor.

He whispered, "If this has been a mistake—"

A tiny click sounded, and a square of the floor—flush with the other boards and invisible—lifted out. From the cavity, Cormac drew out a polished wooden case the size of a shoebox and bound in brass, coated with a film of dust. He set it aside, put back the section of the floor, and pushed the trunk back in place. Tucking the treasure box under his arm, he returned to the trapdoor.

Nick looked wonderingly at the box. "I had no idea. No one did."

"That was the point," Cormac said and gestured down the stairs—he couldn't exit until they did.

Nick guided us back to the kitchen and offered a place on a stainless steel prep table.

I imagined a situation where the box had a key that Cormac and Amelia would now have to hunt down, but it didn't. It did have a trick to unlocking it, though, and Amelia remembered. It was a kind of puzzle box; he ran his fingers over it, sliding a brass knob at each of the corners until the latch at the front of the box clicked, and the lid opened. We all leaned forward.

He took out four small leather-bound journals, wrapped shut with twine; a small stack of loose pages with smudged colored drawings on them; an embroidered handkerchief; and a collection of small artifacts: tiny yellowed envelopes, metal amulets on knotted cords, a carved stick, a star woven out of grass.

"This is what you were looking for?" I said.

"Yes," he said, and sighed. He looked at Nick. "Thank you."

He was staring, expression slack. "You're welcome, I think."

Cormac returned the items to the box, businesslike, focused. Mission accomplished.

Nick was still gaping. "I have so many questions—about the family, the history of it all."

Pausing, Cormac looked at him, impatient. I couldn't tell if the expression was his or Amelia's. "What do you want to know?"

Faced with the question, he seemed at a loss. "What was the family really like? I've heard stories about my great-great-grandfather, that he could be quite the tyrant. What was the house like then? Why did Amelia leave? Where did she go? What really happened to her—how is any of this possible?"

Cormac seemed to gather himself, looking into the

distance, the corners of the room, considering what to say. He wasn't used to explaining himself. But this wasn't about him. "Amelia left because she didn't feel welcome. It's a little weird for her thinking she's got family that might be interested in her after all this time."

"As you say, it's been a long time. The family's not what it was."

As he sealed the box again, Cormac looked around at the kitchen, lips pursed and thoughtful. "She'd been expected to marry a friend of the family, but she turned him down. Her parents—and her brother, I think—never forgave her, so she left because she figured she might as well. She couldn't do anything more scandalous than she already had. She assumed they'd be happy to get rid of her."

Nick turned up a wry smile. "If you'd come to the parlor, there's something I'd like to show you."

We left the kitchen and entered a wood-paneled hallway that led past several doorways with polished molding. Through them I saw dimly lit, sparsely furnished rooms.

In the parlor, though, chairs, sofas, and tables crowded around. When the family did come to visit, this must have been where they spent their time.

Nick brought us to the far wall, decorated with faded red wallpaper in a floral pattern. A couple dozen portraits and photos hung on display—obviously of the family. The square, dark painting of a stern gentleman puffed out in his cravat might have been of

Amelia's father or grandfather. There were paintings of women in luxurious Victorian gowns, their hair perfectly curled and their faces as dainty as dolls. Most of the photographs were black-and-white, and must have been more than a hundred years old. They rested safe in wood and gold-colored frames.

Nick pointed to one of a young woman, stern and unhappy looking in the way that people always seemed in old photographs. She wore a dark, fitted dress, and her hair was coiled under a simple hat. Her face was pale, and the way she looked at something just past the camera seemed particularly sad.

"That's her, Lady Amelia," Nick said. "They never took her picture down, even after word came of her trouble in Colorado. The stories I heard of her—she was a black sheep, the skeleton in the closet that every family has. I'm not sure they understood her. But they never disowned her. Now—it's old history, I think."

Cormac studied the picture for a long time, finally reaching out to brush a finger on the bottom of the frame. He turned his gaze to the rest of the pictures, then the rest of the room, and his smile was tired. "Yeah," he said. "Old history."

Nick made apologies—he had an appointment in the village that afternoon and needed to shut up the house again. We made our way back to the front porch.

He said, "How much longer are you in London for? Perhaps we could meet for lunch or dinner—I'd like to introduce you to my wife and children. I'm not sure they'll believe you any more than I did at first, but . . . I want to give them the chance."

I looked at Cormac, who had insisted that Amelia didn't need her family, just her things. He pursed his lips, his brow furrowed.

"I think we'd like that," he said finally.

"Thanks again for bringing us out and going through this," I said, keeping the warm feelings going.

"I wouldn't have missed it. And do call me if you need anything during your stay in London."

Nick drove us back to the train station—he had the timetable memorized and the next departure was scheduled in fifteen minutes.

Ben had to go and break the cheerful mood. "I don't mean to be unfriendly, but as one lawyer to another I have to ask if you're going to let him walk away with that box or if you're going to claim some kind of ownership. You'd have every right to. We can't prove any of this about Amelia in court."

Nick smiled at him in the rearview mirror. "Mr. O'Farrell, I'm a criminal prosecutor. I think my legal talents are better spent in other pursuits."

"Great, I'm in criminal defense. We should talk."

"Oh dear," he said, laughing.

We said our farewells, and Nick Parker drove off to his meeting. As promised, we were on the train back to London within minutes.

Cormac put the box on the table in front of him and went through the contents again: along with the journals the box held homemade charms made of scrap metal, nails, and the like; lengths of knotted yarn; nuts, acorns, shells, pebbles with holes in them, sea glass in blue and green; dried leaves carefully preserved between folded sheets of paper. They might have been the odds and ends and found treasure that any girl would keep secretly in a box hidden from all prying eyes, especially those of a domineering older brother. But I didn't think so, or I didn't think that was all. It all seemed vaguely familiar—they looked like charms, amulets, talismans. Bits and scraps of magic stored away.

When he finished looking at the pieces and skimming the journals, he put them carefully back in the box, which he sealed, then went back to staring out the window. I couldn't guess what he was thinking.

"You going to be okay?" I asked.

Glancing over, he seemed thoughtful. "Yeah. It's weird. There's Amelia, now her family—a lot more family than I ever thought I'd get."

"Like acquiring in-laws," Ben said, and feigning offense I said, "Hey!"

He backpedaled. "I didn't say there's anything *wrong* with your family, just that there's a lot of them. Cormac and I were both only children, and our folks weren't exactly gregarious. The screaming kids thing takes getting used to." My sister Cheryl had two kids who were firmly into the running and screaming phase. I actually sympathized.

Cormac added, "That, and you see your father killed in front of you you start to think you don't deserve a family."

The train hummed along during the long pause before I ventured, "What do you think now?"

He gave an offhand shrug, glanced at the two of us before looking back out the window. "I think I'm doing okay."

Ben had tensed beside me, watching his cousin. After his answer, he let out a sigh and relaxed again. I smiled, because I thought he was doing okay, too.

I had a sudden thought. "Hey—you should come to dinner tonight. We're meeting Luis and his sister. Just a small group thing. It'll be fun."

"No, I don't think so," he said reflexively.

I looked to Ben, pleading for help in persuading his cousin.

"It's up to you," Ben said. "But you have to eat sometime, might as well get a good meal out of it."

"I just don't think I'm up for much more togetherness right now."

"Mr. Badass hunter guy who isn't scared of anything is scared of *dinner*?" I said. He just looked at me sidelong, smirking.

"She's got a point," Ben said.

"You're supposed to be on my side," Cormac grumbled. "I just don't see the point in trying to . . . domesticate me."

Interesting choice of word. I considered for a minute and realized I would probably never stop worrying about Cormac. "I'm not trying to domesticate you. Just . . . don't you think you should get out more?"

"I'm okay. I've always been okay." He almost sounded like he was trying to convince himself.

I said, "Ask Amelia if she'd like to meet a couple of were-jaguars from Brazil."

The train clacked on the rails as we waited for Cormac's response. His lips were pursed, like he'd eaten something sour.

Finally he said, "Amelia thinks it would be interesting to meet a pair of were-jaguars."

"So you're coming?" I said, bouncing.

He didn't say yes, he didn't say no, but he stopped trying to weasel out of the evening.

Chapter 11

LUIS PICKED the restaurant. Feeling some trepidation, I wondered what trendy/sexy place he'd chosen, and if he would hire a guitarist or violinist or an entire mariachi band to serenade and embarrass me, or have roses delivered, as if any of his come-ons were more than teasing. He wasn't so crass to carry it so far. I wasn't so crass as to let him.

In fact, he'd invited us to a steakhouse, naturally. Simply decorated in a clean modern style, black chairs and white tablecloths, it was filled with the familiar and comforting scents of blood and cooking meat.

"This Luis of yours has class," Ben said at the restaurant's entrance.

"You sound surprised," I said.

"I really didn't know what to expect."

"Now are you willing to admit that my taste in men might actually be pretty good?" I looked at him.

"Well, it used to be anyway," he said, putting his arm around my waist.

Cormac didn't have commentary to add. He kept looking around like he expected something to jump out at him.

At the bar near the front door sat the two young women from the conference who'd asked for my autograph. The ones who confused Emma and me by their apparent lack of presence. They waved at me, still giggling and excited. I smiled politely, trying to get some kind of sense or feel for them and what they were. The food and alcohol smells of the restaurant might have been interfering with my nose.

"You know them?" Cormac finally asked.

"I ran into them at the conference. It's just . . . I couldn't get a scent off them." I wrinkled my nose.

"They're Fae, you know."

"What?" I said, then lowered my voice. "Like Elijah Smith? Like Underhill and Puck and crap?" I tried not to stare, but the young women were looking right at us, and their grins seemed . . . conspiratorial. Not at all cute anymore.

Elijah Smith had advertised himself as a faith healer with the ability to cure lycanthropy and vampirism. What he really did was enslave said lycanthropes and vampires and feed on their powers. He'd been a different kind of otherworldly than I'd ever encountered—fairy, according to the experts. Old-school, ancient stories, nothing cute about him.

We were in England, of course there'd be fairies. I should have known.

Cormac handed me an object—one of the charms

from Amelia's box. An iron nail bent in the shape
of a cross, with a dried-out spring of something bound
to it with twine. A four-leaf clover? When I closed my
hand around it, I had to squint and tilt my head, because a haze filtered my vision, like I'd suddenly
entered a TV dream sequence. The two women glowed,
carrying their own special effects. Also, I could
finally smell them—fresh-cut clover, which clashed
strangely with the cooking meat smell in the rest of
the place.

I might have stared at them all night if Cormac
hadn't taken the charm out of my hand and nudged
me. I blinked again, and the haze vanished, noises
rushed back, and everything was as it should be.

"You okay?" Ben asked.

I must have looked like I'd gone to another world
for a moment. In a sense maybe I had. "It's just . . .
what are they *doing* here?"

Cormac shrugged. "For the conference, like everyone else?"

"Kitty!" Luis called, waving from across the restaurant's main room. He and his sister sat at a table in
a prime spot with a view of the room and through
the window to the street outside. The kind of spot a
lycanthrope would pick, to be able to watch the surroundings.

We went to join them, and I looked over my shoulder at the two women—the two Fae. They had gotten
up and were leaving, without a backward glance.
Maybe Cormac was right, and they were here to enjoy

themselves like everyone else. Their not being human shouldn't have been anything to get excited about. Plenty of people at the conference weren't entirely human.

Luis stood and leaned in to kiss my cheek before I could duck, though the gesture seemed cosmopolitan and harmless, even with the dark look Ben gave me. He and Luis didn't shake hands. Neither did he and Cormac. The two regarded each other warily.

Luis presented his companion. "This is my sister, Esperanza."

She was short and fiery, with a round face and a spark in her gaze. I recognized the family resemblance in those eyes. She wore jeans and a beaded tunic shirt, and her long dark hair lay braided over one shoulder. She smelled of jaguar, like Luis.

We made all the introductions, shuffled a bit around the table, jockeying for seats as Ben pointedly insinuated himself between me and Luis, which meant I ended up sitting next to Esperanza. Ben may have wanted to make sure I wasn't sitting next to the charming jaguar, but it meant I was across from him, and he winked at me, dark eyes flashing. Oh dear. I had suddenly forgotten how to flirt. Cormac ended up stuck at the end of the table, probably by design. He could watch us all, and the rest of the restaurant. He'd probably go the whole evening without saying a word.

"So you're the wolf with the big bad mouth," Esperanza said in a quick voice with a lilting accent. I liked her already.

"That's me. I've heard a lot about you, too," I said, and we both looked at Luis.

"I said you'd get along well because you're both crusaders."

"What's your crusade?" Ben asked her.

"Loggers think half the jungles in Brazil are haunted, because of me. They can't get anyone to work in some sections." She smiled with pride.

"Any of them sue you yet?"

She glared. "What are you, a lawyer?"

"Yes, actually."

"Don't you dare give anyone that idea," she said, pointing.

He held up his hands. "Never."

"What do you do for a living?" Esperanza looked at Cormac.

He hesitated a moment before saying, "I'm a consultant."

"In what area?" Luis asked.

He twitched a smile. "Usually when nobody knows what the hell is going on, they call me."

"So can you explain British politics to the rest of us?" Esperanza asked.

"I have limits," he said.

We ordered a bottle of wine; Luis and his sister argued over labels. We ordered food—all of us wanted steaks, rare as the chef would make them, and the server looked at us funny but didn't say anything. I wondered how many lycanthropes from the conference had eaten here this week. The evening progressed nicely after that as we discussed the conference and whether or not we thought it was accomplishing any-thing, the protests, and the state of public recognition and acceptance of the supernatural in our respective countries. Regarding the conference, the jury was still out—while it was nice that everyone was getting together and talking with relatively little fur flying, so to speak, we'd have to wait until it was over to see what came out of it. The protests bothered us all but we were relieved that no actual violence had come of it, so far. Recognition of the supernatural—that was a stickier question.

"It's turning things upside down," Esperanza said. "We're at what's meant to be a scientific conference, trying to apply logic and science to these questions. And back home attendance at religious services is up over forty percent, and people say the reason is that they're scared. If there's magic and monsters in the world, they want some kind of protection against it, and they're going to church to get it."

Ben said, "One of the sessions I went to yesterday was a presentation by a lawyer from Tanzania who's been involved in prosecutions of murderers of albi-nos. Some people there believe the body parts of albi-nos have magical properties, so people with albinism are killed and dismembered and sold off for potions and good-luck charms. The trade's apparently gotten very profitable over the last few years. He said they've had a tough time getting convictions, but got some help when a well-known traditional healer came out and declared that albinos aren't any more magical than anyone else. He also said that not everyone listens to the guy. Magic's real, people say. Why shouldn't this be, too? As if that justifies killing someone for their hair."

"We think we're solving one problem and five more rise up," Esperanza said.

What a topic for dinner table conversation. I was horrified. I pursed my lips, staring into the ruby depths of my wine.

"Kitty?" Ben prompted.

"I'm trying to figure out how to gracefully change the subject to something a little more cheerful," I said. "Like I wonder if there are any fairy rock bands? Surely if they're eating in restaurants they've got rock bands."

Ben said, "Maybe you're just not looking in the right places. Have you *seen* Prince's videos?"

"No, I think a real fairy rock band would be a little more subtle than that. Like Jethro Tull, maybe."

"You call that subtle?"

"Yeah, you're probably right."

"What did I tell you?" Luis said, leaning close to his sister. "Never a dull moment."

"Hmm, I can't wait for your keynote speech," she said—purring, almost. "What are you going to talk about?"

I closed my eyes and rested a hand on my forehead, a gesture of suffering. "Oppression," I said dramatically.

Dinner was good. Nice, mellow, out with friends, no pressure. Ben may even have stopped glaring at Luis for a few minutes. Naturally, the respite couldn't last.

We'd finished eating and had moved on to coffee and more conversation when activity at the front door caught Luis's attention. He stared, frowning.

"What is it?" I asked, glancing over to see.

"Friends of yours?" he said.

Three men, smelling distinctly of lycanthrope, had just entered and surveyed the restaurant. They were tough guys, in leather jackets, designer jeans, and boots. Two had beards, and all were broad through the shoulders. Moving like fighters, they were shoulder to shoulder, attention out—stalking, like predators. The one in front spoke to the maître d', who nodded toward our table. He shook his head in response, and the trio moved to the bar, where they perched warily, uncomfortably.

"Werewolves?" Cormac said.

"Yeah," Ben answered.

"Problem?" the bounty hunter answered.

They were here looking for me, obviously. But this wasn't the place to start trouble. So far they were just watching.

"Let's wait and see," I answered.

We tried to pretend that the strangers weren't obviously here to keep a watch on us.

Esperanza said, "When you first got here, those two girls at the bar—they were watching you, too."

"No, that was just a coincidence," I said, because I couldn't cope with much more paranoia.

"Right," Ben said. "Didn't mean a thing, they were just fairies."

Luis chuckled. "Really? Like leprechauns and pixies?"

"Not exactly," I said, waving him off. "But yeah, sort of."

His smile broadened. "Makes you wonder what else is hanging around the conference."

I sighed. "Djinn, wizards, gods, goddesses."

Esperanza leaned forward. "Did you say gods?"

My mouth opened to start an explanation, then closed again. Where did I start?

We paid our bill, collected our things, and went toward the door. When the trio of werewolves at the bar moved to intercept us in the restaurant's vestibule, I wasn't surprised. I caught the leader's gaze and held it. His companions flanked him just as Ben and Cormac flanked me. Luis and Esperanza stood aside, wary.

"Kitty Norville," he said. His accent was rolling, quick. French or Italian, maybe. His frown twitched, nervous.

"Yes?"

"I serve the Master of Venice. He sends a message—a warning." I stepped forward, offended, ready to argue; he stepped back and looked away, a submissive move. A peace offering. He wasn't here to fight. "A friendly warning. You do not know what you're meddling with. You do not know the true situation among the vampires of Europe and you'd be better to stay away. Your enemies are powerful."

Wasn't anything I didn't already know. The trick to facing off with another wolf pack was to stand your ground, not flinch, not let your gaze slip for even a moment. He was probably six feet tall, leaving me quite a bit shorter than him. I tried not to show it. "A message like that is a sure way to keep me interested. Like waving a red flag at a bull."

"Please, that is not my Master's intention—"

The front door opened again, letting in a cool breath of night air and a fresh wave of werewolf scent. Caleb and one of his wolves, a shorter man with close-shaven hair and a surly expression, entered, and frowned past me to the other wolves.

"You can step away from her now," Caleb said.

The Italian wolf bared his teeth and his voice burred like a growl. "Stay out of this!"

"You're not the one giving orders here, friend." Caleb didn't have to growl, or show his teeth, and he still managed to radiate anger. In response, the Italian wolf hunched his back, bracing his shoulders like hackles stiffening.

"Guys, stop it," I said, putting myself between them, breaking the line of sight. "Everything's just fine. You don't really want to start something here, do you?"

People in the restaurant were staring. The maître d' had been away from her stand, and hovered nearby, gripping her own hands, waiting for a chance to return.

"You want to take this outside?" I said, indicating the doorway.

Of course, no one wanted to be the first one to move, so I did, pushing past Cormac and Ben, then Caleb and his lieutenant, to finally reach the sidewalk outside. I didn't know how we'd managed to all squeeze into that space. The city air smelled fresh and wild after the closeness inside.

The standoff re-created itself on the sidewalk: the Italian wolves attempting to stare me down, Caleb and his wolf staring *them* down, Ben and Cormac tensed for some kind of action, and Luis and Esperanza lingering on the edges, cautiously watching. We were all anxious, but no one was resorting to overtly aggressive movement. It should have been comforting—it didn't matter where we came from, we all spoke the same body language.

I turned to the alpha of the Italian wolves. "What's your name?"

He hesitated before answering, "I serve the Master of Venice."

"Oh, come on, what's that supposed to mean?"

He shut his mouth, pressing lips into a line.

"Okay. Fine. So this warning . . . is it a generic 'here be dragons' kind of warning or is there something specific I need to be looking for?"

He said, firmly, "Don't meddle. Stay at your conference where you belong. Protect yourself—your pack."

"My pack?"

"Them," he said, nodding at Ben and Cormac. "Your friends. Your army wolf."

Tyler. "He doesn't have anything to do with this."

"You won't get to decide that."

I stepped up to him. "Is something going to happen? What is it? What do you know?"

He backed away, slouching—he hadn't meant to push me, I gathered. He didn't want to fight. He probably hadn't expected me to stand up to him at all. "I—I don't know anything. Just . . . we don't know what's going to happen, none of us do. But the situation—it's dangerous."

"I already knew that."

"Please believe me—my Master sympathizes. He only wants to help."

"I'm not sure he's the kind of guy I'd want help from," I said.

Recovering his confidence—his dignity—the alpha wolf bowed his head in a human gesture of respect. "Then I apologize for interrupting your evening."

He nodded at his two companions, and the trio stalked away, moving gracefully along the street and into the night. We stared after them.

"They must think you're pretty important to be sending you warnings," Ben said.

"I think I need to call Tyler," I said. Not for any particular reason. Just to make sure he was okay. I turned to Caleb and pointed. "And where did you come from? I don't need you babysitting me, you know."

"I wasn't babysitting you," Caleb said. "I was trailing them." He nodded down the street where the Italian wolves had turned the corner.

"Then what were they up to, really?"

"Exactly what that alpha said, I think. Some of the vampires want you staying out of things but are polite enough not to actually bump you off. Nice, isn't it?"

"Real nice," I muttered. "Now I'm going to be worried about everyone for the rest of the week. Even more worried." The shadows all held werewolf packs, vampires, fairies. Who knew what else?

"Think we should follow them, gov?" Caleb's lieutenant said, hands shoved in pockets of his jacket, nodding after the Italians.

"Certainly," he said. "Might be educational."

"You'll call me if you find anything juicy?" I said.

The two British wolves started down the street after the others. Caleb tipped an imaginary hat at me. "Of course."

We watched them leave, and the multitude of shadows left my spine prickling.

"This conspiracy needs a flow chart," Ben said.

"You were right," Cormac added. He wore the closest thing to a grin I'd ever seen on him. "Amelia thinks this is just fascinating."

"Great," I said, and sighed.

Lingering by the wall of the building, Luis and his sister looked like they should have been munching on a bucket of popcorn: wide-eyed, fascinated.

I turned to Luis. "What was that you said? Never a dull moment?"

"I won't argue," he said.

"I'm impressed," Esperanza said. "Handling all

those wolves? That big one was actually cowering, I think."

"It's either that or get eaten. I'd prefer not to get eaten."

"Jaguars are solitary," she said. "Makes it easier."

She might have been right. We started walking back to the hotel. I dug in my pocket for my cell phone so I could call Tyler and see if he'd gotten any mysterious visits or warnings.

When I looked up after punching in his number, the two Fae women stood on the sidewalk in front of me, blocking the way. Without Cormac's charm, they really did look like ordinary women, excitable grad students living it up at a conference. Maybe they were that, maybe fairies had a reason to go to school. But I had to remind myself that they were more than they seemed.

And one of them was holding what looked like a tiny bottle, maybe a perfume bottle with a spray nozzle, and she was getting ready to fire.

I stopped and stared, and the rest of my party crowded in behind me. We all froze, the two women crouched like they were about to run away, us gaping in astonishment. Not many people could sneak up on a pack of lycanthropes—and a human with his pockets full of second sight charms.

"Hi," I said finally, as if they were acquaintances I hadn't expected to run into.

By their crinkling eyes and widening grins, I guessed that they were about to do something with that perfume spritzer, and that I probably wouldn't like it. I brought out a little Wolf, hunched up my shoulders, and stepped forward.

"Okay, just who are you guys and why do you keep showing up in my space?"

"Um . . ." The one with the spritzer hid her hands behind her back. "How 'bout we pretend you never saw us?"

"But—" I stopped again, because a newcomer was standing behind them, and she'd appeared just as suddenly as the first two had.

Tall, striking, she appeared regal despite the patchwork nature of her clothing: scuffed boots, a flowing gypsy skirt, an oversized lumpy sweater, and a faded, lacy shawl. Her golden hair flowed in thick, lush waves down her back. She wore a smile like she knew secrets.

"I'll take that, thank you very much," she said, plucking the spritzer out of the young woman's hand and pocketing it somewhere. "And after all that talk about not causing trouble."

The two fairies weren't giggling anymore. One was biting her lip, the other had her hands to her face, flinching and squinting as if expecting a loud noise. They cringed away from the woman—and who was she? I stole a glance back at Cormac for confirmation; he gave me a single nod. So yeah, she was one of them, too. Even *more* of one.

"Exactly what kind of trouble are we talking about here?" I said. They were avoiding looking at me, and the regal woman had put her arms around them, drawing them close. I had never seen two people look more sheepish.

"Oh, just a little old-school mischief," she said, giving them a squeeze. "A spot of nectar in the eyes, a bit of confusion with mortal affections." She looked at me, and Luis. "Never mind that I told them to stay away."

I needed a second to work out the puzzle. I'd been seeing the two fairies all weekend, so they'd been seeing me, which meant they knew about the history between me and Luis, they way he'd been carrying on, Ben's reaction—

"You mean like some kind of *A Midsummer Night's Dream* shtick? For real?" I said.

The one who'd had the spritzer perked up. "Never gets old! Ow!" she added, when her captor pinched her shoulder.

"We'll just be getting out of your way now," she said and grabbed the two by their shirts to drag them off. They didn't even struggle.

"Wait—that's it?" I said.

She paused, glanced back. "What more do you want?"

I wanted an interview with her for the show. What were their kind doing in the middle of the city? What did they get out of playing pranks on us? On anyone? I realized: I wanted all her secrets. Wasn't going to get them, no doubt. "How do we know they won't come right back and bother us again?"

She pointed at her two charges, who huddled where they were. Convinced they'd stay put, she turned back to me, tilted her head. An odd expression, when she'd been commanding before. My image of her kept changing, even though I hadn't looked away. "You want a guarantee? Or a wish—that's usually what mortals ask for. All right, then—what's your wish?"

One thing popped into my mind, and it wasn't an interview this time. If I could have *anything*, I knew. I didn't even have to think about it. Whether or not she could even grant such a wish didn't occur to me—it couldn't hurt to ask, right? I just had to say it, and if she said no I wouldn't have lost anything, I couldn't be more disappointed than I already was. But if she said yes . . .

"Nobody answer that," Cormac said. "It's a trick."

I hesitated, my mouth open to speak, and realized I could be more disappointed. I took a deep breath to settle myself, and the exhale was a little shaky.

The woman put her hands on her hips and glared at Cormac. "You've had dealings with us before, I see."

"Not hard to read a few stories," Cormac said. He glanced to me. "She'll twist your words, you'd get what you asked for but not what you meant. Or she'd ask for more in return than you could give. Better to ask for a rain check." He spoke with a confidence that I wasn't feeling. "We accept your offer, to be redeemed at a later date."

"You make us beholden to you," the woman—the

leader of them—said, disbelieving. "Do you think that's wise?"

"We'll see," he said.

I hoped he and Amelia knew what they were doing. They seemed to know what they were doing. Did Cormac ever seem otherwise? Would we know if he didn't?

"Well then. I owe you a wish."

"We'll need a token of that," Cormac said.

"You're a demanding mortal." The woman pulled a scarf from some pocket or other with a flourish. Pale gold, wispy, and floral, it floated in her grip as if it might have been a ribbon of mist, until she dropped it in Cormac's outstretched hand, when it became just a strip of cloth.

My phone started ringing. I'd had it in my hand the whole time, set to Tyler's number. I couldn't remember if I'd actually dialed him or not. I stepped away from the others and answered.

"Hello?"

"Hey, Kitty, did you just try to call me?" the soldier said.

"Yeah, I did. I'm sorry, I was distracted."

"You think?" he said, chuckling.

How did I explain the last ten minutes? I didn't. "I just wanted to check in. Have you had any weird encounters? Any more random recruiters or warnings? Vampires hanging around?"

"You mean more than you'd expect at a conference on the supernatural?" He was still chuckling, and I flushed, chagrined.

"Yeah, exactly."

"Not really. But I do feel like I'm walking around with my hackles up all the time."

"Yeah, I know the feeling. Well, let me know if . . . I don't know. You see something weird. There's some bad politics around just now."

"I know the drill. You just look after yourself, okay? I'll talk to you later."

I hung up and returned to the group. The fairies, the regal woman and her two underlings, were gone. The others were looking back at me with bemused expressions to match my own.

"Where'd they go?" I said.

"They just left," Ben said. "None of us really saw them go, but there you are."

And no matter how fast I ran after them, I wouldn't find them. Which didn't mean they also still weren't lurking, spying. I grumbled, "I can't keep looking over my shoulder like this."

"This evening's been much more exciting than Luis promised," Esperanza said.

"What can I say? I know how to have a good time," I said. "What are we going to do with a fairy favor?" My hands itched to touch that scarf, still lying in Cormac's hand. Would it feel like cloth or something else? The hunter unceremoniously wadded it up and shoved it in his jacket pocket.

"Best not to use that word. It annoys them," Cormac said. "As for what to do with it—we'll find out when we need it. This gives us a chance to plan. Maybe mitigate the unintended consequences."

He was right, this was the smart thing to do. I still wondered.

"You had a wish right on the tip of your tongue, didn't you?" Ben said.

"Yeah, I did." I reached for him, and he gathered me into his arms. "And is it me or did that woman look kind of like Stevie Nicks? Is Fleetwood Mac a fairy rock band?"

He pulled away just enough to be able to look down his nose at me. "It's you, and I don't think so."

Chapter 12

MATT AND Ozzie set up time at a recording studio near the convention, making it easier for me to haul in delegates for interviews. I'd record as many interviews as I could through the afternoon and into the evening, assuming I could convince any vampires to show up, which I hadn't been able to do yet. Ned and Emma said no, I didn't know how to get in touch with Marid, Mercedes was out of the question, and the few others I saw hanging around seemed to be spying on me. I'd have asked them for interviews, but they always vanished before I could get close enough. I thought of using the fairy wish to ask for an interview, but I also had an idea of how that would go—not the way I wanted it to.

Matt was with me online. He and the local engineer had arranged a whole techy solution, allowing us to record the show, upload it, and deliver it to Matt, who could get it immediately and be able to edit the show for Friday night.

"Greetings, listeners, you've tuned in to *The Midnight Hour.* I'm your super-vigilant host, and this week's episode has been prerecorded in London, England. Let me explain: I'm here attending the First International Conference on Paranatural Studies, which has brought together hundreds of scientists, academics, and pundits like me to discuss where we stand on the topic of the supernatural in society, and recognition of the same. I've been having a great time, learning lots, and I'm going to report to you on what I've been up to the last few days. I have a whole crowd of fascinating people for you to meet. I'll be talking with a were-jaguar who is an environmental activist in Brazil. We'll meet an attorney from Tanzania working to prosecute those accused of murdering albinos in the name of witchcraft. I've met a music critic who's been tracking down rumors of fairy music in the modern rock scene, a werewolf with a seat in the House of Commons, and we'll be visiting with an old friend of the show, Jules Simpson from TV's *Paradox PI* and member of the Society for Psychical Research.

"As many of you have figured out by now, I really like talking. Sometimes I even like listening. I've been enjoying myself immensely because this week has been full of both. Some stats: the conference has around eighteen hundred attendees from twenty-three countries—not bad for the first time out. The six days of the conference include forty presentations on topics ranging from the supernatural's impact on the legal system and the depiction of vampires in popular culture. You'll forgive me for avoiding that one, I'm sure. I've always advocated shining lights into dark corners and dragging the unknown into the open, and we've spent the week doing just that.

"Right now I have a couple of previous guests with me: Sergeant Joseph Tyler, a veteran of the war in Afghanistan who also happens to be a werewolf, and Dr. Elizabeth Shumacher. I was delighted to discover that they're both here at the conference to discuss what happens when the military utilizes soldiers with nonhuman abilities . . ."

With me egging them on, Tyler and Shumacher talked for an hour. Matt could edit it into a sharp half-hour segment we could all be proud of. Next up was Esperanza, who was happy to discuss her experiences tracking illegal logging in the Amazon basin, and how her lycanthropy—the result of an attack—has helped her rather than limited her. She was articulate and enthusiastic, I hardly had to prompt her at all. The best kind of guest. Nell Riddy, the conference director, needed a little more nursing along, but we still managed to produce a good conversation about how a childhood encounter with fairies put her on the path to studying cryptozoology, and from there to paranormal research.

I might actually pull off entertaining *and* informative with this episode. I was feeling awfully pleased with myself. Of course, I couldn't entirely avoid the bizarre. It wouldn't be an episode of *The Midnight Hour* without it.

"Martin Pearce runs a popular blog, Enchantment

Underground, discussing music and the supernatural. Martin, thanks for joining me," I said.

"Thanks for inviting me." He was young and jittery, bouncing a foot and tapping a hand on his knee. A DJ—anybody in the music business—ought to know better than to make noise like that during a recording. The sound didn't carry, fortunately. Dressed modern hipster, he wore a T-shirt for what must have been a band, though one I'd never heard of, a jacket, and fashionably distressed jeans. He had a regional British accent, northern and industrial if I had my broad strokes right. I'd tracked him down via his blog and invited him on the show.

"You have some interesting ideas about how modern music and tales of the supernatural intersect," I said. "You want to give me the rundown?"

"Yes, right. Do you know anything about, well, the Folk?"

Oh, that he should ask me that now . . . "Fairies, right?"

He squirmed in his chair. "We don't like to use *that* word, but yes, just so. But you've heard of them."

I debated telling him about last night's adventure, but merely smiled encouragingly. "Yes, a bit."

"In the old stories, the Folk love music. Playing it, listening to it, dancing to it. People still play traditional jigs and tunes rumored to come from the Folk. Some stories say they'd use music to entrance people, lure them Underhill, or set them dancing until they collapse with exhaustion. What if that still happens, but on a much larger scale?"

"All we have to do is figure out which bands are torture to listen to," I said.

"Yeah! Well, no, not like that exactly. Today, with as much music as we have, and as many ways to play and distribute it, they must be involved somehow. They'd hardly be able to stay away. Which brings me to the Beatles."

My eyes widened. This hadn't been on his blog; he'd saved it for the show. Awesome. "The Beatles were fairies?"

"Please, don't say that word. Maybe not like *that*. Not specifically *them,* maybe. But all those screaming insane crowds? The reactions they got? No one had ever seen anything like it. They must have had some kind of crazy magic. What if it was a case of elven magic intersecting with modern rock and roll?"

Or maybe they were just really talented songwriters and musicians . . . "Hmm. It would certainly give a whole new meaning to 'I Am the Walrus.'"

"Yeah. Or no—wait a minute. I'm not talking about the lyrics so much as the *effect*."

"The screaming hordes of teenage girls we've all seen in the concert footage."

"The Beatles started an *epidemic* of that sort of thing," Martin said with obvious awe. "Almost had to be supernatural, don't you think?"

I rather thought it may have had something to do with the widespread availability of television ushering in an era of hyped-up pop culture and mass consumerism. But I was willing to humor him.

"You may very well be onto something. Let me

ask you a question: should there be an effect with recorded music, or is it only live?"

"That's the question, isn't it? It would seem to only have an effect on live audiences, but they've sold millions of records. In fact, I'm developing a study that would examine this exact question. If only I can find the funding for it. I've applied for several grants. No luck yet, I'm afraid." He slouched a little.

"I'm sure it's only a matter of time before someone steps forward to help out." Coming on my show certainly wouldn't hurt. I wondered if I'd opened a can of worms.

"That's just it—this isn't frivolous research. It's an *investment.*"

"Oh?"

"Oh yes! If I can figure out what the magical *thing* is, package it somehow, then sell it—can you imagine?"

"Didn't they do that already with the Backstreet Boys? And the Spice Girls?"

He frowned. "Oh . . . oh, someone's already done it is what you're saying?"

Many times over, I thought. "Fairy magic really is the only explanation for some of that music, isn't it?"

"I'm going to have to think about this." He was staring at the microphone, wide-eyed, contemplating whole new vistas of potential, undoubtedly.

"And I think we'll wrap it up there," I said. "Thank you very much for coming to talk with me, Martin."

"Oh—yes. Thank *you!*"

A familiar, back-of-the-neck chill crawled along my spine. *I've created a monster . . .*

My toughest guest came right in the middle of the session, for good or ill. I let the studio staff deal with her, figuring she'd be more at ease. I wanted this woman to *talk*. One of the techs ushered her in and guided her to the guest seat at the other end of the table.

She was human, average, in nice jeans, a blouse and blazer, a thin gold necklace and stud earrings. Her hair was short, dyed dark blond with highlights. In her forties, of average height and build, she looked utterly normal and nondescript. I never would have picked her out of the crowd on any street in any town in Middle America.

I thought about approaching her, to try to get her to shake my hand—or to make her refuse to shake. But I could tell by her frown and the hard edge in her stare how that was likely to go. I let the tech deal with her, fitting headphones and showing her the mike, while I sat back and smiled.

As soon as she was settled, the sound guy gave me a cue, and I launched in.

"I'm feeling a tiny sense of victory in even convincing my next guest to come on the show. But she's here, and I'm very much looking forward to our chat. Tracy Anderson chairs an organization calling themselves Truth Against the Godless, members of which have been out in force picketing the conference. They've gone on record denouncing government recognition and public acceptance of people with supernatural identities. Ms. Anderson, welcome to the show. Thank you for being here."

She and her group had chartered a plane to bring them and their protest banners to London. They'd been planning and organizing to come here for a year. The level of commitment was almost admirable.

Calmly, hands folded on her lap, she said, "I want to make clear that I'm only here because you offer a chance to speak to the audience that most needs to hear our message." She sat as far away from me as she could and still reach the microphone. I had thought she would avoid looking at me at all. But she stared at me, lines of tension around her mouth. I couldn't help but stare back.

"Well, I know I'm taking you away from your busy protest schedule, and I appreciate it," I said.

"My work calls for many sacrifices."

"So does mine, oddly enough. My first question. You're one of the founders of Truth Against the Godless. What prompted you to start this group in the first place?"

"Frankly, we started the group because we were appalled. I find it *reprehensible* that evil has been given such a free rein in today's world. To speak, to act, to corrupt our youth—"

"Evil. I understand you mean something pretty specific by that, and it's not people who set fire to kittens."

She scowled at me. "You know what I'm talking about."

"My listeners may not, so if you'll just spell it out so we're on the same page."

"People like *you*. Werewolves and vampires. Monsters. Satanists. Threats to God-fearing people everywhere."

"I always feel the need in conversations like this to point out how often God-fearing people themselves have been threats to God-fearing people, and everyone else."

"This is exactly what I'm talking about—you think having a platform gives you a right to twist my words. Someone has to stand up to people like you. To denounce you."

"Well, good luck with that. I do need to say, though I always seem to make the mistake that it's blazingly obvious, that part of the whole point of this conference is identifying the underlying causes—and biological implications—of vampirism and lycanthropy. These things have a mechanism. God and Satan have nothing to do with it."

"Oh, but they do! These aren't diseases, they're the marks of Lucifer. It's the same story—science is leading you astray."

"I'm going to ask you the same question I ask all of you who express these beliefs—if I was an embodiment of Satan, don't you think I'd know it? Wouldn't I have some sense of it? Wouldn't I actually, you know, go around trying to do horrible things to people? To be a minion of Satan don't you have to *decide* to be a minion of Satan? I guarantee you I didn't make that choice."

She huffed with apparent exasperation. "You must have done *something*. You may not have consciously *chosen* to become a werewolf, but something set you on that path and put you in Satan's way and here you are, spreading your lies and propaganda."

That actually stopped me for a moment, my jaw opening at the start of a word, only I couldn't decide which one. I didn't think much of her God, if that was the world she lived in.

"You're saying I was attacked and left in the woods to die as *punishment*? Really? What could I have possibly done to deserve that?" My question held a tone of bafflement.

I didn't think she'd actually have an answer for me. I should have known better. "I know this is a personal question and you're probably hoping to keep this secret—but at some point in your life you had an abortion, didn't you?"

If she'd been on the phone I'd have hung up on her by now. The perils of the in-person interview. I needed a moment to shuffle through any number of inappropriate responses, and there were oh so many of them.

I finally leaned back in my chair and regarded her, my expression stony. "So that's what it takes to become a minion of Satan, is it? Good to know. For future reference. So what do men have to do?"

Her lips pressed even tighter. "Mock me all you want, but I'm right. We're *all* right, and you and all your ungodly scientist friends will burn in hell."

"We have to believe in hell first."

"You may not believe in Satan and hell, but they certainly believe in you," she announced, giving a decisive nod.

I had to think about that for a minute before answering, "I don't think that's how that saying usually goes."

"It's still true."

"Actually, I think it's irrelevant. I'm a werewolf. I'm not a bad person. A lot of the werewolves I know aren't. Even a big chunk of the vampires I know aren't bad people. And yet you'd condemn us all?"

"That's right." She beamed like she'd scored a point.

Time to get out while the getting was good. "All righty then. Anything else you'd like to tell my listeners before I kick you out?"

"No. And I'll show *myself* out." She did just that, yanking off the headset and practically launching herself from her seat to march to the door. She turned the wrong way into the hall and had to march back across the doorway in the other direction. I'd have laughed if I hadn't been gritting my teeth.

"And that's a special kind of crazy for you," I said into the mike. "Once again, that was Tracy Anderson of Truth Against the Godless, which has been protesting the conference all week because they think Satan is in charge, or something. I dunno. Let's take a break, and when we come back I'll have another guest on for you."

The recording light went out, and I leaned back in my chair, rubbing my hair.

Matt talked at me from the Skype call on the laptop. "Kitty, why do you love baiting these people so much? You know what they're going to say, and you're not going to change their minds."

"Know thine enemy," I said tiredly. "People have to know the crazies are out there."

"Well, you sure know how to find them."

"I keep thinking if I give them enough rope they'll hang themselves right on the air and I can save my breath."

"If a whole crowd of people like that are protesting out there, you must be having a hell of a time."

He didn't know the half of it, all the crap I wasn't talking about on the air or anywhere else. "It's been . . . interesting. But good. I have to think the good guys are winning."

"Who's defining good?"

Yeah, that was the problem, wasn't it? In her own mind, Tracy Anderson thought she was freaking Joan of Arc. I thought she was a petty little woman with fears so gigantic she had to lash out at *something* to feel safe. Werewolves and vampires were pretty easy targets, all things considered. I almost understood it.

Didn't make it right.

Chapter 13

I FINISHED MY interviews well after dark, and was cranky and in desperate need of some dinner. Another day gone, and the conference was already half over. Despite all my on-air proclamations to the contrary, I felt like I hadn't accomplished anything. But I had to keep up a good front. We were supposed to be saving the world, weren't we? Maybe I ought to set the bar a little lower. The conference was half over, and we hadn't had any riots yet. There, that was something to be proud of.

Ben met me at the studio, and we walked back to the convention. Emma was going to meet us there with the car to take us back to the town house.

"Where's Cormac?" I asked once we'd left the studio.

"Nick Parker invited him to dinner, and he said yes. Apparently Amelia wants to meet the family."

"Huh. That's so weird."

"I don't know. I think it'll be good for him. He actually seems to be developing social skills."

"You mean he can't hide anymore," I said.

"Yeah, that, too."

"Hmm, to be a fly on that wall." I wished them all well. After a hundred years in limbo, Amelia was getting a second chance. A happy ending of sorts.

"How'd your interviews go?" Ben asked.

I sighed. "Maybe Matt can fix it all in post-production."

He chuckled. "That bad?"

I winced. "I can never tell. I got some great people to come in, recorded a couple of really great interviews. We ought to be able to get a good couple of hours of show out of it."

"But?"

"It feels like spitting into the wind sometimes."

"Here I was thinking this whole conference would never have happened without all your work."

"Work, or mouthing off?"

"Yeah," he said and put his arm over my shoulders.

"Thanks, I guess. But is it for the best? Would it have been better if this had all stayed underground?"

He waited a few steps before saying, "I don't know."

I tried to imagine a world in which I didn't have my show—in which I had never announced to everyone that I was a werewolf—and had a tough time with it. I'd still be bottom of the pecking order of the pack at home, the old alphas would probably still be alive, and still beating me up. I'd have never met Alette, Emma, Dr. Shumacher, Tyler, Luis, Esperanza, or a dozen other of my friends. Including Cormac. And Ben would be dead, because I wouldn't have been there for Cormac to bring him to, to save him after he'd been attacked.

I reached around and hugged him. "I wouldn't want things any different." He kissed the top of my head.

We continued on a few more steps, warm and comfortable, before Ben said, "I suppose this would be a bad time to ask you how your speech is coming along."

I groaned. "I still haven't written it. What am I going to do?"

"You can always wing it. That might be kind of fun."

"For who?"

"*I'd* bring popcorn to that," he said, and I fake-punched his shoulder.

We reached the hotel. A few protestors lingered, gathered behind the police barricades and holding their signs. Most of them seemed to have given up for the evening.

Vampire-centric programming would be going on now. I turned my nose to the air and watched the clumps of people that had gathered outside the front doors, smoking and talking while waiting for taxis. A few vampires stood here and there, indistinguishable from other conference attendees, unless you knew what to look for: their skin seemed to radiate cold, and they didn't breathe, though some of them did smoke as an affectation. They didn't have to worry about a pesky thing like lung cancer, after all.

Emma wasn't on the sidewalk, so we went inside to look around. The lobby was still fully lit, busy. All the chairs and sofas were occupied with intense-looking people chatting. I studied the crowd, my nose working to take in scents.

I spotted Emma at the end of a darkened hallway, talking to an earnest, dark-haired man dressed in business-casual. He was a vampire—maybe he'd been at the shindig the other night, but I didn't think so. Thinking Emma had business and I might be interrupting, I held back to wait for her to finish. They had to know Ben and I were there; I hadn't been trying to mask my approach. But she'd crossed her arms, her stance was rigid, and the other vampire had moved close to her, looming. When Emma shook her head and looked away, I had to intervene. If I made a mistake I could be embarrassed about it later.

"Hey, Emma, there you are!" I said in my most chipper blond-girl voice.

The stranger glared at me, maybe hoping he could use his vampire powers to flay me alive. Since I wouldn't meet his gaze, he couldn't do anything.

"Hi, Kitty," she said, eyeing the other vampire. Her voice was even; I couldn't tell if she was happy to see me, pleased at the interruption, or what.

"I'm Kitty," I said, sticking my hand out, focusing on the guy's chest to avoid looking at his eyes. I could just about feel Ben wincing behind me.

I couldn't tell anything about the guy. He might have been Middle Eastern and pale or European and tan. He might have been a newly turned vampire like Emma, or have the dust of centuries in his bones. Whoever he was, wherever he came from, he sneered at my hand and walked away, into the darkness of the corridor behind him.

Emma watched after him, even when he turned the next corner and disappeared.

"Well, he seemed friendly," I said.

"Let's get out of here," she said, sounding tired. She gave Ben a thin smile as she walked past him toward the doors. She didn't even seem bothered that Ben had slipped a stake into his hand. Cormac had probably given it to him—just in case, no doubt.

"What exactly were you planning on doing with that?" I said, nodding to the weapon.

"What do you think?" he said, returning it to an inner jacket pocket.

"This isn't the place or time for that," I said.

"You know what Cormac would say? That you trust them too much," he said.

"No. I trust them just enough. I'm not powerful enough to pose a threat to any of them, and because of my place in the public eye, they can't risk hurting me. In the meantime, we can all sit around pretending like we're friends while we try to get information out of each other. It's all politics."

By the time we joined Emma on the sidewalk outside, the car had arrived and we piled in for the ride back to Mayfair. As much as I wanted to grill her about who that vampire was and what they'd been talking about, I kept quiet. She was in silent, inscrutable mode. The vampire default.

The car parked in the courtyard of Ned's town

house. Another car was already there: the sexy Bugatti from the other night.

"Ned has visitors?" I said.

"Apparently," Emma said, brow furrowed. So she wasn't expecting anyone.

In the foyer, one of the house's staff approached. "Miss, Master Alleyn has visitors and would like you to join him in the study."

"Thank you."

Ben leaned into me. "You're going to try to get yourself invited to that meeting, aren't you?"

"Of course I am."

"One of these days, we're going to take a real vacation. None of the skulking," he said.

That sounded so nice. "Someplace with a warm, sunny beach."

"Vampires don't hang out on sunny beaches. Sounds good to me," he said.

Smiling back at him, I sidled up to Emma.

"Visitors, huh? Anyone I'd be interested in meeting?"

"Oh, probably," she said, then considered a moment. "Why not? You want to come along?"

She led us through the house to a set of double doors made of some rich, polished wood that smelled opulent, and knocked softly before opening it. We entered another manor-house library, filled with books, priceless furniture, and portraits, still impressive if not as grand and packed with amazing artifacts as the house in Dulwich.

Ned and two other vampires sat before the fireplace. One of them was Marid, looking as worn and kindly as he had the other night. He smiled when I entered, as if pleased to see me, and I wasn't sure how I felt about that. Did he see *me,* or did he see another tool in his machinations? The other was the one in the poet's shirt I'd accused of knowing Byron. Tonight, he looked practically modern, in a T-shirt, dark blazer, and slacks. He appeared younger than the others, which didn't mean anything. Raising an eyebrow, he turned to Ned, presumably for explanation.

As always, Ned was at ease in the surroundings, in a frock coat and trousers and silk shirt. "Ah, Emma, excellent." He greeted her with a broad smile. "And you've brought our guests. Ms. Norville, I must apologize, I've been a terrible host, wrapped up in all this other business. But then, so have you, I gather—what exactly were you doing in Sevenoaks yesterday?"

He was keeping tabs on us—I shouldn't have been surprised. I could still be annoyed. Giving him a sweet smile, I said, "It was a personal matter."

"Not even a little hint?" he said, beseeching—teasing me. My expression didn't flinch.

"Are you sure she should be here?" said the younger-looking vampire.

"She *is* intriguing," Ned said. "Marid, what say you?"

"I'd be interested to hear the Wolf Queen's opinion," Marid said.

"I'm not the Wolf Queen," I muttered.

The young one laughed. "All right, color me intrigued."

"Ms. Norville, Mr. O'Farrell. Meet Antony, Master of Barcelona."

"The Antony with the car?" Ben said, thumb over his shoulder pointing to the courtyard, and Antony turned up a hand in assent. Ben smirked. "Nice. Subtle."

"Can we trust them?" Antony demanded of Ned.

"They're *all* intriguing," Ned answered.

"Can we trust *you*?" I said back to him. "Whose side are you on?"

"That's too simplistic a question," the Spanish vampire said, and I wanted to scream.

I laughed instead. "How hard can it be? Are you a good guy or a bad guy?"

He raised a sardonic brow.

Ned said, "Kitty . . ."

I took a deep breath, counted to ten, and groped toward politeness. "I'm sorry for interrupting. What were we discussing?"

Antony's chuckle was nervous. "I must confess, Ned, it's disconcerting to hear a werewolf speak to us in such tones."

"Wolf Queen," Marid said calmly.

"You may convince me yet," Antony answered.

"That's not what you were talking about," I said. "In fact, I'm betting you were talking about Mercedes Cook and who's thrown in with Roman."

Antony made a pointed sigh. "Right. Mercedes and that bastard Jan are here because they want to move against you, Ned. They'll put one of Dux Bellorum's puppets in your place."

"Jan?" I said. "The smarmy guy with the goatee?"

Ned's lips twitched. "Yes. And I've seen no evidence of their intentions. Mercedes would only act if the situation were unstable, and it's not."

"She'll act precisely because you are so comfortable. With London in her pocket, her hold—Dux Bellorum's hold—on Europe would be unbreakable."

Ned shook his head. "I'm not a lynchpin."

"Talbot approached me," Emma said, her clear voice a contrast to the others. They turned, startled by the interruption. "He suggested I start spying on you, Ned."

"Talbot, who is that?" Antony said.

"Talbot is one of Jan's," Marid said.

Antony's expression darkened. "It's a very short step from asking her to spy on you to using her to remove you."

Ned steepled his hands and gazed at the air, distracted. "They targeted you because you're new. A stranger to them."

"They didn't understand that they weren't asking me to betray you, but Alette," Emma said.

"You're Alette's, then?" Antony said. "I don't think anyone knows that. The old girl's still got her hand in it. Good."

Emma turned away, her smile thin, pained.

Ned said, "It's their usual mistake—discounting you Yankees entirely. To think, they all believed Alette mad for moving her household. But the lack of competition overseas made her—and her followers—powerful. I'm curious—what did he offer you?"

"The usual. Second-in-command of London. I'm not old enough to want that kind of power. They'd give it to me, then destroy me with it."

"I'm very glad Alette sent you to me, Emma love." He caught her hand and kissed it lightly.

"She wanted me to learn," Emma said, sounding young and tired. "I'm not sure she had any idea I'd get caught up in all this."

By way of interruption I said, "I had my own encounter last night. Werewolves saying they served the Master of Venice delivered a message telling me to stay out of things, for my own good."

"They even sounded worried about us," Ben added.

Ned nodded thoughtfully. "Worried that you wouldn't be safe, or worried that you're powerful enough to cause trouble?"

"Who knows," Ben said.

"Filipo hasn't said a word all week," Antony said. "What side does this put him on? And why talk to her?"

"Maybe he's a fan," I said, shrugging. "The whole thing makes me more curious, not less."

"You certainly are something of a wild card," Ned said.

I crossed my arms. "You really think Mercedes will try to replace you as Master of London?"

He shrugged. "I've no idea. I'll be on alert, certainly. But this is about more than London."

"It's the public question, Kitty," Marid said. "So much has been revealed. How much, then, do we con-

tinue to hide? Is hiding even the right response anymore?"

"Exactly," Antony said, pointing. "We bring the
fight to the public, then no one can hide."

"You're in my territory now," I said, quirking a
grin. "I can tell you all about publicity."

"Do you advocate it?" Marid asked.

"Jury's still out," I said.

Antony said, "Right now the most visible public
vampire is Mercedes Cook. She's beautiful, amiable,
charming, has given dozens of interviews—and she's
a follower of Dux Bellorum. We have to counter that,
get one of our own in the public eye."

"You have someone in mind to be your first public
vampire?" I said. "'Cause you know, I could help
out with that. It's not too late to get in on this week's
show."

They all looked at Ned, who rolled his eyes.

"It's perfect," Antony argued. "Cook was already
famous before she declared herself. It endeared her to
the public. Ned can do even better than that—he was
famous four hundred years ago! She's an actress,
you're an actor—who better?"

"I will have Shakespeare, Marlowe, and John Donne
scholars camped on my doorstep for the rest of eternity.
Do you have any idea what I'd go through?" Ned said.
He leaned conspiratorially toward me. "I married Donne's daughter, did you know that?" I hadn't.

To get a scoop like that, to be the one to help Ned
Alleyn go public as a vampire . . . my talk show

personality was absolutely drooling. But the rest of me knew it wasn't that simple.

"It only works if people believe you're really Ned Alleyn," I said. "Can you prove it? Link the person you are now with who you were then?"

"That won't be the issue," Ned said. "Mercedes Cook has endeared herself to the public because they don't *have* to believe that she's four hundred years old, or older. She rose to fame in current living memory. She says she's a vampire and it makes her a novelty, but it doesn't make her threatening. Try to tell that same public that an Elizabethan actor is still alive—it's not merely fantastical to the average person, it's frightening. I'm willing to listen to the argument that more of us need to become public figures. I'm not willing to agree that that person ought to be me. There are better choices."

"You're being stubborn, Ned," Antony said.

"I'm also right," he answered.

"I think I agree," I said. "It would be like a grave opening up and the occupant climbing out. Too creepy."

"Kitty's made a career of public relations," Ned said. "We would do well to listen to her."

"You're a coward, Edward Alleyn," Antony said.

"I'm also over four hundred years old. There's a correlation. Besides, I don't see how that matters. It's not as if Mercedes is rallying the masses to the cause of our enemy."

"Not yet," Antony said. "But if she already has the

majority of us on her side, there'll be damned little to oppose that when the time comes."

"You talk like this is going to be a real war. Not a metaphor," I said.

"It is," Antony said, as if it was obvious.

"And you think it's coming soon."

"Don't you?"

"Depends," I said. "Soon on your scale or mine?"

"Soon on a mortal scale, Kitty," Ned said. "Dux Bellorum has exposed himself these last few years, revealing himself to people like you, who are—or at least were—outside the Long Game. He's gathering power. It can't be long."

I sat on a chair at the edge of their circle, leaning forward. Ben stayed behind me, hand on the chair's back. I could feel his warmth radiating.

"What's he planning, then? Everyone I've talked to about the Long Game says it's leading to something, that there's an endpoint. What are we talking about? He enslaves all the werewolves? Destroys all the vampires? Overruns nations with his hordes? Runs for president? Does anyone have any idea?"

"'And there were voices, and thunders, and lightnings; and there was a great earthquake, such as was not since men were upon the earth, so mighty an earthquake, and so great.'" Ned the orator intoned the words, which filled the room, and the house, echoing through the foundations.

"That's not Shakespeare," I said.

"No," Marid said. "It's the Book of Revelation."

Oh. Well then. "Okay. So we're talking Biblical. That still doesn't tell me anything."

"If we knew, we'd be able to stop him, wouldn't we?" Antony said.

"We'd prefer to stop him before we reach that point," Ned said. "None of us really wants to find out what he has planned."

The conversation reached a lull; maybe we were all contemplating the possibilities. It was enough to turn any party somber. I had an urge to call Cormac to ask his advice, interrupting what was no doubt a nice domestic scene across town. But I wasn't going to ask him in front of the vampires. I asked myself, as I often did when I was stuck in a situation I couldn't seem to solve: What would Cormac do? What did the true hunter's extinct call for in this coming war?

Cormac would say to go after Roman until we completely smoked the bastard. Trouble was, we'd tried that one before. Maybe we had to come at this a little more defensively.

I straightened, caught their attention, spoke. "In summary, you're worried that London is in danger from Mercedes and her allies, and you don't know who to trust among the vampires. So why not turn to the werewolves? Ally with them."

Antony chuckled. "I don't mean to sound rude— I'm happy to listen to any and all recommendations of course—but what can the werewolves possibly do to help?"

I managed to keep my voice calm. "Caleb has

united the werewolves of the British Isles. They can help you."

"Ah, yes, you've gone and met Caleb all on your own. When were you going to tell me about that?" Ned sounded genuinely put out. As if he wasn't the greatest actor of his generation, able to sound however the hell he wanted.

Flatly I said, "You never asked. As I was saying, the werewolves here are independent, not under your thumb at all—"

"Because I don't need them," Ned said. "Caleb understands that. We don't bother each other. It's an equitable arrangement."

"You don't need each other, either, I understand. Rick in Denver and I have the same deal—except we go a step further. We help each other, because the city is stronger when we work together. That's how we've kept Denver out of Roman's hands."

"Werewolves aren't that powerful," Antony said.

I spread my arms. "Hey, I'm the one who broke up your party the other night."

"Regina Luporum. Hmm," Antony said, tapping a finger on his chin, considering.

Facing the ceiling, I growled. Ben patted my shoulder and kissed my cheek. "You brought this on yourself, hon."

"Fine. I quit."

He just grinned at me.

"Perhaps she's right, Ned: you should arrange a meeting with Caleb," Marid said.

London's Master regarded me with a narrowed gaze. "Kitty, perhaps you should arrange the meeting. Since you two apparently get along so well—"

"I wouldn't say that—"

"If I approach him he'll think I'm conspiring. He won't trust me. But if you mediate . . ."

"But you *are* conspiring," I said.

"Yes, for all our benefits," he replied.

I'd practically asked for this, hadn't I? I put my hand over Ben's and glanced at him. "What do you think?"

"I think it's worth a try. You've said it before—the more people are keeping watch against Roman, the better."

I pulled my cell phone out of my pocket and walked to the other side of the room to make the call.

His greeting when he answered was practically a bark, designed to make the listener cower. I resisted the urge and tried to sound annoyed. "Hello to you, too. It's Kitty Norville."

"I can hear that. What sort of trouble have you gotten yourself into?"

"Nothing yet. I've volunteered to mediate. Ned Alleyn wants a meeting."

"He does, does he? What for? Going to try to convince me that due to current turmoil I need to put myself under his protection? For my own good and the good of my wolves, of course."

"Sounds like you two already had that conversation."

"What's he want, then?"

"I believe he wants to discuss an alliance." Smiling

pleasantly, I turned to look at Ned, who was watching me with a raised brow.

"Now I'm confused. What are you all playing at?"

"Agree to a meeting and find out."

The rumble over the line might have been distant static, or his growl. I hoped I dangled enough bait in front of him. He had to be curious.

Finally he said, "All right, but we meet on my turf. Hyde Park in an hour. My people have used the park for emergencies before—we can disable enough of the CCTV cameras to create a protective blackout."

"I think that sounds entirely reasonable."

"And just him. He can bring flunkies to stand watch, but when it comes to talking it's just the two of us. I don't want any of those other Masters there."

"As long as the same applies to you, I expect. A few flunkies, and that's it."

"He'll never agree to terms I set. Just watch."

"We'll see you there, Caleb." I clicked off before he could harangue me further. "There. Meeting set." I relayed the details.

Ned pursed his lips like he'd tasted something sour. "I was hoping we could meet someplace a little more . . . sheltered. Like here, for example."

He'd overheard the whole thing. Just meant less for me to explain. "I think he has every right to avoid that. You're not worried, are you?"

"Don't worry Ned," Antony said, smiling. "We'll be there to back you up."

"Ah, no you won't," I said. "Caleb said just Ned. You all have to hang out somewhere else."

"Isn't that a bit unreasonable?" Ned said.

"Not to mention presumptuous," Antony said. "We agreed to the meeting with certain assumptions in mind. Who are you to undermine that?"

"A werewolf?"

"Exactly! The nerve—"

"Get used to it," I said. "If this is going to work, you have to treat Caleb and me as equals. If you can't do that—why are we even here?"

Antony slouched back in his chair, glowering.

"There there," Ned reassured him. "Humility is a lesson we all have to learn."

"Remind me again—why are we listening to her?"

"Because she's faced Dux Bellorum and lived to tell about it. Pay attention, Antony."

They planned among themselves, which of Ned's followers should tag along as bodyguards, and how close Marid and Antony could get without violating Caleb's terms.

"I assume you and I are going to this?" Ben said, leaning in close and whispering. We couldn't guarantee that the vampires didn't hear us, but we could make the attempt at privacy.

"I'm the mediator, right?" I whispered. "You know, this makes me seem a whole lot more badass than I actually feel."

"Just keep playing badass and you'll do fine."

"Thanks, dear."

Chapter 14

I HAD A sudden need to look up where the Jack the Ripper murders had taken place. Not near Hyde Park, it turned out, which was only mildly reassuring. At night the place was spooky enough to start my imagination running. The nearly new moon and gas lamp–looking lights on posts gave the wide lawns and straight paths a sepia tone cast: gray, orange, murky. Stands of trees ringed the area like sentinels, and the buildings beyond the park seemed unnaturally far away.

I was a creature of the night, I wasn't supposed to be afraid of the dark. Not that it was the dark I was afraid of—it was the *other* creatures of the night.

Caleb had chosen a spot almost in the center of the park, where several paths converged, and some distance away from the Serpentine, the long, winding lake on the south end, where someone could easily be trapped in case of an ambush. Not that he was thinking in those terms. He probably just wanted to be in a place with good visibility, where he could watch people approach.

Ben, Ned, and I followed one of the paths, then cut across the lawn, roughly in the area Caleb asked us to wait. Emma stayed home; Ned was worried at the interest she'd drawn from Jan's flunky and wanted her safe. He had four other vampires standing guard. Marid and Antony promised to stay out of the park, but they didn't say where they would be. I hoped they didn't spook Caleb. What was I saying, could anything spook Caleb?

"This would be nice if I weren't so twitchy about it," Ben said, scanning the shadows.

The place was quiet, peaceful. We could go for a run—the four-legged kind even—and not feel the press of the city. Lie together on the grass and watch clouds passing in front of the moon. But yeah, twitchy. Caleb and his wolves were on the way; I could sense them, a touch of wild on the air. We were in their territory, and Wolf wasn't happy about it.

"Well, we're here," Ned announced. Bundled in a coat, face up, hair ruffled, he was a shadowed figure in the dark, perfectly at home and not at all nervous. "And no werewolf. I'll give him ten minutes, then give up on him."

"Here he is," I said, nodding.

Caleb and three men approached on one of the other paths. He spoke to his companions briefly, and they broke off, cutting across the lawn to take up some kind of perimeter lookout. Ben watched them go—keeping a lookout on *them*.

Britain's alpha werewolf closed the distance with

an easy stride, as if he'd happened to meet friends on the path during a casual stroll. But his gaze was focused, his shoulders tense.

I smiled at him. "We thought maybe you changed your mind at the last minute."

"Naw, I wouldn't miss this. You bossing the bloodsuckers around? Priceless."

"I do what I can."

"Ned," Caleb said flatly.

"Caleb, good of you to come." The vampire offered his hand. The werewolf considered it a moment, as if thinking of biting it. He finally shook it in a civilized manner. "Kitty said you disabled the security cameras?"

"Of course I did. We're not stupid, no matter what you lot think of us."

Ned pouted, but his eyes crinkled with amusement. "Don't be cross. I had to ask."

"You wanted this meeting. Why?"

Ned answered, "There's a war coming, we both know it. There are forces that would destroy what we've worked for, and destroy *us*. I would like to prevent that and I assume you would as well. I believe we can no longer approach this conflict defensively, as insular entities."

Caleb studied him for a long moment. I was about to interrupt when he finally answered. "That all sounds very fine, but my only concern is keeping the isles stable. You sound like you want to bring a war to our doorstep ahead of schedule."

Ned said, "If we're strong enough, the war may not come here at all. We might even consider launching an offensive."

"Have you been giving him ideas?" Caleb said to me.

I winced. "I might have made a suggestion or two."

"I knew you were trouble."

"Here's the thing," I said. "This isn't about territory, this is about building an army to withstand Roman. To raise a defense that he can't touch. If he solidifies his power in Europe, what does that do to your stability?"

The werewolf frowned. "You're staging World War Two over again, you know that?"

I considered that a moment. The comparison seemed too easy to make. Maybe there was a reason for that. "I guess I am. So how about it?"

"You remember the Blitz, Caleb?" Ned said.

"Before my time, but I know the stories," he said. "The city's werewolves could see and move in the blackouts, and they weren't easily injured by falling debris and shrapnel in the bombing. They organized, became Air Raid Wardens, walked patrols, and arranged rescues of survivors buried in fallen buildings. They could smell them and guide the rescue crews to them. The city's alpha at the time, a hoary old monster without a lick of patience, punished any wolves caught hunting or killing in the chaos."

Ned said, "I gave the wolves who patrolled the run of my properties so they always had a safe place

to go, rations that no one else had access to. I organized—"

"Give yourself a bloody medal, why don't you,"
Caleb said.

Ned pursed his lips. "I'm merely demonstrating
that we can work together to protect the city because
we've done it before."

"This isn't the Blitz."

"Not yet," Ned said.

Even I thought that might have been overstating the
case, except for the voice in the back of my head that
said, *What if he's not?*

Caleb might have been asking himself the same
question, the way he scowled.

Ned continued. "The turmoil surrounding this conference of Ms. Norville's has convinced me that I can
no longer watch events from the sidelines. Our two
tribes working together must be stronger than the sum
of our parts."

The werewolf gave him a sour look. "You talk high
and mighty, sir, but you're no Churchill."

"I knew him, you know."

Caleb turned away, scowling dramatically.

"What do you think, Caleb?" I said.

"I'm willing to consider an alliance. But an alliance isn't strategy. How do you expect—"

A long, strained howl echoed from a distant part of
the park, then cut off abruptly. A warning.

"That was Sam," Caleb said, listening, ear cocked.
"He's meant to be watching the east approach."

"That sounded like trouble," Ben said.

"Yes," Caleb said.

We all faced different directions, scanning the edges of the open space.

"Might I suggest moving indoors?" Ned said. His town house was maybe ten blocks away.

"It's too late for that, I think," Caleb murmured.

The figure of a man, shirtless and barefoot, came toward us across the lawn from a distant row of trees. He was fast, powerful, running with a long, loose stride that had an animal quality to it, easy and fluid. One of Caleb's pack—the lieutenant who'd been with him the other night. The alpha trotted out to meet him.

"They got him, they killed Sam," he said to Caleb. "They went right for his heart, he didn't have a chance—"

"Who is it, Michael? Who got him?" Caleb held the man's head steady and made him look in his eyes. The wolf, Michael, was struggling, gasping for breath, his muscles tense. All his instincts were telling him to shift, but he was holding on. "Was it vampires or wolves, Michael?"

"Both, Caleb. Both!"

Chapter 15

MICHAEL LOST control, doubling over and hugging himself, groaning as his wolf fought free. Caleb knelt with him, hand on his shoulder, steadying him as he fought the last of his clothing. Bronze-gray fur rippled across Michael's back, and his face stretched.

The instinct to Change spiked through us.

"Keep it together," Ben murmured, for my benefit or his I couldn't tell.

"Kitty?" Ned asked cautiously.

"We're fine," I shot back. "Where are they? I don't smell them."

"They're moving downwind of us," Ben said. We stood back-to-back, our natural posture in the face of danger.

"Caleb, how many are there? How many did he see?" Ned said, but Michael's last moan turned into a growl of warning.

"He saw enough, likely," Caleb said.

Ben looked at Ned. "Well, Churchill, have any ideas?"

"If I'm not mistaken, they're hoping to corner us, attack us all at once. Bloody and decisive."

"There's a reason I'm the alpha of this territory. They're not going to win this," Caleb said. "Michael, call them."

The wolf had been pacing back and forth before his alpha, ranging forward and circling back. His ears were flat, his lips drawn back. Tipping his head back, he howled a series of long warning notes.

"That going to be a problem when people start calling the police about wolves running wild in Hyde Park?" Ben said.

"They'll say it was kids messing around. It's happened before."

The open, sloping lawn meant we had a good view in every direction. The position might not have been as defensible as I liked. Behind walls would have been better.

"Here they come," Ned said.

Four wolves ran, bodies rippling, strangely liquid, shadows flowing across the lawn. They approached at a wide angle, aiming to converge on us. At the same time, three more wolves, stretching legs to make huge strides, came obliquely to intercept them.

"Those three are mine!" Caleb called. They were all just shapes, creatures from a nightmare, multiplying.

"I should Change," Ben said. "I can fight better if I Change."

"Too late," I said. "Stay with me."

The two waves of animals met each other, bodies crashing, pale teeth bared and flashing in the dark. Their snarls cut like rasps on wood.

I looked behind us, because no way would a pack

of wolves have launched an attack on just one front. Sure enough, two more rocketed from the back of the hill, in beautiful motion, without a wasted step. They aimed toward Ned.

The vampire waited calmly on the crest of the hill. He'd taken off his coat, laid it on the grass, and rolled up his sleeves. Ben and I ran to join him, reaching him as the wolves did. Three against two—not terrible odds. But this was going to hurt.

The two of us jumped at one of the wolves, tackling him, using our weight to pin him to the ground. The wolf was ready for us and writhed, twisting back on himself, flexing every muscle to wrench out of our grasp. He snapped; his teeth caught on my arm, and I hissed at the pain. I managed to grab his ear and twist; he yelped, then jerked out of my grip. Ben was trying to turn him onto his back, but the wolf kicked, digging claws into us, and tumbled away.

Ned had pinned the second wolf with a knee and wrenched back its head until bone snapped. The wolf fell limp. Our opponent jumped on him, and we scrambled to help. Moving so fast he blurred, Ned swung around and punched from the shoulder, striking the animal in the eyes, knocking him over. That gave us a chance to grab him. I leaned an elbow into the wolf's belly, Ben dug into his rib cage, and Ned, once again, took hold of the head and twisted. This one collapsed, too.

They weren't dead—they didn't shift back to their human forms. They'd heal from the broken necks. But it would take a while.

"I thought you had this one," Ned said, nudging the unconscious wolf with a toe.

"Yeah, well," I muttered. We weren't fighters, just stubborn.

The battle continued down the hill. Caleb was the only human figure among the swarm of battling wolves. More had arrived since we turned away. Growls rumbled; I could feel them through the ground, as well as the impacts of dense bodies slamming into each other. Teeth ripped at flesh; fur, spit, and blood flew. A couple of wolf bodies lay abandoned—one panted, bleeding from a gash in his side. The smell of it was thick, sour. Caleb crouched near this one, snarling, slashing with clawed hands to drive off enemies who came too close.

"What a mess," Ned said with a sigh, marching down the hill and into the swarm. One of the wolves turned toward his approach, dark eyes gleaming, and let out a sharp bark. A couple of the others who were still standing looked up, and they all ran at the vampire, ignoring the attackers slashing at their heels.

This wasn't a general attack; it was a suicide mission aimed at Ned. Not that he seemed concerned. When the lead wolf jumped at him, he sidestepped in a blur and punched the animal in the gut. Yelping, the wolf toppled. Ned kicked him for good measure.

I was about to run and help—or at least try to help—when Ben gripped my arm.

"We're missing something," he said.

Michael had told us he'd spotted both vampires and werewolves. So where were the vampires?

"Where are they?" I said, panicked. He shook his head, scanning the park on all sides.

The vampires had sent the wolves to scatter us, soften us up, before they came in to clean up the mess. Antony and Marid were out there somewhere—surely they'd heard the warning? Couldn't they take care of it?

"Wait a minute," Ben said, and nodded to one of the paths beyond a stand of trees. "Smell that?"

I had a hard time smelling anything apart from the slaughter, the sweat and adrenaline of the battle nearby. But I tipped my nose up and the air brought me a touch of cold, of death.

"I can smell them but I can't find them," Ben said.

"Let's go." I tugged him forward and we set off to find the trail.

The first of them hid among the trees, surveying the battle. I recognized him from the convocation the other evening—not one of the delegates seated at the table, but one of the henchmen standing guard. That meant he wasn't ancient, which meant we might have a chance of taking him out.

We wouldn't be able to sneak up on him, but if we attacked as fast and hard as we could, we might get lucky. We had a few tricks on our side.

Ben pointed, and I nodded. Circling around, I approached from the front. Ben continued on, softly, stake in hand.

Yelling, I ran straight for the vampire. Head down, I reached with my hands, curling my fingers as if they were claws, charging as a werewolf might attack. The vampire didn't even look surprised. He merely narrowed his gaze and twitched a smile.

Then his eyes widened as Ben drove the stake into his back.

The vampire had time to cough and clutch at his chest. The point hadn't gone all the way through, and he craned his neck to try to look over his shoulder, but Ben remained hidden. The vampire dropped to his knees. He didn't decay, didn't turn to ash and dust. Instead, he slumped over as his skin dried out and turned gray, leathery, drawing taut over sharp bones. He hadn't been old at all—a few decades at most.

I'd pulled my attack short to watch. Ben stood before me, holding the stake, staring at the shrunken vampire, looking about as surprised as the vampire had.

"We did it," he said, blinking.

"That wasn't so bad," I said. "Maybe we can do it again."

Ben fell backward, yanked by a shadow into the trees, the stake knocked out of his hand by his attacker. Growling, I sprang after him.

The vampire loomed over Ben's prone form. Tall, broad, dressed in a T-shirt and slacks, he was another of the bodyguards from the convocation. So where were the leaders, the guys in charge? I wanted to find *them*.

Teeth bared, he hissed at me. Gripping Ben's throat, he pressed down—Ben slashed at his chest with fingers that were becoming claws, ripping at the fabric. I charged, making no attempt at an elegant attack. This was all about momentum.

The vampire was ready for me when I crashed into him, hands up, taking hold of my shoulders and turning, so that we tumbled together, scrabbling to be the one on top of the pile. I didn't know what I could do next, but it didn't matter, because the vampire had let Ben go.

The guy looked big and powerful; I expected him to be strong. I didn't expect him to feel like a block of lead settling on me. That vampire strength pressed down, and I couldn't seem to get the leverage to slip away from him. Reaching for Ben's dropped stake seemed unlikely, but I tried. Meanwhile, that open mouth and those vicious sharp teeth sank closer to my neck.

I wouldn't panic. He couldn't kill me by biting me and taking my blood. Not unless he took it all.

The vampire grunted, an instinctive burst of surprise in a creature who didn't have to breathe. Ben was hanging off him, arm braced around his neck, trying to pry him off me. Nice thought, but strangling him wasn't going to do any good. It did give me a chance to knee him in the gut. It felt a little like kneeing a wall.

Without a stake, or holy water, or something, we weren't going to get out of this fix. Ben still hung on, strong enough to stay with the vampire if not strong enough to rip his head off bare-handed. His face was flush with effort.

I reached for his eyes, an act of desperation; if I could claw them, scratch them, blind him—hurt him, even a little bit, as unlikely as that seemed—we'd be able to regroup and try the next thing. I couldn't get a grip. The vampire twisted his head, snapped his teeth, and when he caught the skin of my forearm, he tore. Blood streamed down to my elbow; a length of skin hung loose.

Snarling, I punched at him, or tried to. Ben, his own growl burring in his throat, had done the same from the opposite direction, which only served to mildly rattle the vampire.

"Ms. Norville, Mr. O'Farrell, move aside," a newcomer commanded.

I'd have liked to. It was easier said than done. Then, once again, Ben fell, yanked back by a shape in the darkness. He let out a bark.

A cane swung above me, striking the vampire's head, sounding like a beat on a hollow melon. The vampire fell, and I scrambled away. If I had hit the vampire like that, even with werewolf strength, the guy probably wouldn't have noticed.

But Marid was holding the cane.

The guy was on his back now, and Marid didn't give him a chance to recover enough to sit up, much less stand. Moving next to him, he stepped a booted foot across his neck. Then Marid set the sharpened tip of the wooden cane on the other vampire's chest and leaned.

"No, no, no—!" the prone vampire managed to gasp before the cane's point broke through skin, then through ribs. The vampire arced, muscles contracting at once, and flailed like a bug on a pin before going limp, his skin turning gray and desiccated, leaving an aged corpse stuck to Marid's cane.

Marid stepped on the dried-out chest and used the

leverage to yank out the cane. A puff of ash rose up. Marid didn't glance back.

"Ben?" I asked, looking.

He was picking himself up, brushing himself off, and his scowl hinted at a foul mood. "I hate vampires."

"Present company excepted, I'm sure," Marid said, donning a crooked smile.

Ben huffed, and asked, "You okay?"

I was frowning at the gash in my arm. "Nothing a little time won't heal."

"Jesus," he muttered, coming at me and holding my arm up to study it. He pulled me close and dropped a kiss on my cheek. A big chunk of tension drained away at that, and I breathed in Ben's scent.

Marid leaned on his cane, regarding us with amusement.

"Thanks," I said, over Ben's shoulder. Marid waved me away with a tip of his hand.

"How are we doing otherwise?" Ben said, keeping hold of my hand.

I listened and couldn't hear anything that sounded like fighting. When I tipped my nose to the air, the only blood I smelled was my own.

"Almost finished," Marid said. "We're cleaning up now. We managed to drive them off."

"How many did we lose?" I asked.

"Two of Caleb's pack, and one of Ned's Family," the vampire answered. "Not bad, all in all."

"But not good," I said, and he shrugged. I hoped

Caleb was okay. I wanted to find him, to see if I could do anything to help.

The three of us went back to the path, and from there to the hill where we'd started. We let Marid walk on ahead.

"I'm glad Cormac wasn't here," Ben said softly.

"He'd have been okay." I wasn't sure how convincing I sounded.

"I worry about the day he isn't," he said.

"Well, that's what family does." It wouldn't matter if Cormac was a corporate drone or a firefighter. We'd still worry.

"If he ever gets bitten, if a werewolf ever infects him, he'll kill himself. You know that, right? If it had been him instead of me who'd been bitten that night, he'd have just shot himself." Many years of worry strained his voice. Cormac had been hunting werewolves a long time.

"That was before Amelia," I said. "You think maybe she could change his mind?"

"Or drive him even more crazy."

The others had gathered at the top of the hill. The meeting might have been going on, uninterrupted, if there hadn't been so much blood and sour sweat on the air, smells of death and fear. Bodies—naked, human—lay on the sloping lawn. A wolf with a human companion—another werewolf—moved around the area in a patrol.

Ned watched the tableau. He was holding his left arm with his right, and I had to study him a moment to figure out why. His sleeve hung in tatters, and the arm inside was likewise shredded. A wound like that, there should have been more blood, but the shirt still shone white, and the flesh underneath was strangely clean. Vampires didn't have much to bleed. Still, the skin and muscle hung in ribbons, pale and pink, torn away from the shoulder, rent in jagged tears by claws and teeth. An ivory gleam of bone, the round joint of the shoulder, shone through. A wolf hadn't just attacked, it had hung on and gnawed. Ned seemed strangely unconcerned.

Antony and a pair of vampires from Ned's Family also stood nearby, keeping watch.

"Are you all right?" I said to Ned.

"This is nothing," he said. "What about you? I could smell you coming fifty yards away."

I looked at my own arm, which in contrast to his was red and dripping. The swathe of pain throbbed in time with my pulse.

Ben unbuttoned and pulled off his shirt. Taking my arm, he used the shirt as a makeshift bandage, tying off the wound and mopping up blood. The pressure settled the pain to a dull roar.

Caleb stood a few yards away from us; his eyes shone dull gold. Rage contained. He cupped a cell phone in his hand, pressed to his head. "I've got a cleanup," he said. Then, after listening a moment, "More of theirs than ours." He clicked the phone off and shoved it in a pocket.

"I have people who can take care of that," Ned said.

"This is my territory, vampire, I can handle it."

"I think there's enough mess for both of you to clean up," I said. Even I thought I sounded tired.

"You two all right?" the alpha werewolf asked. He didn't seem tired at all; rather, he seemed ready to go another round.

"Yeah," I said.

"Anyone who isn't needed here should get indoors," Caleb said. "Ned, you, too. Get that fixed." He gestured at the injured arm.

"I can help—"

"We're supposed to be working together. Isn't that what this is all about? We work together, I trust you, you trust me. Try to keep blowups like this from happening. Keep the buggers out of our city." He shook his head. "I'll be at your place in twenty minutes."

"All right, then," Ned said.

Ben touched my arm and nodded down the path; I caught the scent just before they appeared—a new group of werewolves, burly, broad shoulders built up from manual labor, five-o'clock shadows from being up all night. Caleb approached them, and they ducked their gazes in submissive greetings. In moments, they went for the bodies, slinging them over their shoulders. The visual—these strong and silent men carrying off naked, bloodied bodies—was surreal, definitely criminal.

"He's right," Marid said, after we'd watched a moment. "We should go."

Chapter 16

THE GROUP of us trooped back up the path in the other direction, to Ned's town house. Before we left the park and the blackout area created by the disabled CCTV cameras, Ned adjusted his coat to hide his ravaged arm. To anyone watching, via camera or otherwise, we'd look like a group of acquaintances walking home after a night out. Actually, Marid, Ned, and Antony probably wouldn't show up on the cameras at all. I stuck close to Ben.

Back at the town house, Emma came running into the hallway from the parlor.

"How did it go?" she asked.

Before I could answer, Ned closed and locked the door and shrugged off his coat so that she had an excellent view of the injured arm. Emma gasped, bringing her hand to her mouth. A very human gesture.

Recovering quickly, she pointed vaguely to the back of the house. "I'll go get something for that."

"That would be lovely," Ned said, a weak smile shifting his beard. "You might find some bandages for Ms. Norville as well."

"I think I'm just about healed," I said, unwrapping Ben's shirt from my forearm. The wad of torn fabric had become a crusty mess. I frowned at it, then frowned at my arm. Sure enough, a fresh scab colored an angry, healing pink ran down the skin. When I flexed the muscle, it hurt, but not as much as it had before. Go go super healing.

"I'll just throw that away for you," Emma said. I handed the bloody shirt to her, and she ran back down the hall and disappeared around a corner.

"What exactly does one do to fix something like *that*?" I said to Ned, nodding at his own injury. Then I remembered. "Wait a minute, you're not going to ask me to help with the first aid, are you?"

"One would think you'd been in such situations before," Ned said amiably.

"You mean have I had injured vampires beg a pint off me? Yeah."

Ben looked at me. "Wait a minute, what?"

Ned narrowed his gaze. "I can fend for myself, never fear. Let's retire to the library, shall we?"

Infuriatingly, Antony was chuckling. "She's a bit jumpy," he said to Ned, leaning in to whisper. As if I couldn't hear him.

"You can hardly blame her."

"I hate vampires. Did I mention that?" Ben whispered at me.

I patted his arm. "Several times."

He frowned. "I'm going to find a new shirt. I go through more shirts on these trips . . ."

Before he left to go upstairs, he leaned in for a

kiss, which I gave him. His lips were warm, comforting, and sent a flush to my toes. I wanted to curl up with him right now—best way to heal. Soon . . .

When Ned settled into a big armchair by the fireplace, he actually winced and sighed. So he was in pain. I hadn't been able to tell. He arranged his arm so it didn't have pressure on it, ripping away the last of the sleeve and baring most of his torso. He had the body of a middle-aged man—a healthy middle-aged man in good shape, but the sparse hair on his chest was gray, and the skin was loose. Ben returned wearing a clean white T-shirt at about the same time one of the human staff brought a tray with tea and finger food, some kind of breaded meat pies. I wanted to dump the whole plate of them into my mouth. It made me think Ned was used to entertaining tired, injured werewolves.

Emma returned, carrying a pint glass in both hands, stepping carefully because it was filled almost to the rim with dark, viscous blood. She knelt by the chair, hovering, concerned, and Ned took the glass from her without spilling a drop.

Giving the rest of us a glance, he said, "Pardon me," then tipped the glass to his lips. He drained it in a single go, throat working as he swallowed, not needing to stop for a breath. He kept the glass upturned for what seemed a long time, letting the last of the blood drain into his mouth. The tangy, heady odor of the liquid permeated the room. My nose wrinkled, and my shoulders tensed.

I hadn't noticed how pale Ned had turned until the

infusion endowed him with a flush that started in his face and moved downward. Drops of blood began to seep from the wound at his shoulder. Where blood had poured from my wound, the liquid seemed to co-alesce along Ned's. Clotting along the skin and mus-cle, it built up, took on shape, faded in color, melded into the jagged skin at the edge of the wound. The healing seemed to happen both very slowly, and all at once, like watching plants grow on a time-lapse film.

He closed his eyes and relaxed against the back of the chair. Flexing his hand, new muscles tensed and released. The arm was almost back to normal, only a fine web of pink scars revealing the injury.

"That never gets old," Marid said. "It's marvelous."

"Hell of a cure-all," Ben said. He offered me a meat-thing. "Hors d'oeuvre?"

I scowled at him. I couldn't decide if I was starv-ing, or if I'd lost my appetite completely.

A banging sounded from the door to the court-yard. The noise was slow, loud, steady, like someone was trying to break in.

"That will be Caleb," Ned said. "Emma, will you let him in?"

She frowned. "He'd be happier if you met him."

"He'll see me soon enough. This isn't the time for status and posturing. He can put up with an underling showing him in." He opened his eyes and looked at her. "You're not an underling, you're a protégé. It doesn't matter if he doesn't understand that."

She pressed her lips and returned to the hallway.

I expected an argument and didn't want to miss anything. The door squeaked open, footsteps pounded, and Caleb marched into the parlor, stopping in the doorway to glare at us.

Ben and I both stood, an instinctive response to the anger Caleb radiated. His expression held challenge; we didn't know if it was meant for us.

"You okay?" I said, testing.

Caleb looked away, and I relaxed. So did Ben.

"We need to talk," Britain's alpha said to Ned.

"Yes," the vampire answered. "Sit down. Have some tea."

I preemptively poured another cup from the still-warm pot. Sighing, Caleb found a chair that seemed strategically located in the middle of the room. He had a good look at us all from there.

As I brought him his tea, he pulled a flask from an inner coat pocket. Before taking the cup, he poured a measure of what smelled like whiskey into the tea, put the flask away, took the cup from me.

What an amazing idea. Why hadn't anyone told me about that?

"I want to try that," I said, returning to my seat next to Ben, who shushed me.

The china teacup looked fragile in the werewolf's hands.

"It was awfully convenient," Caleb said. "Them knowing exactly where we were meeting and likely what we were meeting about."

Ned shrugged his coat back on, making him appear

more whole and in charge. "You're implying something."

"They knew," he said. "Somebody told them."

The anxiety that we'd struggled to hold at bay returned. We glanced around the room, studying each other—did we have a spy?

"Do you have an idea who?" I said to Caleb.

"I've got a few," he answered.

My own thoughts tumbled over possibilities, mostly asking myself the question, how well did I trust these people, really?

I trusted Ben. He'd sat back to listen, an intent focus in his gaze that had more to do with his lawyer side than his werewolf side.

"Not many of us even knew about the meeting," Ned said.

I shook my head. "That's not true. A lot of us did. There's you, Marid, Antony, me, Ben, Caleb, Caleb's wolves—"

"And your girl, Emma," Antony said, looking at the young woman still standing in the doorway after letting the alpha in.

A number of accusing gazes turned to her, and the temperature in the room seemed to drop with the chill of it. Even Ned's gaze narrowed, studious. She straightened, her brow furrowing, eyes shining.

"Now hold on a minute," I said, as if I could do anything to deflect their attention. "Why her?"

"She said they approached her," Antony said. "This evening, at the conference."

"Would she have told you about it if she was actually working for them?"

Detached, objective Ben said, "She'd have had to say something because you saw her. If she didn't you would have."

"No," I said, shaking my head. "Ben, you were there, you saw her—did she look like she was being subverted?"

"No, she didn't. I'm just being the lawyer."

I turned to Ned. "I don't think it was her. You're looking at the outsider for a suspect. It's what everyone does."

"It wasn't me, I swear to you, Ned." Emma was shaking her head.

"It could have been me," I said. There, that distracted them. They all turned their gazes on me, and the attention felt like a physical blow. "I wouldn't have had to tell them—they'd have just needed to follow me. I go everywhere, talk to everyone. Geez, I've been tracked, stalked, and pestered this whole conference. They could have had someone standing next to me and I wouldn't have known."

"Well," Caleb said. He drained the last of his tea and set it aside. "I've got one of their injured wolves trussed up in the van outside if you'd like to have a go at him. He's probably not awake yet, but it shouldn't be too much longer. He ought to be able to tell you."

Ned raised a brow. "And why didn't you say this earlier?"

Caleb's smile showed teeth. "Wanted to see you lot squirm."

Marid laughed.

Caleb stood and moved to the door. "Ben, Kitty. Care to help?"

Not really, but wolves were the muscle. Even he had that habit. I glanced at Ben, who raised an eyebrow—an uncommitted look. He was leaving the decision to me.

"Let's go," I muttered, leveraging myself from the chair yet again.

"I'll get the door," Emma said and started to leave with us.

"Maybe you'd better stay here with your Master, love," Caleb said. His tone was flat, his gaze a wall revealing nothing. No sympathy, no accusation, nothing for her to react against. Frowning, she stepped back.

She *hadn't* told anyone, she wasn't a spy, I was sure of it. But the way they all looked at her, pinning her to the wall with their glares—they all thought it possible. Was I just being naïve?

The trio of us went outside, where one of Caleb's wolves opened the back door of a dark SUV.

A naked man, a white guy in his twenties, lay on the bare, carpetless floor of the vehicle. He was one of the werewolves Ned had disabled with a snap of his neck. Now, he seemed to be sleeping. Healing, I gathered, though I didn't want to know how long it took—or how much pain it involved—to heal from a broken spine. I'd cracked my pelvis in a fall a little while back and that was bad enough. It had taken a full night to heal. The man's hands and feet were tied with plastic zip ties, as if they expected him to wake up and fight.

I couldn't smell a touch of blood, either on the man or in the back of the car. They really had known how to clean up. I couldn't help but be impressed. Back in Colorado, in the years when the pack had a lot of infighting—before I took over—there'd been bodies. Usually, they got dumped down one of the countless caves and abandoned mine shafts scattered in the foothills outside of Denver. Occasionally, there'd be a body in the city needing to disappear. I didn't know if my pack could clean up a fight of this scale. We hadn't had any fatal fights for a long time. I worked hard to keep it that way.

"Right, let's get him inside," Caleb said.

"What are you going to do with him?" I asked.

"Crack him like a nut," Caleb said.

I looked at Ben again. Like I kept waiting for a different response from him.

The henchwolf cut the zip tie at the prisoner's hands, and Caleb grabbed one of the arms. He called to Ben, who took hold of the other. They each hauled an arm over their shoulders, lifting him off the ground. I didn't have much to do but watch. Maybe call a warning if the guy started waking up.

We returned to the parlor, where Caleb and Ben dumped their burden in the middle of the floor. The man groaned. Alive and awake. My hackles rose, a tightening down my back.

Emma had retreated to another chair near the fireplace, between Ned and Marid. She looked small and young, slouching in on herself. I wondered what they'd been saying to her, if they'd been conducting their own early interrogation. Antony stood farther off; he looked like he'd been pacing.

Caleb gripped the man's hair and yanked back, showing his face to the room. "Wake up, you."

I couldn't decide if I wanted this to be successful or not. If this guy did know what had set our enemies on us, was I ready to hear the answer? It didn't matter if I was ready or not.

Ben moved close to me, our arms brushing. "Torturing him isn't going to work. He'll know we have to kill him one way or the other."

Justice, Wolf growled. This man would have killed us—me, Ben, whoever else he could have, all on the orders of some vampire like Mercedes Cook. This was justice.

Didn't mean it was going to be pretty.

"I don't know if I can watch this," I said to Ben.

"Will you lose face with these guys if you don't?"

"Yeah, probably." And I wanted to be here when he talked. I'd stay. I thought of saying something about how this was going to mess up Ned's very nice, very expensive carpet. Likely, Ned didn't much care.

Still propping his head up, Caleb slapped his captive across his face a couple of times. Not hard, just noisy and startling.

He flinched suddenly, batting at Caleb with his freed hands, but when he tried to scramble back, to put himself in a position to fight, his still-bound feet tripped him and he crashed to the floor, flopping.

Caleb let him struggle a moment before grabbing an arm and twisting it back. The werewolf cried out in frustration and bared his teeth.

"Settle down, there," Caleb hissed in his ear. "There's nothing you can do, so you might as well let it all go."

The man gave a wordless moan and kept thrashing, or trying to, anyway.

"Ned," Caleb said. "It's your turn, I think."

Oh—on the other hand, this wasn't going to be messy after all.

Ned rose from his chair, adjusted his coat, brushed imaginary dust off its hem, and arranged himself as if about to step on stage. He commanded attention; no one would ever guess that he'd been injured. I expected him to launch into a soliloquy.

Instead, he knelt before the captive, seeming to regard him with scientific curiosity as the man flailed in a panic. Finally, Ned took hold of the man's chin. Making a deep-throated noise of denial, the werewolf squeezed his eyes shut, straining to turn away. Ned merely closed his hands around either side of the man's face, put thumbs over his eyelids, and pried them open.

"Hush," Ned breathed. "There, now. Don't fret. It'll all be over soon."

The werewolf froze. Slowly, his muscles relaxed—tension actually seemed to seep out of his body. His jaw hung open and his eyelids drooped as he met Ned's gaze, and fell into it.

"That was a splendid little offensive you and your friends mounted in the park just now."

"No," the man said, chuckling sadly. His accented voice—he might have been German—was haunted, dreamy. "It was a mess. Rushed."

"Oh?" Ned feigned curiosity.

"We were just supposed to be watching . . . sur-surveillance." He sighed, tried to shake his head, but Ned wouldn't let him break his gaze.

"Watching who?"

"The American bitch."

I never knew whether to take that term figuratively or literally.

"I think I need to get that on a T-shirt," I whispered to Ben, who quirked a smile.

"Who else were you tracking?" Ned asked.

"Mexican delegation. The Indonesian doctor. The wolf soldier." I tensed, my instinctive, protective reaction at the mention of Tyler. The prisoner continued. "It's no secret where they're staying. But when the bitch went out with you all . . . we called it in."

"Called it in to whom?" Ned asked.

"Jan."

"He's holding your leash?" The werewolf nodded, and Ned went on. "You were ordered to watch Kitty

Norville, then. You didn't get your information from anywhere."

"Her. Her mate. We tracked them."

"Why target them?"

"Not them. They're in the middle of it . . . but not important. Follow them, secure the target."

Ned raised a brow and seemed genuinely intrigued. "Oh? Who, then?"

The werewolf smiled, a conspiratorial edge showing even through the trance. "Edward Alleyn, Master of London."

"Am I to take it, then, that Jan saw the opportunity to remove a foe from the field and sent everyone he could muster to attack?"

"Too good a chance to miss," he said. "You're the obstacle. Without you, the rest would fall."

"Well." Still holding his gaze, the vampire absently stroked the man's face. "How do you feel about that now?"

The werewolf's body tensed, straining against the grip that held him. Anguished lips pulled back from teeth, and he snarled. But the gaze held, and the werewolf didn't struggle. The vampire shifted his grip, twisted, and snapped. Neck broken twice in a night. Had to suck.

But I had a feeling he wasn't going to wake up from this one.

Caleb dropped the limp form to the carpet and brushed his hands. "First London, then the world, is that it?"

"And it wasn't Emma who told, right?" I said.

"No," Ned said, looking at the young woman. "But you understand, we had to ask."

She'd collected herself, sitting straight and calm, not letting the least emotion flit across her face. She tipped her chin up in acknowledgment, that was all. A gesture she'd learned from Alette. Ned must have recognized it, too; he turned to hide a smile.

"*I* didn't think you'd really done it," Antony said, spreading his arms. "It was just a possibility."

"This cannot stand," Ned said. "Any neutrality they've enjoyed, they've lost."

"So the war begins," Marid said. "At last."

Ned shook his head. "They'll go to ground when their minions don't return. Move to new lairs. It'll take time to find them, and it's getting too close to dawn to search."

"Dawn's a perfect time to go after vampires," Ben said. "Get 'em when they're woozy."

All the vampires gave him a look, even Emma.

"It's a perfect time for *you* to go after vampires," Ned said. "But I intend to twist Jan's head off myself."

"I can track them," Caleb said.

"How?" Ned said roughly, skeptical.

Caleb curled a smile for him. "They've got their wolves standing guard. Like they always do. I may not know where the vampires are, but I can find their wolves."

Antony stepped forward. "Then we'll attack—"

"No," I said. I started pacing, trying to catch a thought before it fled. "If we know which of the werewolf guards have moved, we'll know who was in on the attack—which of the Masters are allied with Jan and by extension Mercedes—"

"And therefore Roman," Ben said.

"So we can attack," Antony reiterated, frowning.

"That's not the point," I said. "An attack is going to end up like the one we just had, lots of fighting with no real result. We can't take the vampires on their home ground so there's no point fighting their wolves. We don't *want* them fighting us, we just want—"

"We want them to leave," Caleb said. "Kitty's right. My folk and I killed eight werewolves tonight. You lot can have your war, but it's us that keep dying, and I'm sick of it. Go after your vampires, but I won't let you go through more wolves to do it."

"That's just it—we can talk to the wolves. Oh, we can do this," I said. My thoughts had caught up with my subconscious. Wolf and I both knew what to do here. We just had to prove to them that we were the stronger alpha, smarter even than their Masters. And they'd listen to us, right?

Ha.

"Caleb," I said. "We have to find them. I need to talk with them—all of them."

"You think they'll just stand still to listen to you? Are you daft?" Ned glared, but I stood my ground. I was right. I was sure I was right.

"Don't underestimate her ability to talk," Ben said, his expression wry. He was enjoying this, the bastard. "It's her superpower."

"I don't believe you," Ned said. "I don't believe you can manage this."

"Caleb," I said. "Will you help?"

His smile turned toothy. "I'm in. I want to see this. How about it, Ned? Give us your blessing, won't you?"

"Do I have a choice? As soon as the sun rises you'll do what you want, am I right?"

"You'll just have to trust us," the werewolf said. "Isn't that what this is all about? Look at us—working together."

"We should get going," I said, my eyes bright, my nerves jumpy. Cormac—we had to call Cormac and let him know what was happening. Maybe he'd have some advice, however unlikely that seemed. He was used to shooting, not talking.

Caleb nodded, and we headed for the door.

"Before you go," Ned said. "You mind if we take care of this one for you?" He pointed at their prisoner.

Caleb scowled at the inert body. "Be my guest."

Apparently, advocating for the benefit of werewolves in general was one thing. But this one had attacked him and his people. Sympathy was forfeit. I couldn't say that was the wrong attitude.

"Marid, have you eaten tonight? Would you like a bit?" Ned said, nudging the unconscious werewolf with a booted toe. "Antony?"

"I think you're still in need of a boost, wouldn't you say?" Antony answered.

"I daresay there's enough for all of us to share."

Antony actually rubbed his hands together.

"That's it," I muttered. "I'm out of here."

"I'm sure we could *all* share," Ned said. "The four of us will only take his blood, after all."

He was only being polite. I glanced at Ben, whose face had gone scrunched up, bemused. It was what happened when your stomach turned and your mouth watered at the same time.

"I don't . . . *eat* people," I said.

"Not at all?" Antony said. "Ever?"

I paused, wincing. Bringing up the issue ignited the memory of a taste on the back of my tongue, flesh and blood, the iron warmth of it squishing between sharp teeth, gulping down my throat. It wasn't even my memory, it was Wolf's. I hardly remembered it, except that the sensory detail had never gone away. "Just that one time."

Ned gave me an inquiring look. "You? Really?"

"The other one was just a nibble . . ." I really did have to stop and think about how many people I'd taken a chunk out of. I put a hand on my forehead. The night had gotten very long indeed.

"I'm not sure I know about the other one," Ben said, looking at me with . . . curiosity? Admiration?

"It was that guy in Montana," I said.

"Ah."

"Ms. Norville, you are constantly intriguing," Marid said, leaning on his cane. Even Caleb regarded me appraisingly.

"I really think it's time for us to go. You guys have

fun." I grabbed Ben's hand and pulled him from the parlor.

Emma put a hand on my arm in the doorway. "Thanks. For sticking up for me."

I shook my head. "They were just grasping at straws. I don't think they were serious."

"Ned would have killed me himself if he thought I'd turned spy." She gave a nervous hiccup of a laugh. "I didn't want to be a vampire. I thought I'd rather be dead. I can't tell you how many times I almost opened the curtains at dawn to kill myself. But now, it's almost funny. I don't want to die."

"Good," I said. I touched her hand, surprised as I always was at how cold she was—she had no heat, no blood of her own.

"It should be night in D.C. by now," she said. "Do you think I should call Alette? Tell her what's happening?"

"I think that's a good idea," I said. "Let me know what she says."

She stayed behind to take part in Ned's leftovers. I didn't want to see it.

Back in the hallway, Caleb waited for us. When footsteps sounded in the back foyer, we all jumped, then stalked forward. I had a sickening vision—that Jan and Mercedes had anticipated us, sent their own attack first—

We met Cormac coming in through the back door, smelling of the city's chill nighttime air. He studied us with curiosity. His shoulders tensed—all the surprise he showed.

"There's been a fight," he said.

Was it that obvious? Caleb must have changed his clothes on the way over—he was clean. Ben had on a new clean shirt, but rusted streaks of dried blood still marred his face. Most of the blood was mine. My shirt and jeans were torn, soiled with mud and grass stains. I was cradling my injured arm, which sported an impressive red welt where the wound had been. Cormac would know it had happened recently.

"You two okay?" His voice was calm, and he eyed Caleb with suspicion.

"Yeah," I said, and Ben nodded. "I just got a little cut up."

"I should have been there—"

"No," Ben and I said at once.

"It's good that you weren't," Ben said, finishing the thought for both of us. "It was all werewolves, and you don't have any guns—it was a mess."

Cormac considered, then nodded. "Right. Want to tell me what's happening then?"

"You trust him?" Caleb said. "He's not one of us."

"We trust him," I said, my gaze on Cormac.

"You can't bring him in on this," the alpha said.

"If there's trouble, you're not leaving me out," Cormac said.

I wanted to tell Cormac no. To protect him. He would say he was doing the same. We were a pack, right? I looked at Ben, who didn't seem inclined to argue. But he and Cormac had been a team for a long time. Including him no doubt seemed natural.

"All right, then," I said. "Introductions: Cormac,

this is Caleb, alpha werewolf of the British Isles. Caleb, this is Cormac. He's—" Words failed me, as they usually did when I tried to describe him.

"He's family," Ben said.

They regarded each other, gazes suspicious, yet curious. They both obviously had questions that they weren't going to ask. That was fine. I just had to be sure I kept myself in between them.

A couple of Ned's house staff worked at night, natch. The driver, Andy, and one of the housekeepers, Sara. She was in the kitchen; I begged some extra tea and snacks from her, and she seemed happy to provide.

The four of us retreated with our spoils to one of the smaller rooms in the back of the house. It was cozy, with chairs pulled up around a fireplace where a heater had been installed. We could imagine we were alone. The vampires would retreat to a set of basement rooms when dawn came.

"Tell me what happened," Cormac said.

We explained our evening, talking over each other in a couple of places with our own take on events. The shadow conference of vampires had turned violent, one faction rising up to try to take out Ned. Cormac sat back, listening, hand on his chin.

"My first thought?" Cormac said. "Get out. You're outnumbered. They got the jump on you once, they're not going to just stop. You want to stay safe, get out, get home."

"He's got a point," Caleb said. "You're not so bad after all."

"You don't think they'll just follow us?" Ben said. "Send another posse after us?"

"There's that. But you'd be on your home turf."

"Or we could stop them now," I said. "The plan isn't to fight. We want to sow a little dissention in the ranks."

"You're going to try talking them out of this war of yours, aren't you?" Cormac said. He held a cup of tea, the vintage china looking out of place in his calloused grip. He wrinkled his nose at the liquid, but drank anyway. Maybe Amelia would help him develop a taste for the stuff.

"It's not my war," I muttered. "But yeah."

"I think she's got a chance at it," Caleb said.

"In my experience, werewolves don't stand still long enough to listen to much talk," he said, setting the cup down.

"You didn't see her earlier this week, at the convocation," Ben said. "I think they were all so surprised they didn't know which way to jump."

"Yeah," the hunter said. "That sounds about right." Caleb made a gesture as if to say, *you see?*

"What do you want me to do?" Cormac said.

Stay in the car? "Keep watch? You know the kind of defenses panicking vampires are likely to have. We don't want any surprises."

"Just what do you know about panicking vampires?" Caleb asked.

"They're like anything else," Cormac said. "You corner them, they get stupid."

"When this is all done, would you mind letting me buy you a pint and wring some stories out of you?"

Cormac just smiled.

Caleb rose from his seat and said, "First thing to do is check in with the scouts. That'll give us some idea of who's on the move and where we should go next. If you'll excuse me." He drew his phone from a pocket and scrolled through its numbers as he left the room.

Cormac gazed after him. "Alpha of the British Isles, you said? That's impressive."

"Yep. Don't look at him like you're staring through gun sights," I said, and he chuckled.

"By the way, where've you been?" Ben asked. "Dinner with the Parkers couldn't have lasted until four in the morning."

"No. They have an early bedtime with the kids and all, so we went out looking for ghosts."

I had to ask. "Like, real ghosts?"

"Amelia wanted to check up on some spots she knew from before. The Tower, along the river, Whitechapel."

"Jack the Ripper?"

"Among other things, yeah."

"Huh." He wasn't going to keep talking unless I prompted, and I was dying to know. "And . . . how did the dinner go?" Ben and I leaned in to hear the answer.

"It was . . . awkward," he said. "Not bad. But you know, trying to make small talk channeling someone's dead relative . . ." He made an annoyed movement like he had an itch on his back. "I keep asking how I got myself into this. Stuff like this, what I've been doing? Nice dinner at home with the family?

Never would have thought of it." His expression was confused, wondering. Like he really had just woken up from a nap and found himself in another country. "Anyway, his wife got out the photo album and Amelia ID'd faces in old pictures. Broke a little ice that way. The kids are cute. For kids, you know."

And that was almost as astonishing as Amelia hunting for ghosts in Whitechapel.

Phone in hand, Caleb returned, smiling, a gleam in his eye like a wolf who's spotted prey. "We've got our first stop."

Chapter 17

CALEB DROVE us to a neighborhood in south London called Brixton. Dawn hadn't yet broken, but the sky had paled to a gunmetal gray. Soon, it would become light. Shadows played strangely.

"Not the best part of town, is it?" I said, whispering. We'd passed street after street of row housing, endless three-story buildings of brick walls stained by decades of soot and graffiti. They might have been a hundred or more years old, but they looked tired and decrepit rather than quaint.

"Depends on who you are and why you're here," Caleb said. His focus wasn't on me, but out and around, scanning his territory. "Some vampires like staying in neighborhoods like this. Helps them keep their cover. They certainly don't mind a little thing like crime rates. I suppose we could have brought along your soldier friend for more backup."

"No," I said. "I want to leave him out of this." Tyler had his own problems, he didn't need to fight my fights, too.

After turning the next corner, Caleb nodded. "Right, there he is."

He was one of Caleb's lieutenants, a man with dark skin and a shaved head. In his midtwenties, he was tall and broad, tough. Pure enforcer, though he ducked his gaze and slouched when Caleb looked at him.

The British alpha parked on the street and rolled down his window. "Find anything?"

"Don't know just where the fangs are holed up, but there's a pair of wolves patrolling the end of the block. I stayed downwind of 'em, they haven't spotted me."

"Whose?"

"Solomon's."

"Good man," Caleb said. "Let's walk, shall we?"

The four of us got out of the car.

"Which one is Solomon?"

"Master of Istanbul. You probably met him at your fancy meeting."

Which one at the convocation had he been? It didn't matter. We could chalk him up to Roman's side, now.

"Cormac, maybe you'd better wait here," I said.

"I'll be fine. They won't know I'm there."

I believed him. "Just stay back behind the others."

"Here, take this with you." He offered me a slender dagger tucked in a black leather sheathe. If I pulled the knife out, looked at it, the metal would wink, edged with silver.

I shook my head. "I don't need that."

"It'll give you authority," he said.

"I don't need it. I don't want to take a chance of having it used against me."

"It'll make me feel better," he said.

"No." I glared and walked away.

"Don't take it personally," Ben said to him.

"You want it?"

"Hell, no. I'm likely to trip and cut myself on it."

Cormac standing guard with his silver daggers should have made me feel better. But I had this sneaking worry that he was right, and that we would need the weapons.

I'd learned to carry myself with a straight back, my chin up. To move as if I was powerful, no matter what I felt. A far cry from the old days, my earliest time as a werewolf when I cowered at every stray noise or cold glance. A far cry from before I became a werewolf even, when I was a pampered college kid willing to go along with whatever flow was carrying me. I wondered sometimes—if I'd been stronger then, would it have prevented any of what came after from happening?

I had to work to show any confidence here, on a street with no lights, with blackened and broken windows staring down on me, where the air smelled unfamiliar and a distant shattering of glass distracted me. Ben walked at my side, unflinching, and I couldn't tell if he was faking it, too. Cormac was, as he had indicated, out of sight. Surveying from a secure location, an ace in the hole.

Caleb's enforcer followed us, and he ducked his gaze when I looked at him.

"There he is," Caleb said, nodding ahead. I turned my nose to the air, smelling. Our quarry didn't just smell of wolf; he carried a trace of his Master's scent with him, too. "You want to do this or should I?"

Ben's fists clenched, and he tensed, ready to pounce. They all expected this to turn out badly, didn't they?

"I'll do it," I said evenly. This was my idea, right?

"What about me?" Ben said.

I squeezed his hand. "Stay close."

"Kitty. Be careful."

I moved ahead. The others fanned out in a protective arc behind me. I could hear their steps on the asphalt, even the soft hush of their breathing. We were a pack on the hunt.

A figure darted ahead of us, crossing the street. A second one prowled in the shadows of the row houses, looking like he wanted to try to flank us. We were in the wide open; we'd see anyone trying to get the best of us. The guards probably hadn't been expecting a frontal assault.

"Hey!" I called. "I just want to talk!" My voice echoed along the empty street as if we were in a cave. Even the clouds hung low, ceiling-like.

"Talk. To say what?" The one moved from the shadows, coming to face me in the middle of the street. He kept glancing over his shoulders, probably looking for the inevitable ambush. He was powerfully built, broad shoulders, defined muscles along his arms, visible under short sleeves. He showed teeth when he scowled.

"Calm down. I really do just want to talk."

"Don't move any closer," he said. His accent was

precise, as if he'd learned English rather than growing up with it. I stopped advancing. But I also wouldn't lower my gaze.

"You ever think about leaving? Walking away from this? From Solomon?"

The werewolf huffed a nervous chuckle. "And do what?"

"Whatever you want."

He shook his head, like he thought I was joking.

"You know you're just cannon fodder, right? You stay with him, you'll get killed eventually. Messily, probably. You know what happened at Hyde Park tonight?"

"That's not normal."

"How many of your pack did you lose tonight?" He scowled and didn't answer. "There's a war coming. It may get to be normal. You might want to ask yourself if you're on the right side."

He fidgeted, nervous, and ducked his gaze, just for a second.

"You don't owe him anything," I said, pressing.

"He looks after us—"

"By using you to fight his battles?" I raised a skeptical brow. "Solomon serves Dux Bellorum. He may have told you that Dux Bellorum's army has no opposition. That the coming war will be easy to win. But they're wrong. Because we're here to stop him."

"This is a trick—"

"No. We're just tired of werewolves killing each

other. Especially for people like Solomon, Mercedes, and Jan."

I didn't need an answer from him. I didn't expect him to drop everything and follow me. I just wanted him to think. Turning, I gestured to Ben and Caleb, indicating it was time to leave.

Then Solomon's guard said, "I remember you at the convocation. You don't fight. Is that it? That you don't want anyone to fight?"

"Oh, I fight. When I need to. But you're right, I'd rather avoid it."

"Because you're weak?"

"Because I'm lazy. Essentially."

I'd hoped for a laugh. At least a smile. His curled lips remained in a snarl. "This is a trick."

He backed away. Out of the corner of my vision I saw his partner paralleling him along the houses. They both retreated, without turning their backs to us.

"I think it's time to go," Caleb said.

We fell into step and jogged back to the car. By the time we reached it, Cormac had reappeared.

"Where were you?" I asked him conversationally, in a tone that I hope also said, *told you so*.

"I was there. Saw it all."

"What, were you invisible?" Could Amelia do that, I wondered?

"How about just not noticeable."

I decided I didn't really want to know.

Caleb gave his lieutenant instructions, and the man went back to the shadows he'd emerged from, to guard this corner of their territory. The alpha returned to the driver's seat.

"This is bloody useless," Caleb said. "They're not going to listen to you."

"He listened," I said, determined to believe my own words. "He didn't start a fight, did he?"

"I don't know," Ben said. "I think you got to him."

"We just have to shake things up a little," I said. "What's the next stop?"

"Njal," Caleb said. "My scouts say he's holed up in Chelsea. Can't bear to slum it, the git."

In my mind, this was the most important stop on the list. The two werewolves in chains at the convocation belonged to him. If I could only shake up one vampire's household tonight, convince the werewolves to leave their Master just once, this would be it.

We drove in silence, back north into London's interior neighborhoods.

Chapter 18

THE CONTRAST between this neighborhood and Brixton couldn't have been more profound. Even in the misty dawn, the rows of ornate town houses and well-groomed parks seemed picture-perfect. The low, wrought-iron fences had fresh coats of paint, the façades were clean and elegant. Not a smudge of graffiti in sight.

"His guards have staked out the next block," Caleb said. "Same routine, I take it? Walk in until we flush 'em out?"

"Wait," I said, focused out the window to a stray shape that had moved in the morning shadows. "Let me out here."

"What are you on about?" He slowed the car.

"I saw something. They've spotted us, let me out."

"Kitty—" Ben said. The car had stopped, and I was already out.

I breathed deep and caught only a hint of werewolf. The air moved wrong, and felt wet and heavy in my nose. But they were out there. Caleb had parked, and he and Ben moved in behind me. Cormac was around, I was sure, but again stayed out of sight. They wouldn't interfere, but they had my back. I didn't have to worry about anything but what lay in front of me.

The street narrowed, curved, funneling into a small square, hemmed in by town houses. Even narrower lanes led away. I wasn't quite hemmed in without escape. The lair had to be nearby.

Several werewolves were watching me from sheltered places around the square. Only watching.

"I have a message," I called out. "Once I've said what I need to, I'll leave. No trouble." Their scents were musky, tangy with adrenaline, with fear. Some of them were in wolf form, fur bristling, panting.

"Tonight's battle was just the start. But this isn't about us, it's about the vampires. They should fight their own war, don't you think? Instead of using us. That's my message: our fight isn't with you. You don't have to stay. If you leave, trouble won't follow you. Your Master's already picked sides, and he's already finished. But you don't have to go down with him." I felt a little ridiculous, calling platitudes in an empty street, unable to gauge my audience's reaction. Couldn't be too long before someone called the cops, in a neighborhood like this.

Nothing happened, no one answered.

"Like I said," I added finally. "It's just a message. Think about it." I turned to leave.

"Where are we supposed to go?" a man called in accented English.

The same question, and that was the problem,

wasn't it? Did they only stay because they didn't have anywhere else to go? If I could just get all these people together . . .

I shrugged, wishing I could produce a magical floating island where we could all live in peace. Yeah, right. "Where do you want to go?"

"No matter where we go, we are in someone's territory. In someone's reach."

Europe was crowded, in other words. "Maybe someone would let you in. If you talked to them. Made a deal. It has to be better than this."

The speaker emerged into the light, and my breath caught. He was the male wolf, the one in chains who had lain at Njal's feet. He was dressed now, shockingly ordinary in jeans and a sweater. But he still wore a metal-trimmed collar around his neck.

So did the lean wolf who padded beside him. The woman, his mate. She lowered her head when I saw her, hanging back, pressing herself to her bipedal companion. His hand reached down to brush her fur. He was protecting her; everything he did was to protect her.

"I'm listening, because you wouldn't fight," he said. "You understand."

My voice stretched thin with sympathy. "You have to get away from him. You know that, don't you?"

"He cares for us. In his own way."

"You're not pets."

He looked away, like he didn't believe me. "You don't fight. Why are you trying to start a war?"

My smile felt bitter. "Oh, I didn't start this."

Four others had emerged, arranging themselves in the square behind the man. Two were in wolf form. Their ears were up, listening. Their postures were wary. Even the humans had stiff shoulders and taut expressions.

"You're a pack. If you left together, looked to yourselves for leadership instead of that jerk of a vampire—" I shook my head. It had taken me years to learn that lesson. I couldn't just rant at them and expect the lightbulb to turn on.

I turned to walk away. Looking at them—at those collars—made me too sad.

"Wait!" he called. He'd stepped forward; his mate moved with him. "Could you—could you take us with you?"

How much courage did it take for him to ask that question?

"Harald, you can't," said one of the others, reaching. "He'll find you."

"She can protect us. Look at her."

What exactly did he see in me? I felt tired, running on adrenaline. On desperation. I imagined metal rods down my neck holding my chin up. I looked to Ben for help. He gave a small shake of his head—not denying, but expressing confusion.

I suppressed a laugh. "You don't get it. This is about taking care of *yourselves*."

"You—" The man nodded over my shoulder; Caleb stood there, his glare still, neutral. "You are the alpha of this territory? You'll let us stay, then. I ask for . . . for asylum." He set his jaw.

"Harald," his comrade called again. Harald didn't look back. His fingers twined into his mate's coat, and she whined softly.

Caleb's expression didn't change. I wanted to say he was angry, but I didn't know him well enough to decide for certain. Silently I pleaded with him, wishing for telepathy, *Say yes . . .*

"I'm not in the habit of taking in strays," he muttered. "But in the interests of the cause . . . You'll behave? No double-crossing?"

Harald shook his head. "We are not so clever. I just want to keep her safe." He rubbed a hand over the wolf's head. The poor woman had her ears back, her tail between her legs. She was terrified. But she trusted her mate.

"Come on, then," Caleb said with a sigh.

The defector inched forward carefully, obliquely, moving around us instead of toward us. His mate was even more tentative, hunched over and padding carefully. He had to urge her forward. Caleb didn't look at them, didn't make so much as an aggressive flinch— they might have fled at the least discouragement. But Caleb was thoroughly self-possessed. An alpha to admire.

"Anyone else?" I called to the others.

The remaining wolves fidgeted, gazes darting, but none moved forward. In fact, after a moment, they faded back to morning shadows. They weren't going to try to steal back their pack mates, and they'd have to wait until nightfall to report to their Master. Good.

Ben moved beside me, regarding the two defectors

who stood near Caleb. She was still cowering. Harald managed to look simultaneously miserable and resolute.

"I'm suddenly feeling grateful," Ben said. I glanced at him, questioning. He shrugged. "For choices. For big open spaces. For you."

I knew what he meant. *There but for the grace of God . . .* I squeezed his hand.

"Now, what am I going to do with you?" Caleb said, his tone as tired as it was annoyed.

Harald studied his feet. "If you have a place for her to sleep . . ."

"I think we can manage that," Caleb said. "Let's get out of here."

"Thank you," I said as we walked back to the car. The two new wolves trailed us, wary and showing deference. I tried not to keep looking over my shoulder at them, which would only make them more nervous.

"Don't tell anyone I've gone soft," he muttered. "But maybe this'll start some rumors, encourage some of the others to desert as well."

"We can hope."

Cormac joined us by the time we reached the car, and I didn't look for where he'd appeared from. The way he moved was almost vampiric, but it was probably just a charm of Amelia's. Harald and his mate jumped when they saw him, and Caleb murmured reassurances at them.

With the newcomers, the car didn't have room for us all, and we agreed that the priority should be getting the defectors to safety. Caleb would take them to one of his pack's safe houses, and the three of us would continue on our own. He gave me his list of contacts and locations, apparently more confident in my abilities now that he'd seen the plan in action.

"I have to give you some credit. This may work," he said.

"There's a vote of confidence," I said.

He winked. "Never had a doubt, love. Now, off to play good Samaritan and check on my own wounded. Call me in an hour."

"Yes, sir."

Somehow, in the last half hour, daylight had arrived in force. The cloud cover made it impossible to spot the moment when a shadowy dawn had given way to full day. But the sky was bright now, if overcast. The vampires would be sleeping. And have no idea what we were up to.

Caleb's scouts had tracked five vampires who'd moved their lairs. We assumed Mercedes didn't have a lair of her own—she'd always traveled light and alone, not weighed down by a household. Able to manipulate others to get what she needed. We had three left, took a cab to the next one, and the last two were within walking distance of there. Morning traffic had begun to clog the roads; we moved carefully.

At one of the five lairs Caleb and his people had tracked—Petra's, the woman in the glamorous gown, Mistress of Krakow—we couldn't find the wolves standing guard. We spent half an hour wandering the neighborhood, making our presence known. No werewolf guards appeared, leaving me no one to talk to. They might have fled, or they might have decided to stay out of sight. Didn't matter, because we didn't have time to linger.

The last two visits went much like the first: we found the guards, they stopped long enough to listen to me—my actions at the convocation had earned me that. But I couldn't tell if what I said made an impact. I was able to add rumors to what I'd said before: that I'd been able to rally some of the other werewolves, that Roman's base of support was crumbling, and they had better consider our offer of amnesty—a chance to escape—while they still could. So only two wolves had defected for sure, and they were a special case. This whole escapade was about propaganda, wasn't it? If I was wrong and my plan failed entirely, I'd have other problems to worry about.

By then, some of the clouds had burned off, blue sky broke through, and the morning blazed, maybe as sunny as this country ever got. Wandering on a hunch, I led Ben and Cormac out of the neighborhood of our last encounter, down a couple of curving streets, and stumbled on the astonishing vista of Trafalgar Square.

"I think I need to rest a minute," I told them and wandered across the plaza in front of the National Gallery to sit on the steps at the top of the square. I resisted an urge to cower before the huge bronze lions looking out, guarding the base of the immense column that bore aloft a nautical statue of Admiral Nelson—

indistinct from this distance. There were also fountains, neoclassical architecture on every corner, block after block of impressive façades stretching all the way down Whitehall. If I wandered that way, I'd eventually get to Big Ben, Parliament, Westminster Abbey . . . Never mind the column and statue, this one square—this whole city was a monument.

I'd been in old places—old by American standards at least—and had been in beautiful places that made me sigh with pleasure. But I had never felt the weight of history settle over a place the way I felt it here, solid and daunting. I shouldn't have—this was a modern city, with traffic jams and crowds of people on their ways to jobs or events or important rendezvous. It smelled like a city, exhaust, concrete, asphalt, combining in a haze. But the buildings were all so old by my admittedly narrow American view. The columns and domes and plinths and everything were done unironically. Then came the layers. Behind a neoclassical theater was the preserved basement of a medieval church, and around the corner from that a row of houses that had been destroyed in the Blitz and replaced by a park, and yet another corner once held a statue placed by a king eight hundred years ago as a monument to his dead wife. Norman castles, Renaissance palaces, Victorian parks—they all lived here together.

This city had been a city for two thousand years, and I could feel that with every step I took. Bits of all that time were still here, alive, even if it was just in the form of collective memory.

I wondered if being in London was a little like being a vampire.

Ben settled on the step next to me, resting his elbows on his knees. Cormac stayed standing, keeping watch.

"You're thinking very deep thoughts, I can tell," Ben said. The sunlight exposed the exhausted shadows under his eyes, and a pallor to his skin. I wondered how bad I looked.

"Yes," I said, and left it at that.

"Do we have any more conspiracies to initiate right at the moment?"

I had to think about it a moment. "I don't think so. Not right at the moment."

"Then can I vote that we try to get some sleep?"

I couldn't remember the last time I'd slept. No wonder my brain felt like cotton. "I think that's an excellent idea. Cormac?"

He stood a little ways off, sunglasses on, looking over the scene, frowning.

"Some days I think that nothing ever changes," he said. Or Amelia said. The thought could have come from either one of them.

We caught a cab back to Ned's house in Mayfair.

Chapter 19

IF I managed a couple of hours of sleep, it was because I curled up with Ben. Lying with his warmth around me and his scent in my nose made me feel like I was home and safe. The feeling didn't last, and I woke up with a start, remembering what we'd done during the dawn, and wondering how it would turn out.

First thing, I pulled out my phone and called Tyler. "Hey—are you okay?"

When he answered, his voice held laughter. "Even my mom isn't this worried about me."

"Yeah, well, your mom isn't here dealing with vampire and werewolf politics. Some of these guys have their eye on you."

"Yeah, I've spotted them lurking around. I get to feeling like I'm in a spy movie."

"Tell me about it. But they haven't approached you—haven't tried to draw you in?"

"No—just the straight-up human government people have been doing that."

"Good. Okay."

"I'll be careful, Kitty. I promise," he said, and we signed off.

If anybody could take care of himself, it was Tyler.

I still had to deliver my keynote address at the conference tomorrow. I had a million things I could say—that was part of the problem. I wasn't sure it mattered anymore. On the other hand, part of me wanted to run straight to the conference, get on a PA system, and tell everyone to stay in their rooms and lock their doors. That might have been an overreaction. Then again . . . I felt like I had to warn people. *We fought a battle last night, I spent the morning sowing chaos . . .*

I returned to the conference at noon, after an argument with Ben and Cormac. I was too visible, they said. I shouldn't go because the conference made me too much of a target. I argued back, that going would prove that we hadn't been scared off. When that didn't work, I said if I went to the conference—on my own, even—we could use me as bait to draw out our enemies. That suggestion didn't go over so well.

Then one of the werewolves from last night—one of Solomon's, not the one who spoke but the one who'd kept to the shadows—showed up at Ned's gate asking for help. We called Caleb, Ben waited with him, and Cormac and I went back to the conference because I wondered how many werewolves—who didn't know where we were staying, for example—might show up there hoping to find me. Not because they wanted to hurt me, but because they needed help.

We let Andy drive us this time, for speed. The protestors were still out front, loud as ever, their voices like the crashing of waves. Andy dropped us off at the side entrance to avoid them. I didn't even want to look at them.

Side by side, Cormac and I marched to the lobby. My nerves felt like they trembled; I wanted to growl.

"You should have stayed back at Ned's," I said. "All these lycanthropes, and you don't have any way to defend yourself—you'd be safer."

"Didn't know you cared," he said.

I stopped. "I care."

He wouldn't look at me, and I didn't know what to say after that. I sighed. "I know you hate it when we get all overprotective, but—"

"No." He shook his head, gaze downturned. "It's just I'm used to being the one taking care of everyone else. I—sometimes I think I'd be better off if I moved away. Different city, different state. If I wasn't around anymore and you didn't have to worry. But . . . that would be worse, wouldn't it? We'd all still worry but we wouldn't be there to check up on each other."

"Yeah," I said.

He gave a curt nod and continued down the hallway. I hurried to follow.

The first person I saw in the lobby was Luis. As nice as he was on the eyes, I didn't want to deal with his flirting right now. I had to get the first word in, warn him what was happening—and convince him to take it seriously—before he could start batting his eyes and kissing my hand.

"Luis, I need to talk to you—"

"Kitty! I need your help," he said. He wasn't smiling.

"What is it?"

"It's Essi—Esperanza. She's in the middle of it, and I can't get her to let it be. The protestors—they know who she is because of her work with the conference. If she gets stuck—I don't know if she has a way out. She won't listen to her crabby little brother but maybe she'll listen to you."

That wasn't even the disaster I was expecting. "Let's go," I said, taking his arm to push him forward, leading the way.

We couldn't see a way out of the lobby's front doors—a crowd of people was blocking them. The local fire marshal was going to get involved if this kept up. We'd have a hard time even getting to the front doors—the crowd was getting larger.

"Back around," I said, and took off in a run, back for the side entrance.

"Kitty!" Cormac called.

The two of us outran him. Instinct took over; I didn't even think about it.

Hundreds of people gathered, running down the street as if drawn by the noise, the sheer energy of it. A police siren sounded nearby. Once outside, we stayed close to the building and eased toward the street in front, pressing past people, working along the wall. We rounded the corner.

Wolf bristled, snarling behind the bars of her cage, and I had to stop to catch my breath, to quell the instinct to simply turn and run away. Too many people, all pushing together, shouting. And Esperanza was in the middle of it? What must she be feeling?

Ahead of me, Luis looked back. "You okay?"

"I hate this, but yeah," I grumbled.

Frowning, he'd hunched, his shoulders tense, grimly pressing forward into the crowd. I grabbed his elbow in an effort to keep close to him, to be sure we weren't separated. He clamped his arm to his side to keep me there.

The crowd surged like a live thing. We were making progress until something happened in front, and a wave of flesh and angry attitude pressed back. We had nowhere to go because people had closed in behind us. Luis shouted for his sister. I was just barely tall enough to see to the tops of people's heads, but no farther, even standing on my toes. But we kept moving forward, Luis pushing on, a cat on the hunt. I kept my gaze on his back, ignoring the hordes pressing on every side. I was trapped. I wanted to howl.

The people around us were all ages, male and female, shapes, sizes, and builds. The words they shouted came out muddled, blurring into one another, and I couldn't read any signs—most of them were up front, where it was easier to hoist them. I couldn't tell which side of the debate we'd ended up on. Somebody, or several somebodies, reeked of garlic, like they'd bathed in it. Maybe they had. No one recognized me at least.

Ahead, a space opened, a place on the street where the crowd ended. Striped police barricades kept people corralled. I heard a voice shouted through a bullhorn—authoritative, a police officer maybe. Cars with flashing lights parked on the other side of the street, also keeping the crowd corralled. Luis called Esperanza's name again, and we were close enough to the front of the protest to hear words.

Luis elbowed past people and pulled me the final step to the barricade.

Esperanza was on the other side of it, shouting, hands in fists at her sides, teeth bared. "You don't have that power! If someone stands here and tells you they're a human being, a *person,* you don't have the power to argue with that!"

"You are *not* a person, you are not a human being! You're not *like us*!" He was a young man in jeans and a T-shirt. Sweat matted his hair, and his muscles stood out. He brandished a sign on a stick, waving it above his head as if it added to his voice: ANIMALS ARE NOT PEOPLE.

God, this was so wrong. Both of them had crossed their respective barriers, but hung back, arguing across an open stretch of sidewalk, as if kept to their side of the protest by magnetism. Where were the cops? I saw the cars, the lights, heard the bullhorn— they were trying to push forward, I thought. I hoped.

"Esperanza! We need to break this up!" I shouted. "Now, before the cops get here!"

"Essi, listen to her!" Luis added.

She glanced back at us. Strain marked her features; her mouth hung open, her teeth slightly bared. She was hunched and tensed in that cat-like manner, like Luis.

Luis reached his hand, held it out despite being jostled by the crowd behind him. Everyone was shouting; the sirens were loud. Esperanza nodded, then. She glanced back at her heckler, spit at the asphalt near his feet, and turned to reach back to Luis.

Someone from the other side ran forward, tipping one of the sections of barricade in his effort to get past it. He was also young, also scrappy—and he held a bucket in his hands. He moved like an attacking predator, head down, arms reaching.

"Esperanza, get down!" I shouted. Too late—she was looking at the attacker. Everybody was looking at the sudden burst of movement across open space.

The man threw the contents of the bucket, an arc of thick, red liquid that splashed in a wall, hit Esperanza in full, and continued on to spatter a swathe of the crowd on either side, including me and Luis. People around us screamed.

The stench of it filled my nose, making me sneeze. I fought past the initial shock and horror to identify it: cow blood. Plain old cow blood. Nothing more sinister than what you found on the average butcher block, which was probably exactly where this came from.

Not that that mattered. He might as well have thrown kerosene on a fire.

The taut fury marring Esperanza's features, the hiss she let out, weren't human.

The crowd was in motion, and its tenor had changed. Instead of a slow press, an ebb and flow, people surged in a panic, away from the source of the attack, away from the blood. Luis went the other direction, toward his sister, and I followed. He knocked down the plastic barrier and leapt for her, far more agile and graceful than a normal person would have been.

I wasn't a jaguar who could leap and turn on a dime, but I could put my head down and power through. We both reached Esperanza and grabbed her before she could pounce at her attacker. Luis took her arms, held them back, and locked her in an embrace; I got in front of her, hands on shoulders, holding her back, blocking her view. The man with the bucket, now empty, stood in the middle of the sidewalk, regarding his handiwork with wide-eyed bafflement, as if he hadn't expected everyone to actually start screaming.

Luis was speaking rapid, steady Portuguese close to Esperanza's ear. Her skin was hot under her clothing, tingling against my touch—close to shifting. Her glaring eyes had turned emerald—she might not even have seen her brother.

"Luis, we have to get her out of here."

He'd already hoisted her into his arms, cradling her. She struggled, batting him with a hand that now bore claws. I hovered close, both to grab her if she broke free, and to shelter them from the screams and shouts of the mob as I guided them to the nearest doors at the hotel's lobby.

Without the barricade, the two groups of protestors came together, merging into a riot. Somebody fell, smacking into my back—Wolf turned to snap, until I yanked her back. Had to stay human. Had too much to do, too much to go wrong.

The bullhorn was close, now. Somebody was yelling to stop. I assumed they weren't yelling at us.

One of the doors ahead of us opened up; Cormac held it, clearing the path for us, urging us inside. He was right where he needed to be, to come to the rescue. The warm air of the hotel lobby had a corporate, carpeted scent that stabbed through the turmoil. I steered Luis toward that smell, our escape route.

"Thanks," I gasped.

"This way," Cormac said, pointing to a room—a bellhop station or maybe just an office or small meeting room, I couldn't tell. I pulled Luis's arm and pointed to the shelter.

Cormac shouted, a path cleared, and we moved forward.

Another familiar face emerged from the crowd of onlookers—Dr. Shumacher. "Can I help?"

I couldn't think of very many people I'd want helping in a situation like this, but she was one of them. She'd seen out-of-control lycanthropes before. The four of us lunged into the room, and Cormac slammed the door.

After the mob on the street, the room was very quiet. It was small, no more than ten feet across, carpeted, empty, lit by fluorescents. It could have held a small conference table and a few chairs, or served as luggage storage.

Luis set Esperanza on the floor. She was still batting at him, and he was doing a good job ducking, but she'd gotten a swipe across his cheek, three rows of cuts dripping blood. The wound was hard to differentiate from the smears of cow blood that covered us all.

Her whole body was rigid, braced against itself, and she was gasping for breath. Traces of fur gave her brown skin a sheen. She was trying to keep it in, to hold it together. Luis held her close, still whispering in their language.

"Thanks," I said to Cormac and Shumacher.

The scientist stood by the door, watching with her neutral, clinical gaze. "Her shifting under duress in public would have been a disaster."

"Good thing it didn't happen, then," Cormac said.

Got that right. If she'd shifted in the middle of the crowd, the odds of her getting out without hurting anyone, even by accident, were slim. At least here, with friends looking after her, she had a chance of staying safe and in control. I couldn't tell if she was right on the verge of shifting or not.

"You two might want to stay outside for now," I said. "Just in case."

Even Cormac didn't argue, and they both stepped quickly outside and closed the door.

I pressed to the wall, ready to help if needed but wanting to stay out of the way, to avoid upsetting her precarious balance. If she was going to shift uncontrollably, she'd have done it by now, I thought. But I didn't know her well enough to tell. Luis did, and he continued holding her, cradling her. Were-jaguars didn't have packs like wolves. I didn't know if the contact would help. Then again, maybe it would, not because he was another were-jaguar, but because he was her brother.

Using the hem of my shirt, I wiped at the blood spattered on me, which didn't help to clean it up, really. So my shirt instead of my arm was bloody—hardly seemed an improvement.

Finally, Esperanza sighed, slumping in Luis's arms. Her skin had lost the sheen of fur, and her hands were hands, with human fingers and fingernails, resting on her lap. Luis continued whispering at her, murmuring at her, until she seemed to fall asleep. He tried to clean some of the blood off her face, using a corner of his shirt. Didn't have much more luck than I had.

When he finally looked at me, his face was ashen and lined with worry. "That was too close," he said.

"Is she going to be okay?"

"Pissed off when she wakes up, but yes. I think so."

I opened the door, let Shumacher back in and introduced her to Luis, who thanked her. Esperanza started to rouse, as if from a brief fainting spell, her face creased, struggling to sit up. She said something in Portuguese, and Luis reassured her.

"You might want to stay here for a time," Shumacher said. "At least until that crowd clears out a little. Your friend is standing watch, keeping people out."

If I focused, I could still hear shouting. I settled in

to wait. Shumacher pulled a cell phone from her jacket pocket and made a call. She waited for an answer, and waited. When the number went to voice mail, she left a message.

"This is Elizabeth Shumacher, there's been some trouble outside the hotel and I just wanted to touch base. Please call back when you get this."

"Who?" I questioned. She looked worried.

"Sergeant Tyler," she said. "I hope he's all right."

"He probably just missed the call," I said.

She made another call. "Yes, can you call room twenty-four eighty, please. Thank you."

Again, she waited, and waited. Again, she left a message when no one answered.

"When was the last time you saw him?" she asked me, putting her phone away.

"I talked to him on the phone this morning; he was fine then."

"You haven't seen him at all since?"

"No."

"Neither have I," she said, frowning.

"I'm sure he's fine. He probably went out sightseeing." I didn't sound convincing.

A catalog of possible disasters scrolled through my mind. Some of those protesters may have gotten out of hand and taken direct action. Any supernatural bounty hunters in town may have decided to gun for him. I'd have pointed to the local werewolves if I didn't know Caleb. Then I thought of the vampires— Mercedes hadn't been able to get to me. What if she'd decided to go after Tyler? I didn't even know where to start.

I had to stave off the panic and remind myself: Tyler was ex–Special Forces. Highly trained, very badass. He could take care of himself. Someone would need a huge amount of know-how, not to mention firepower, to take him out.

"He's a tough guy, Doctor. There's probably a logical explanation." But my own instincts were screaming at me.

"He wouldn't just *leave*, Kitty."

"Is something wrong?" Luis asked.

Esperanza groaned. "Yes. I need a shower. Badly."

"Friend of ours. A werewolf, Joseph Tyler." I turned to Shumacher. "Can we check his room?"

"Maybe we should."

Esperanza was ready to move, so we decided to leave our shelter, chaos outside or no. Getting to her feet with Luis's help, she seemed tired, as if she had actually shape-shifted and run wild rather than merely threatened to. She'd used all her strength to keep that from happening. She looked awful, sticky blood soaked into her clothes, matting her hair, streaking her face. She looked like she'd come out of a war zone.

"You okay?" I asked, not because I thought she was, but I didn't know what else to say to her.

Wincing, she nodded. "What kind of asshole does something like that? Most people wouldn't know right off it was cow blood."

"I don't know," I said. "He probably just wanted to shock people."

"Well, I hope he's happy," she said, with a bitter chuckle.

Actually, I hoped he was in jail right now. What were the odds? I took the time to make a call of my own, and held my breath until I got an answer.

"Kitty," Ben said. Single word, heartfelt greeting. "Where are you? I saw what happened on TV, CNN was broadcasting. Are you okay?"

Oh, so everyone saw that. Great. "I'm fine. Luis and Esperanza are safe. Cormac's here with us. But there's another problem. Can you get over to the hotel right now?"

"What's wrong?"

"I don't know." I sighed, thinking of Tyler, looking at Esperanza. "Maybe everything."

Chapter 20

THE STREET outside the hotel, visible through the lobby doors, was oddly clear of people. Everyone had fled, or the cops had cleared everyone out. The barricades lay toppled. A car was parked across the way. Trash was scattered, and a dark, wet splash marred the sidewalk—blood from the attack. Here in the lobby, groups of two or three people stayed close together, talking low and nervously. A couple of them glanced at Esperanza, staring. Cormac glared back, and they turned away.

"Essi, we should get out of sight," Luis said, and she nodded.

"Call me if you need anything," I said.

Arm in arm, they hurried to the elevators.

Shumacher went to speak with a manager at the front desk.

I waited, scratching at the streaks of blood drying on my skin, staring out at the eerily deserted street. We had to make sure Tyler was okay. Maybe Jan and Mercedes couldn't target me, but they could target him.

Then Ben appeared, stepping out of Ned's car, which had just pulled up to the curb. I wanted to rush to meet him, but I waited. I could be calm. But my hands itched until he was standing in front of me, and I could grab his hand. He squeezed back, and glanced at Cormac as if checking him for damage.

"We can't get ahold of Tyler," I said.

"You think something's happened?" he asked. I shook my head to say I didn't know.

Shumacher turned away from the counter. "They'll let us into his room with someone from security."

A woman in a nicely pressed suit with a hotel name tag pinned to the jacket lapel came through an office door behind the main desk, joined by a man in a security uniform.

Together, we went to the elevators.

Tyler's room was on the third floor—second floor, in British-speak. Probably the lowest floor he could possibly get a room, which would have appealed to his werewolf side—closer to the ground meant easier escape routes. The elevator ride up was claustrophobic, anxiety-ridden, and thankfully short. We spilled out, and I looked back and forth down a long corridor—two possible routes.

The hotel manager took the lead and guided us to the farthest room on the left. She swiped a key card three times without being able to open the door. I almost shoved her out of the way to try it myself, but on the fourth try the lock clicked and the door opened inward.

Dr. Shumacher was about to push past her and enter

the room when the security guard suggested they both step back, so he could enter first. "Mr. Tyler, sir?" he called in.

No one answered.

The officer entered, then Shumacher. I'd have crammed in right after, if the officer hadn't turned around and ushered us both straight out again.

"What?" I said, trying to look past him, to see into the room.

"I need to call the police," the guard said. "We've got a crime scene here."

"Oh my God, he's not—"

Shumacher shook her head. "No, he's not there. But there's obviously been a struggle."

"He was kidnapped?"

She didn't answer, but she'd gone pale and clasped her hands. The officer was speaking on a phone, Ben was at my shoulder. The hotel manager hovered, looking lost and worried. I leaned on the door frame, to see as much as I could without stepping inside. The room was dark, the curtains drawn. The bedspread lay in a heap on the floor at the foot of the bed. The TV had fallen off the dresser, and the mirror on the wall was cracked.

Closing my eyes, I took a deep, slow breath.

Tyler had been living in the room for a week, and his scent—his distinctive imprint of fur, skin, and wild—lay thick on the air. On top of that, I caught the barest hint of blood. Not a lot—the trace from a cut, that was all. And then, on top of *that*—

"Can you smell that?" I murmured to Ben.

"Like someone spilled a medicine cabinet?"

The odor was even fainter than the blood, but nonetheless distinctive—antiseptic with a sickly floral overlay. "Did they drug him?" I said, trying to be still, letting my nose work to take in as much air as possible.

"Maybe. Whoever it was was human," he said.

He was right—not another werewolf, and not a vampire. The invaders had made an effort to cover their scents, probably wearing gloves, boots, and masks and the like. There'd been more than one of them, but the individual marks were a tangle, too faint to make out.

"We have to find him," I said.

"The police should arrive soon," the security guard said. "They'll want to talk to you all, if you wouldn't mind waiting."

We didn't have time to wait. Someone had taken Tyler—when had it happened? Where had they gone? We had to track him down, as soon as we could—

"Give me your phone," Ben said. Blinking, I handed it to him, watched him scroll through numbers, pick one, and call. "Hi, Nick Parker? Ben O'Farrell here, from the other day? Yeah. I wondered if I could ask you a couple of questions about CCTV footage. Yeah, the police are involved, or will be soon . . ." He walked a few steps away for privacy. I heard Nick's answer buzzing through the speaker; he was too soft-spoken for me to make out words.

Cormac said softly, to keep the others from hearing, "Even if there is footage, you really think the cops will be able to find him?"

Of course he was right. It wasn't that the cops couldn't ordinarily find a kidnapping victim. They just might need help with this one and not even know it. The sooner we got that help . . .

Ben returned, clicking off the phone and handing it back to me.

"What'd he say?"

"He's got some contacts with the police. He'll find out what he can and keep us in the loop." He shrugged, as if in apology for not being able to do more.

I made a call of my own. Fortunately, he answered right away, saving me those few seconds of anxiety.

"Caleb? It's Kitty."

"If this is another scheme of Ned's—"

"It's not Ned. Tyler's missing. Someone's taken him."

"Taken him? Who? Where?"

"I don't know—if I knew I wouldn't need help."

"Settle down. Is it the vampires?"

"In broad daylight? Besides, we didn't smell any in the room. Really, it could be anyone."

"If the vampires—their minions, I mean—took him out of some kind of revenge for last night, he could already be dead."

I shook my head. "I have to think that he's more valuable alive."

"Sounds like a tracking job, then. We'll get on it. Where was he taken from?"

I explained the situation. Caleb and his people knew the city, would have the best idea where Tyler might have been taken. They were the best people to look for him. It was hard, though, leaving it in their hands.

The next couple of hours went too quickly, or too slowly, depending. I changed my mind minute to minute. Either way, it was a blur. Police, uniformed and plainclothes detectives, and forensic technicians descended on the room in a swarm and herded us into yet another bare office for interviews. They asked us about the last time we saw Tyler, we told them, and they asked who we thought might have wanted to do Tyler harm. That was the problem—I had to explain how difficult doing him harm actually was, and that the perpetrator had to have known exactly how.

The list of suspects I gave the poor overwhelmed detective was very long and ranged from foreign militaries to anti-werewolf extremists to vampires.

"Vampires?" the detective said, unhappily. "How am I meant to look for vampires?"

"Before sunset, in a room with no windows?" I said, and she glared at me.

The police finished their interviews, took our phone numbers and contact information, asked us not to leave town, and let us go.

Then we hunted.

In the back of the hotel, at one of the service entrances, we caught Tyler's scent, along with that human, vaguely medicinal smell from the room. They'd taken him out the door here. He was probably already unconscious. And then—nothing. The trail vanished.

"Probably loaded him into a car," Cormac said.

"What do we do now?" I asked, looking back and forth down the small, empty side street, as if they had just turned a corner.

"The security cameras had to pick up something," Ben said.

I paced, back and forth, over ten feet of sidewalk.

"Kitty," Ben said, meaning to be soothing, probably. The tone annoyed me.

I pulled out my phone and called Caleb again. "You find anything yet?"

He sounded growly even over the phone. "Of course I haven't, London's a big city. Have you even got an idea of where to start?"

"No. They apparently drove him somewhere."

"Then he could be anywhere. We're hunting, but there are a lot of strange werewolves in town just now."

"Okay. I know you're trying. Thanks."

"Kitty. If he really was snatched, they've got him stashed someplace we won't be able to smell him. You understand?"

He was giving up before even starting. No—he was warning me. Being realistic. "I know. Thanks," I said, and we hung up.

We had to be able to do something. I wasn't going to just let him go.

I called Dr. Shumacher for an update. The police

hadn't told her anything yet, but she'd called the American embassy to report Tyler's disappearance, and the authorities there promised to put their considerable resources into the search. We called Nick Parker again, and he did have some news. Ben and I both listened, heads together, the phone between us.

"I'm with a friend who works in CCTV evidence, which means I'm probably looking at this footage before the DI on the case, but don't tell anyone. A camera on the street behind the hotel shows a gray SUV with tinted windows parked by the service door you indicated, four hours ago. The car stays there for ten minutes while three men offloaded a bundle from an industrial laundry hamper. The bundle could hold a large person."

"Can you ID the car? The people? Can they track it?"

"That's just it," he said. "We can reasonably confirm that your friend was taken from the hotel. But the men are wearing scarves over their faces, and the car's registration plate has been covered with tape. They could very easily have driven to the next block, pulled the tape off, and blended into traffic. The make and color of the car are common enough it'll be difficult to spot them. We're looking at CCTV footage from surrounding areas, but it'll take time. I'll let you know if we find anything more."

He was going through a lot of trouble for us, which was kind and a little heartbreaking. "Thank you."

With such slim clues to follow, I tried to reconstruct what had happened. They'd caught Tyler by surprise in his room. They must have said something reasonable to convince him to open the door—there hadn't been any sign of a break-in. Once inside, though, they must have revealed themselves, and he'd struggled, but they had some way of quickly over-powering him. Tranquilizer darts, probably—I'd seen them work on werewolves before. They'd loaded him into one of those hotel laundry bins, taken him down a service elevator with no one the wiser. And it had all happened four hours ago. What were we doing four hours ago?

The riot. Luis and I had been struggling to the front of the crowd, and the attack on Esperanza had come right around then.

"Was it a setup?" I said out loud, wonderingly.

"Was what a setup?" Ben asked. "What are you thinking?"

"Crazy conspiracy theory," I said. "The same time Tyler was being loaded into the car, the riot was break-ing out in front of the hotel."

"A distraction?" Ben said. "It would sound crazy if it didn't actually make sense."

"What are we dealing with here?" I continued, thinking aloud. "Whoever took Tyler also has the wherewithal to instigate riots?"

"It would have just taken the guy with the bucket of blood to tip that crowd over the edge," Cormac said.

I called Nick again, told him about the correlation with the riot, and suggested looking for the guy with the bucket of blood. He might be a thread back to whoever had Tyler. Nick said he'd pass the information along to the police.

We walked back to the front of the hotel, but I didn't know where to go from there. The police were working on it. We'd followed the leads we knew to follow. Caleb was searching—without a lot of chance of success, but still searching.

It wasn't enough.

I stopped, and Ben and Cormac stopped with me, turning to look.

"Cormac," I said. "We have a fairy wish to use."

Ben chuckled. "You think that's for real?"

Cormac ignored him. "You sure you want to use it on this? We might be able to find Tyler without it."

"Alive?" I said, and Cormac didn't answer. "Yes. I can't think of anything better to use it on."

"You're both talking like this is actually going to work," Ben said. "There's magic and then there's . . ." He paused, a sour taste puckering his mouth.

"And then there's fairies. Yup," I said.

Chapter 21

CORMAC SUGGESTED moving into the open, to make it easier for the Fae to hear us. We deferred to his wisdom. Hyde Park was a few blocks down the main road from the hotel. I kept touching my phone, checking for calls that I might have missed, but hadn't. No one had called to say that they'd found Tyler and everything was okay. The sun was sinking, the shadows growing longer, twilight threatening. The vampires would be awake soon, and I didn't know if that was a good thing or a bad thing.

The park was as gorgeous as ever, a startling oasis in the middle of the city. Joggers were out, along with people walking home after work, and others playing with dogs who looked at us askance, ears flattened, knowing something was off about us. One, a bristly German shepherd, barked until his owner pulled him away, giving us a muddled apology, Bruce wasn't normally so rude, and so on. We avoided the dogs as best we could.

Cormac led us to an out-of-the-way glade, near a

stand of trees, and—a statue of Peter Pan, depicted as a slender, elfin child playing a pipe. He might have brought us to the spot on purpose.

Cormac pulled the scarf out of a jacket pocket and handed it over. It tingled in my hand. Was it just the shimmering texture of the fabric, or something more?

"What do I do now?"

"It's the Fae. Make a wish," he said.

"Just like that?" Ben said.

Coiling the scarf around my hands, I closed my eyes and thought about finding Tyler. Wished I could find him, right now, nearby, whole and unharmed. I drew a breath, smelled the grass, trees, the contained nature of the park hemmed in by the odor of city. Heard traffic, footsteps, a barking dog. Ben and Cormac standing still, breathing softly. It all felt so incongruously calm.

Something hit me from behind, like someone shoving in a crowd. I jumped and looked.

The young women from the conference and the restaurant, the ones who'd started the whole thing, stood arm in arm, looking at me, grinning wide, their big eyes shining. Daisy and Rose.

"Where'd they come from?" Ben hissed, looking around in a panic.

"You wouldn't understand," said a newcomer, who also seemed to have appeared from thin air, but might have walked from behind the stand of trees, except that I hadn't heard or smelled her coming. And I'd been listening.

Wearing a beaded skirt, a shapeless blouse, a shawl that seemed to be made of flower petals, and an annoyed expression creasing her elfin face, she was the regal woman from the other night. Now, at dusk instead of full dark, she reminded me of sunshine and distant meadows. Her clothing seemed old-fashioned but new at the same time. Her hair appeared to have flowers woven in it, but I couldn't tell what kind. They were tiny, and shimmered.

"I need help," I said starkly, holding her scarf out to her.

"You mean you're not going to ask for a castle or a bag of gold? Hmm."

"Would we have waited to ask if we were?"

"Yes, of course. You're the clever kind. At least, *you* are," she said to Cormac, who remained standing quietly with his hands in his pockets. "You and the one inside your head."

He narrowed his gaze and pursed his lips.

"Can you help?" I asked.

"Help with *what*?"

Focus, had to focus. It wasn't easy. "A friend is missing. Joseph Tyler, he's a werewolf, he's been kidnapped. A lot of people are looking for him, but he could be anywhere. Can you get him back?"

"And that's your wish? To get him back?"

"Yes. Rescue him. Alive, safely, in one piece, and sane." I blinked earnestly, hoping I'd covered all the bases.

She smirked. Clearly, I was pushing.

"Your wish is to retrieve one soul in this whole wide city," she stated, making it sound like a done deal. I glanced at Cormac, hoping for confirmation that this was good, that I was doing it right. He hadn't said anything, so I had to be reassured that I wasn't inadvertently selling my soul. I could see how it would be easy to do. She seemed so *nice*.

"Hand it over," she said, holding out her hand, shaking it. I laid the scarf across her palm.

She flourished the fabric and tossed it into a pocket—or somewhere. At any rate, it was gone. Clapping her hands, she called, "Girls. Call the troops. Werewolf in trouble. Go!"

The two—henchwomen? Sidekicks?—ran, but I couldn't have described exactly where they went. The woman smiled as if pleased. I hesitated to ask any other questions.

"Shall we look at the stars?" She settled onto the grass, lying prone, looking up. The sky had darkened to a royal blue, but I couldn't see any stars past the glow of the surrounding city.

We hesitated, but she pointed to the ground insistently, and how could we refuse?

We must have looked ridiculous, the three of us looking on, awkward and uncertain, with this odd woman lying in the grass, her clothing splayed around her.

"Is this really going to work?" Ben leaned toward me to whisper.

"I don't know," I said. "Cormac?"

"Hard to say. Anything can happen."

I took out my phone; still no calls. I had to resist calling Nick and Caleb yet again; it couldn't have been more than twenty minutes since the last time I called. They wouldn't have found anything new.

"Look, there! The evening star!" The fairy queen pointed off at a forty-five-degree angle.

I wouldn't have thought any stars would be visible in the middle of the city, but she'd found one, a single point of light, twinkling. Like a comforting hand on my shoulder.

"Actually, I think it's an airplane," Ben whispered.

"Oh, fie." She pouted.

I lasted about five seconds before I started tapping my feet. I cleared my throat a little. "Do you have any idea how long—"

"*Everyone's* looking," she said. "It's hard in the city, with all its iron. We cope—it's better than the alternative, after all. But these things take time. You know, it isn't that we're particularly good at granting wishes, or finding things or, well, *anything*. Playing tricks, maybe. But we pay attention. We find the loose thread that everyone else misses and *tug*. It makes us look so very clever."

We three humans clumped together and waited.

"Amelia's loving this," Cormac said.

"At least someone is," I muttered.

The sound of laughter filtered from . . . somewhere . . . and the two giggling women tumbled onto the grass next to their mistress. Again, I couldn't have said where they came from, just that they *arrived*.

The queen sat up and put her hands on her hips. "Well? Where is he?"

One of them scrunched up her face, almost tearful. "It's full of iron, we can't get any closer!"

"Fie," the queen said. "But you found him? Show me where," the queen said. The three of them huddled together, faces bent. I couldn't hear a thing. When she looked up again, she seemed determined. The two junior fairies beamed with pride.

"You couldn't get him," I said.

She held her chin, eyes crinkled with thought. "There has to be a way, I can't just leave a wish hanging like this."

"Um . . . can you tell me where they found him?" I said. "That'll be good enough."

Someone jogged on the path, and I froze, wondering how I was going to explain all this, but he never turned his head.

"You're saying I just have to tell you where he is, not fetch him."

"That's right." Hurry, hurry . . .

She said, "It's down the river at least five hops, then you have to wiggle up a bit, to one of the places where there isn't a single tree left—"

Cormac pulled a map from his jacket pocket, unfolding as he went. "You think you could point to it?"

Her gaze darted over it and she pursed her lips. "Hmm. How novel." After a moment, she pointed. "There."

Well east of the city, downriver. Just a spot on a map.

I frowned. "I don't suppose you have an address?"

She crossed her arms and pouted. "Addresses, bah. By the way, have you asked yourself whether or not I might be lying?" She was smiling, but it wasn't pretty.

"I'd be no worse off than I was before," I said, and she slouched, the wind taken out of her sails. Wings? She didn't seem to have wings, not that I could see anyway. I sighed. "This has to be right. Thank—" Cormac squeezed my arm and shook his head. You didn't thank fairies. Hmm.

"Right. This'll work," I said, and the queen offered a brief, mysterious bow.

I called Caleb. "I think I have a location for you. A place called Creekmouth?"

His voice sounded tinny, distant, like he was in a car. "It's an industrial park, part of the port system. That's not good," he said. "Where'd you get this information? How do you know he's there?"

"Um . . . fairies told me?"

He sounded surprised. "And you trust 'em?"

"They owed me a wish."

"Ah, right," he said.

"You believe me? Or, you believe in fairies?" I asked.

"I knew they were out there," Caleb said. "Though it doesn't do for a bloke like me to run around saying he believes in fairies. The thing you've got to remember about them—they're not human, so don't think you understand them. You, me, Ned, Marid, all of us—we all started out human and were changed. We might turn out quite different, but you can still suss us out at the heart of it. But them? They never were human."

"We've been having this conference on the paranormal and we missed this whole part of it that isn't even *human*?"

"Not my concern," he said. "Where are you?"

"Hyde Park," I said. "The Peter Pan statue."

"Typical," he huffed. "Walk north, you'll end up at the Lancaster Gate tube stop, we'll pick you up in about fifteen minutes."

"How far away is this place?"

"It'll take time to get there," he said. "I've got a couple of people I can send to scout ahead."

It would have to be enough. I shut off the phone and looked around to say good-bye to the queen and her folk, but they were gone.

I blinked at Cormac and Ben. "Where'd they go?"

"Vanished. Poof," Ben said, flicking out his fingers.

"Just like that?" I said.

"Hard to tell," Cormac said. "I wasn't quite looking at them."

"Yeah," Ben agreed. "I thought I just glanced away for a minute."

That shouldn't have surprised me at all. "We have to get moving, Caleb's going to pick us up."

Nightfall gave the mission even more urgency—we'd be dealing with vampires soon. Njal would know that Harald and his mate had left him. Other vampires would call on werewolves who were no longer there.

When we got to the intersection, the lights and traffic nearly blinded me after the relative peace and darkness of the park. I spotted Caleb when he flashed headlights, and we piled into the back of the car. Michael, one of Caleb's wolves, occupied the front passenger seat. They nodded at us in acknowledgement.

"You all right?" Caleb asked.

"Yeah. For now. How are Harald and his mate?"

"Her name's Karin. Poor kid, too scared to even talk, but she seems relieved to be here. They're safe, still resting. I've got someone staying with them who's very good at this sort of thing."

"Good." I sighed.

Caleb knew his way around the city and steered confidently through the maze of streets. I was lost in moments. Nothing in this city was set up on grids. I imagined London's citizens laying out medieval streets based on curving them around random trees, barrels, horses, whatever, that they didn't want to bother moving. What other explanation could there be? He managed to avoid the worst of the evening traffic, until we were on a wide—even relatively straight—highway. The central congestion of the city gave way to suburbs, parks, industrial sections, dockyards. I caught glimpses of the river now and then, a wide, dark band reflecting lights.

The phone rang. *Now* I hear from everyone. "Hello?"

"Kitty. Ned here. We have some catching up to do, I think."

"Yeah. I don't even know where to start."

"I'm hearing some very odd rumors. Did you really rescue those two wolves from Njal?"

"I guess we did," I said, bemused.

"I'm getting visits, calls—foreign Masters wanting to know if I've really withdrawn neutrality, why Masterless wolves are running around, why their own wolves are standing up to them, asking them to keep out of the war. They've been talking to each other, haven't they? And Vidal of St. Petersburg asked if I've really killed Roman. I admit I was cagey with him, and he seemed so pleased . . . Whatever you did this morning has everyone flustered."

I closed my eyes, enjoying a second's worth of victory. No one knew what was happening—our enemies couldn't unite. We'd bought ourselves time. Maybe even allies. Any of the Masters who'd been waiting to see who was stronger in the coming conflict might side with Ned, now.

"I hope . . . I hope this works out," I said.

"'Stiffen the sinews, summon up the blood, disguise fair nature with hard-favour'd rage,'" he said. "Where are you and your pack now?"

"In a car with Caleb, heading east to look for a friend who's gone missing."

"Your Sergeant Tyler, yes? What happened?"

"He was kidnapped out of his hotel room earlier this afternoon. We're following a lead that says they've taken him to Creekmouth."

"That isn't good."

"That's what Caleb says."

"You'll need help."

"Any you can spare. But you'll never get there in time, they have a huge head start, it's miles away—"

"Oh, have no fear at all about that." His tone held a wicked smile.

"What—"

He hung up. I stared at my phone.

"That was Ned," Ben said, a statement. "What's happening?"

"I'm not sure," I said, frowning. I wanted to blame my exhaustion and muzzy-headedness on jet lag but wasn't sure I still could, a week later.

While I'd talked to Ned, Caleb had gotten a call, and had driven the last mile or so with his phone pressed to his ear. He put it in a pocket and glanced at me in the rearview mirror. "I think we've found him. But we don't have a lot of time."

"What? Why not, what's happening?"

"I told you there's a shipping dock—they may be trying to smuggle him out of the country."

Chapter 22

WE LEFT the highway and turned into a clutter of warehouses. This wasn't the pretty postcard, touristy part of London. This was east of the city, along the river, past the bridges and castles and giant Ferris wheel and twenty-first-century development. London was still a busy international port, full of big steel warehouses, concrete docks, cranes, industrial sites, refineries. It seemed otherworldly, like we'd entered some industrial hell. A dystopian Terry Gilliam film.

Caleb switched off the headlights and stopped. Michael immediately left the car and trotted a ways out, turning between a pair of buildings.

"He'll meet up with my scouts," Caleb said.

"How many people do you have here?" Cormac asked.

"Two, plus Michael. Stealth will have to make up for numbers in this fight."

Cormac made a noise, and I couldn't tell if he was satisfied or not. Me, I always liked stealth. If we could sneak in, grab Tyler, sneak back out . . .

I didn't expect it to be that easy.

The rest of us left the car and moved into the shadow of the nearest building, out of the streetlights. Cormac held an object hidden in his hand, some charm against the dark.

A container ship, a hulking form just visible between buildings, was docked some distance down. Tyler's captors could load him onto such a ship from here, take him anywhere, and we'd never get him back.

"This isn't a real good environment for us," Ben said.

His nose was flaring, wrinkling as he took in the smells in the area—oil, fuel, concrete, steel. Nothing natural intruded. I thought I should have been able to smell the river, the rich waterway of the Thames, but the air in that direction smelled of oil and volatiles, tainted and poisonous. The only scent in the mix that even resembled nature was a trace of rat and pigeon droppings. An industrial lamp sent out a circle of light gone hazy in the mist. Over the course of the evening, the clouds had returned.

"Not our territory, not our habitat. It *sucks,*" I said.

"A dead zone to people like us. Another good reason to bring Tyler here. I'm surprised your fairies were able to find him," Caleb said.

"We asked them to rescue him, but they couldn't get this close," I said. "Too much iron."

We listened, tense and alert, all senses turned outward. I suddenly wished Cormac wasn't here. If our enemies sent lycanthropes, if any of them bit him . . .

"All we need now is the zombie apocalypse," Ben said.

"Zombies don't exist," I said. "Not that kind of zombie, anyway."

"What?"

"The brain-eating zombie—those are movie zombies. They don't exist. On the other hand, Haitian voodoo zombies totally exist."

"How do you even figure these things out?" he said.

"Long story."

"I guess so."

Caleb raised a hand; I looked to see what had caught his attention. A short-haired woman, small and athletic, young and jumpy, approached. A werewolf, she seemed at ease in a tank top and shorts, even in the chill air.

"We think we found 'im, gov," she whispered to Caleb. "Spotted their car."

"Lead on, then," he said, wearing a proud smile. "Jill has the best nose in the south of England."

Single file, we followed her, winding a path among the buildings. Ben, I noticed, had moved to put Cormac between us. Maybe an inadequate shield, but a shield nonetheless.

We stepped slowly, carefully, wolves on the prowl, pausing often to survey the air. I couldn't smell much besides oil, concrete, and our own party. A couple of times, Caleb signaled to his three scouts. Michael returned, paralleling us on a different path—keeping watch on Jill.

When Ben let out a stifled yell, we all dropped into defensive crouches.

"Where the *fuck* did you come from!" Ben hissed to the figure behind him.

"You ought to keep your voice down," Ned said in a stage whisper.

He should have been almost an hour behind us. "Wait a minute. How—"

Ned put a finger over his mouth and shook his head.

"Not funny, Ned," Caleb said, glaring.

The vampire said, "I brought half a dozen of my folk with me, along with Antony and Marid. Ought to help, don't you think? I thought you'd be pleased."

"Tell me you didn't bring Emma," I said in a sudden panic.

He had the grace to look startled. "Good God no, she's just a child."

He hadn't put her in harm's way yet, he wouldn't start. The relief I felt at the news was painful.

"Anyone ever tell you you have a flair for the dramatic?" I said.

"Ha," he answered flatly.

We moved on, and I wondered how much more of this exacting progress we had to make. Patience . . . if you waited long enough, still as a pond, the deer would come to you. For the fifth or sixth time, we paused at a corner to scout the lay of the land. The scouts returned to confer with Caleb. Jill said she thought Tyler was being kept in a building at the very end of the street. Ned, who remained like a statue, agreed with her. We still hadn't met any guards or opposition, which was starting to make us all nervous. It was only a matter of time.

We should have expected it when a shot fired with an echoing crack.

"Aw, Jesus!" Michael stumbled and fell, clutching his shoulder. We pressed the wall.

He moaned around grit teeth. "Caleb, it's silver, oh God—"

"Michael." Caleb pulled his lieutenant into shelter with the rest of us. Jill and the second scout, Warrick, huddled together. A second shot fired, but no one cried out, so it must have missed.

"Silver bullets," Ben hissed, and got in front of me, pushing me into a doorway. And Cormac got in front of *him*.

Wolf thrashed, beating herself against the bars of her cage, and I had to swallow her back, taking deep breaths to pull her inside. She wanted to run, to flee—it was the only response to such a deadly enemy. Get as far away from the silver as possible.

But we couldn't do that. I huddled with Ben and tried to hang on to myself.

Michael let out an even more pain-racked groan and curled into a fetal pose. Caleb held tight to him, cradling him. He couldn't do anything else. A very long time seemed to pass until Michael's shivering stopped, until he was gone. Caleb, Warrick, and Jill all had hands on him, touching him, for his comfort and theirs, sending him on his way.

Ben found my hand and squeezed tightly. My other hand found Cormac's arm. He stood before us both, a shield. He had a chance of surviving being shot with a silver bullet.

Only Ned seemed unconcerned, unaffected by the scene. He gazed out, and up. "I believe I see him. If you'll excuse me."

And he was gone. Just gone, like shadows vanish when the lights turn off. The scream came a scant moment later. I shivered.

We waited; I caught the touch of chill air the moment before he reappeared.

"There are four more of them watching the small warehouse on the next block. They're human. Some brand of mercenary I should think. The warehouse is filled with heartbeats."

Not vampires, then. "Whose mercenaries?" I whispered.

"I didn't ask," Ned said. "I thought we were in a hurry."

"We are," Caleb said, voice low, gravelly. "I'll kill them all."

"Leave them to us," Ned said and paced away. I saw his retreat this time, or thought I did, until he disappeared into the next set of shadows.

Caleb's expression was sour. I touched his shoulder, which was tense, hard as steel.

"They can stand up to silver bullets," I said to Caleb. "Our job is finding Tyler."

We should have been in forest, with familiar, earthy smells, trees blocking out the sky, the trails of our prey fresh as spring. Caleb said he'd show us where he and his wolves ran on full moon nights. After we got through all this, I'd take him up on the offer. It would feel like a vacation.

Carefully, cautiously, ducking around corners, constantly scanning our surroundings, we moved onward. I kept waiting for the sound of gunfire, knowing it would still startle me when it came, no matter how ready I thought I was to hear it.

"There," Jill finally said, nodding to the next doorway. The building was low, only one story, made of prefab steel walls with a slanted roof. It might have been offices or storage. It didn't seem to have windows.

I took a deep breath and still couldn't smell Tyler.

We waited for what seemed a long time, but no guards appeared.

"Is it clear?" I asked.

Her eyes closed, Jill took a series of long, quiet breaths. "Two guys on the other side, I think. Human."

"Armed with silver, no doubt," Caleb muttered. "Door's probably locked to boot. They'll hear us coming no matter what."

"There another way in?" I said.

"Other side," Jill said. "But the SUV's parked there. That door's probably worse than this one."

We still had no idea how many—or even what—we were facing here.

"I'll go," Cormac said, gathering himself to continue on.

"No," Ben said.

I shook my head. "They'll shoot you same as us."

The hunter's expression didn't change. "We hit this door. I can give you maybe twenty seconds to get their guns away."

"How?" Ben said.

"I'll take care of it."

I snorted. "Does Amelia have some hoopy spell for that?"

"*I* have lock picks. Amelia has the distraction. Assuming the wolf is right about there only being two guys."

Caleb said, "Can you really get the lock?"

"What is it, a dead bolt? I think so."

"Then Warrick and I will get the guards. You two"—he pointed at Ben and me—"stay put, cover our backs."

Cormac nodded. "When I give you the signal, cover your eyes."

I reached. "Wait a minute—" But the three of them moved off, and Ben held me back. It made sense from a tactical standpoint. Caleb and Warrick were bigger, tougher, and no doubt way more experienced fighters than we were. I still felt like I should have been the one on the front line.

"What's he got planned?" Jill whispered. She was just a puppy—couldn't have been more than twenty. She crouched, balancing on one hand, bouncing a little. I swore I saw the ghosts of pointed ears prick forward with interest.

"I don't know," I said.

Cormac pulled lock-picking tools from his jacket pocket. I winced—I could hear the scraping from here. The guards on the other side of the door would be waiting for them. They were all dead. I almost ran over and told him to stop, that we would find another way, that Tyler wouldn't want anybody—anybody else—dying for him.

"Tell me he knows what he's doing," I whispered to Ben, who just shook his head.

Then Cormac nodded to Caleb and Warrick, who turned their heads, shading their eyes.

It happened quickly: Cormac kicked open the door, raised his hand, and a blinding white light flashed before him, floodlight bright, filling the room inside. The two werewolves rushed in. The sounds of fighting, a few meaty smacks, were brief. Cormac lowered his hand, closed his fist, and the light faded.

He may have picked the lock, but that spotlight spell was Amelia's. The guards may have been waiting for someone to kick in the door, but they certainly hadn't expected to be blinded in the next second.

"Brilliant!" Jill said. No pun intended, surely.

When Cormac looked back and waved, the three of us moved up to join him.

A single work lamp hung in the back of the room, giving off just enough light to see comfortably. The room was small, maybe the size of a garage, and might have been used for storage once. A few empty cardboard boxes lay around the periphery, along with some crumpled packing paper. Two men, hulking guard types in black fatigues, lay writhing on the ground. One of them was already tied, hand to foot, arms wrenched behind him, with what looked like nylon cord. Caleb stood on the second one's neck while Warrick trussed him up—the cord looked like it came from the guy's own pockets, part of his own inventory. That had to hurt.

Their guns, mean-looking assault rifles, were tossed aside, against a far wall. Cormac eyed them thoughtfully.

"Don't even think about it," Ben said.

Inside, the smells were clearer. People had been moving in and out of the warehouse all day. I caught a trace of lycanthrope—wild, wolfish—as well as the chill that meant vampires had been here. One of Ned's spies? Or an enemy? The guards from the front of the warehouse must have heard us. They ought to be pounding through any minute. So where were they? Step by soft step, I moved to the next door against the opposite wall.

"Kitty!" Cormac hissed, and I held back.

"Warrick, watch them," Caleb said, pointing to the guns. The werewolf picked one up and held it on the two mercenaries, who stopped squirming in their effort to loosen their bonds.

Cormac studied the door, its handle, and the crack of light between the frame. "It's not locked."

Jill came close and took another of her long, quiet breaths. "Werewolf—maybe your man. He's not alone."

Great. The other guards weren't storming us—they were waiting for us to come to them. The next room was well lit—Cormac's trick with the flare wouldn't work again. Maybe we could rush them. Without getting shot.

This was why I preferred talking my way out of dodgy situations.

"Everyone take cover," Cormac said, hand on the handle ready to pull it open. The rest of us stood against the walls, waiting. I watched him take a breath, then another. Counting to three. Then he swung back, pulling open the door.

Nothing happened.

Inching forward, I reached the edge of the door frame and very carefully leaned around to look. Ben held my arm, as if he could yank me back when the gunfire started.

The next room was like this one—concrete, abandoned. In the middle of it crouched Tyler, fully conscious, muscles tensed, ready to spring. Another black-garbed guard lay crumpled in the corner, knocked out, a bruise marring his slack face.

"Tyler!" I said, falling into the room.

For a short moment, his lips pulled back in a snarl, and his eyes gleamed. Then recognition flashed.

"Kitty," he said and heaved an exhausted sigh, and I skidded to my knees on the concrete floor. I touched his arm, brushed my hand over his nearly bald head, and let him take in my scent. Anxiety eased out of him, and he leaned into me.

"They miscalculated the dose," he said. "I don't think I was supposed to wake up yet."

"Do you know who did this?"

"Private security, decently trained." Tyler nodded a greeting to Ben and Cormac. Caleb and Jill fanned through the room, standing watch, covering the doorway we'd come through, looking forward to the next one, leading to yet another room.

"The ringleaders are in there," Tyler said, tipping his head to the door.

"How many?" Cormac asked.

"Three, I think. Human and vampire. I haven't seen them since I woke up, and my nose isn't working too well."

Once again, we braced for the inevitable battle that would come swarming through the door any moment. It didn't happen. It kept not happening. I couldn't even hear anything in the next room.

They, whoever had taken Tyler, knew they were busted. They were fleeing, and if we waited, we'd lose them. I walked straight for the door, stalking like Wolf had cornered her prey.

"Kitty—" Cormac called after me.

"At least stand back when you open the door," Ben said, rushing to join me. He got to the door first, gripping the handle ahead of me. "Ready?"

I stood on the other side of the door frame and nodded. He turned the handle, yanked open the door, and got out of the way.

We waited for a few breaths, a handful of heartbeats, and I tried to catch a scent of what was waiting for us inside. No gunfire responded, so Ben and I eased around the door frame.

Dr. Paul Flemming stood against the far wall,

looking just like he did four years ago: thin, mousy, bureaucratic, with a well-worn jacket over nondescript shirt and trousers.

"*You,*" I hissed, and lunged.

Ben grabbed my arm, and I nearly wrenched it out of the socket trying to pull away. I didn't care. Snarling, I charged again, flopping to try and break free from his grip. He used both hands and might have yelled at me to calm down, but I wasn't listening. My vision, all my senses, had narrowed to a tunnel that focused on Flemming, and my mouth watered at the thought of putting my teeth around his throat. I had him, if my too-cautious mate would just let me go, I'd *kill* him—

"Look at that, she's gone nonverbal. What the bloody hell did you do to her?" The British alpha stood at my other shoulder, and I growled at him, too.

Flemming had flattened himself against the steel wall and stared at me with white-rimmed eyes. Wasn't so calculating now, was he? See how he did when I ran claws down his face—

Ben got in front of me and pressed. "Kitty, you're not helping. Snap out of it before you lose it." He put his face in front of mine, catching my gaze and projecting calm. I gave another halfhearted lurch to break out of his grip, but he was a wall. Settling slowly, I tried to unclench my hands. He moved aside, but kept his arm across me—just in case.

Finally, I looked at Flemming without losing my temper entirely.

"So," I said, flatly as I could, to keep from yelling. "What's your story this time? Got another silver-lined cell all set up? What were you going to do to him?"

His chin tipped up, an effort to stay calm. "I—I wasn't going to hurt him."

"Like you weren't going to hurt me?"

"You weren't hurt—"

I growled and lunged again—Ben caught me, like I knew he would. His voice in my ear was calm. "I'm going to call the police," he said. "He'll be extradited to the U.S. He'll get what's coming, okay?"

"Don't," Caleb said. "Don't call them just yet. Not 'til we get what we need." He had a curl to his lip.

Caleb and Cormac were in the room; Tyler was with Jill, who was helping him to his feet; Warrick stood guard behind us. We were three rooms in, and based on the size of the warehouse we had to be nearly at the other side. The next door should have been the last. It was open, just a crack.

Flemming eyed the cracked door, as if he thought he could make a run for it. He'd spent half his career studying werewolves; he had to know better than that. We fanned around him, wolves on the hunt. His breathing had become rapid.

"Where are the rest of the guards?" I asked.

"I—I don't know. They're supposed to be here—"

"Who's really behind this, Flemming?" I said. "You didn't get these resources on your own."

The detritus here was different than in the other rooms. Instead of empty cardboard boxes, a couple of

plastic crates were stacked in corners. A card table
with several chairs around it showed the remains of
an Indian takeout meal, wrapped in a plastic bag. I
paced, to investigate. Flipping back the lid of one of
the crates, I found coils of nylon cord, vials of clear
liquid and tranquilizer darts, handcuffs that gleamed
silver. Everything you'd need to catch and hold a
werewolf. I shook my head at it all.

A black leather attaché case was shoved under the
table. "Yours?" I said to him, kicking it. He'd taken
on the aspect of a prisoner of war, his jaw clenched,
silent.

I pulled it into the open and started digging.

Flemming actually had the nerve to reach. "You
can't—"

"We can make you disappear, if we like," Caleb
said cheerfully. Flemming slumped back to his place
on the wall.

In the case's outside pocket I found a bundle of
standard-looking documents, forms with boxes to fill
in with names, addresses, dates. Customs declarations,
shipping manifests. Buried in the bottom of the pocket,
I found a bundle of passports. I flipped through them
quickly—three, including one for the U.S., were for
Flemming alone. A British one had Tyler's picture in
it, but a different name. Probably to help smuggle him
out of the country, and get him into another.

A name appeared over and over again on the paperwork—as a contact person, the owner of goods to
be shipped, the authority by which money changed
hands. I assumed it was Flemming's alias. Except . . .

"Who is G. White?" I asked Flemming.

He swallowed hard, moving his lips as if preparing to speak. For all the good it would do him, surrounded by werewolves as he was. We could smell the lies.

Hand on chin, gaze thoughtful, Ben said, "Cormac . . . Amelia . . . check something for me: What's the Latin word for *white*?"

"Albus," Cormac said.

Couldn't possibly be a coincidence . . . "Albus. Albinus. Gaius Albinus?" I murmured. "G. White, is that who you're working for?"

Flemming said, "He's a foreign investor, heads a private security firm. It's perfectly normal—"

I said, "Have you met him? What's he look like?"

"I don't know why you're asking—"

"Tell her," Ben said.

"He . . . he's about my height. Lean. Dark hair, close-cropped. He always wears a long dark coat—"

"Oh, my God," Ben murmured.

It was Roman. I showed Flemming a mix of emotions, from rage to despair. "Do you have any idea who you're working for?"

"I told you, a foreign investor—"

He had no idea.

"What would Roman want with Tyler?" Ben said.

"Ready-made werewolf soldier, trained in the American Special Forces. He'd be priceless," I said. Gravity must have suddenly doubled, I felt so tired, so slow.

"Who's Roman?" Tyler said. He'd come to stand in

the doorway. "And why would he think I'd work for him?"

"He's a vampire, a very old one," I answered. "He wouldn't need your cooperation, he'd just need you." We hadn't called the police yet. Surely Ben would let me at Flemming now. I said to him, "He conned you into recruiting for him—"

"He funded my research, that's all—" Flemming said.

"And you still think it's okay to kidnap werewolves for that research? Have you learned *anything*?"

"It's necessary—"

"Bah." I flung a hand at him and turned away. "You'd better call the cops in before I have a go at him."

Ben already had his phone in his hand, but Caleb put his hand over it, lowering it from his ear.

"Give us a chance to get out," Caleb said. "I don't want to have to explain our handiwork to them. Not to mention Ned's."

"Ned probably owns the cops," I muttered.

"Kitty?" Tyler said. "What's it mean? What were they planning to do with me?"

I couldn't even look at Flemming again, however much I wanted to scrutinize him, to get *him* to tell Tyler exactly what he'd planned. I'd lose my temper for sure. I said, "Use you, control you, throw you into battle. Make you train others. The same damn thing."

"It's an awful lot of trouble to go through," Caleb said.

Maybe. But with Tyler's training and expertise? He wasn't just werewolf cannon fodder. In a fight, he was worth ten of the rest of us.

"Doesn't matter now," I said. "He's in a lot of trouble back home."

Flemming quailed, his voice trembling. "You won't get away with this. I have friends—" The cliché must have come instinctively.

"Your G. White isn't going to come save you," I said. "Whoever your allies were in this, they've left you."

Caleb went to the crate of equipment and drew out a pair of handcuffs. "I'll truss him up a bit, so he doesn't get the idea he can just walk out. Jill, we'll go back and get Michael and bring the car 'round. *Then* we can call the cops."

"Yes, sir," she said.

Along with Ben and Cormac, Tyler and I moved to the door and waited. Cormac opened it wider, looking out. The SUV from the security footage was parked outside. A hundred yards away, lurking like a mountain in the dark, a freight ship was docked on the river. If they'd gotten him on there, Tyler would have just vanished.

Caleb left Flemming lying against the wall in handcuffs. The scientist seemed relieved, somehow, as if assured that the werewolves weren't going to tear him apart on principle.

He caught me looking at him. "Who is Gaius Albinus?"

How to explain, in a sentence or less, without shouting? How to tell Flemming just how far in over his head he was without realizing it, so that I could savor his reaction? My lips turned in more of a sneer than a smile. "Dux Bellorum. Do you know what that means?"

"Leader of war. It's a title for a general," he said.

"That's right. Same guy, and he's collecting allies. Servants."

"That sounds very dramatic," he said. "But I work *with* people. Not for them."

I laughed bitterly. He'd probably been telling himself that his whole life. In our last encounter, he'd had help catching me. No way he could have pulled that off on his own. He'd made a deal with a vampire, Alette's lieutenant in Washington, D.C. He caught me, and in return Flemming gave him a security contingent to help him destroy Alette and take over the city. I don't think there'd been any question in Leo's mind who came out ahead in that bargain. Too bad it had backfired. Even Flemming saw that in the end. But he hadn't learned a damn thing since then, and here he was, working with vampires again.

"You don't even know how much you don't know," I said.

"The police will let me go," he said. "I won't be extradited. I won't be tried. I haven't done anything wrong."

"Haven't done anything—only if you believe that werewolves aren't people."

The expression he turned to me was so matter-of-fact, my breath caught. So, that was where we stood.

Tyler and I went to stare out the door with Cormac and Ben.

"That's what you get for baiting the guy," Ben said, putting his arm around me and pulling me close. I snuggled against his warmth.

Caleb and the others seemed to take forever with the car. Then I remembered they had Michael's body to retrieve.

"This Dux Bellorum," Tyler said, his voice low, weary. He still smelled ill, the tranquilizer lingering in his system. "Am I going to have to keep worrying about him?"

"Probably," I said, leaning my head on Ben's shoulder. "But knowledge seems to be the best defense. He won't be able to sneak up on you again."

All of us were running on next to no sleep, frayed nerves, and spent adrenaline, and we fell into silence. Even the room behind me had become especially quiet, as if Flemming had fallen asleep.

But when I looked in on him, he was gone.

At my shocked gasp, the others turned.

"Where'd he go?" Ben said.

Tyler went on the move, pacing this room and into the next, examining it, sheltering behind the doorway before glancing into the third room.

"He couldn't have gotten away without making any noise," the soldier said.

"Then where is he?" I asked. I took a slow breath,

smelling. We should be able to track him, even with the diesel stink of the place. But all I sensed was a horrible, unnatural chill . . .

"Kitty," Cormac said, pointing out to the street.

Tonight, Mercedes wore green, a lacey camisole that set off her creamy skin and blood-colored hair, and loose silken slacks that fluttered in the breeze coming off the river. She was such a contrast to the surroundings, managing to remain haughty, imperial.

Standing across the wide street between warehouses, she held Dr. Flemming braced beside her. He was dead weight, seeming to hang on her arm like a sack of potatoes. The effort didn't strain her at all.

She waited until she knew we were all looking, then tilted her head to give Flemming one of her charming, winning stage smiles. "You are a miserable failure," she said, and dropped him. He fell in a heap.

I would have sworn that she turned and casually strolled away, high heels clicking on the asphalt. But when I ran after her, shouting, she was already gone. She'd turned a corner, transformed into a shadow, or simply vanished.

The others' footsteps pounded behind me, catching up. I stopped at Flemming's body, turned him over on his back.

He blinked at me and grasped weakly with still-handcuffed hands. His mouth worked, but he had no air left. A ragged, three-inch gash tore into his neck, opening a major artery. Scarlet lipstick smeared the skin around it. She hadn't drained him completely.

But she hadn't left him enough to survive on. Bastard had finally dug himself in too deep. He had just enough life left to look me in the eyes as he died. He seemed . . . confused.

"Kitty." Ben touched me.

"I was so angry at him," I said weakly.

"Let's get out of here," Ben said. "Maybe we can take Caleb up on his offer to go for a run somewhere."

Somewhere far away from this concrete pit. Someplace with trees, grass, wide open spaces, wind in my fur.

The sound of an engine echoed, and Caleb's car pulled around, headlights off. He left the engine running, got out, and looked around. "Well. This is a mess. Not to mention the pile of unconscious mercenaries we found by the main road—that's where all the guards went. Ned's doing, no doubt." Bemused, he hitched his thumb over his shoulder to indicate the direction.

I hardly had the energy to be relieved at the news. "We should go looking for her," I said. We had to stop her. Somehow. I couldn't seem to find the energy to stand.

Ben's hand squeezed on my shoulder, and he pointed behind us, to the corner of the building we'd found Flemming in. A different corner, a different shadow than the one Mercedes had disappeared into. This time, Ned emerged. The chill of his being was almost indistinguishable from the nighttime chill in the air.

"Look who we found," Ned said, stepping into the open, illuminated by a streetlight. He seemed to have chosen the spot, as if walking into the circle of a spotlight on stage. Marid and Antony followed him. Between them, gripping his shoulders, they dragged Jan. They wouldn't let him get his feet under him, and he scrabbled ungracefully to keep his balance. Marid had a grip on the captive vampire's hair and wrenched his head back.

Ned considered the scene around us. "Oh, you've all been busy, haven't you? Sergeant Tyler, I presume?"

The soldier, standing nearby, raised his brows in a question.

"You got him," I said stupidly, nodding at Jan.

"Yes, we did." He beamed.

"What about Mercedes? She was right here. Did you see her? She killed Flemming." I pointed at the body, as if they hadn't seen it.

Marid shook his head. "Only Jan and his hangers-on. Mercenaries, a handful of lesser vampires. Are you sure it was her?"

I growled. Ben's hand closed on my arm, a gentle warning.

"If it was her, she's gone now," Ned said. "And you know what they say about a bird in the hand." He leered at Jan, who flinched back, but Marid and Antony held him fast and seemed happy to do so.

"But—" Mercedes was the mastermind. The direct lead to Roman. If he was the general, she was the master sergeant.

This was exactly how she'd planned it, I realized. Mercedes sacrificed Jan. Like a herd of deer leaving a weaker member behind for the wolves, she'd let him get taken, a distraction, while she made her escape. And the vampires thought they were so much better than us. I could almost feel sorry for the merely decades-old vampires who kept taking metaphorical bullets for these old bastards.

Grinning, Ned stepped behind Jan with the air of an executioner.

Jan started yelling. "The bitch is right, it's Mercedes you want! It's all her, I'm just . . . just a foot soldier. She can lead you to Roman!"

"Even if that's true, you think I'm going to just let you go? *Really?*"

"I can help you!"

With Marid and Antony bracing his arms, Ned curled his arm around the vampire's head, a mockery of an embrace, and wrenched until the bone cracked.

Jan kept arguing, as if the injury hadn't happened. "You need me! This is a mistake! I have a thousand years of experience at your command! Edward, listen to me!"

"I never have before, why should I start now? Because you *ask?*"

Ned was still wrenching, twisting Jan's head, until the vampire's face looked along his shoulder, then over it. Vertebrae crunched again. His voice finally strangled to gasping silence as his windpipe kinked shut. His head faced backward now, and Ned kept on, as if muscling open a water main. The skin furrowed, stretched, tore. Ned dug in his fingernails to help it along. The tendons on his hands stood out. Impossibly, Jan still twitched, struggling.

I looked away before the head came off, but I heard it, tendons popping, wet tissue slurping apart. The thud as the body dropped. When I found the stomach to lift my gaze, Ned tossed a melon-sized bundle toward the warehouse wall. The body lay at his feet. The stringy, ragged gash where his head should have been didn't bleed at all.

We all stared, silent as snowfall.

"I thought you were joking," I murmured.

Evenly, Ned said, "Mr. Bennett, I'm sure you have a stake on your person I might borrow?"

Cormac was already holding the sharpened rod of wood, in an overhand grip, ready to use. He seemed to consider exactly how he ought to give it to Ned. I tried to develop instant telepathy—*don't argue, he just ripped a guy's head off!*

Cormac tossed it, and Ned caught it.

Vampire bodies disintegrated when the vampire was destroyed. The decay of the grave caught up with them at last. Jan's body . . . the flesh of his hands was pale, but creamy, with the faintest rosy flush, evidence of his last meal.

My throat closed, choking on bile. Jan was still alive, in some form.

Ned drove the stake through Jan's chest, and that finished him. Only a smear of ash remained of the vampire. The three of them, Antony, Marid, and Ned, were congratulating themselves, laughing and telling some hundred-year-old inside joke. Celebrating like they'd already won the war. And these were my allies?

Ben was right. We needed to get out of here. Too many bodies, too much of a mess. But I was curious. I crept forward to study the stain on the asphalt that used to be Jan. Even his clothes were gone. Sure enough, though, a leather cord had fallen off his neck when Ned did the deed. The nickel-sized Roman coin tied on the cord was old, dark with tarnish. I only found it because I was looking for it.

"Ned?" I said, picking up the cord, watching the coin dangle. "We need to smash this."

His smell fell, the jubilation quelled. He studied it, fascinated. So did the others.

"I've never seen one of these," Antony said.

"Probably for the best," Ned murmured.

Caleb had a hammer in the trunk of his car. I used it to smash the coin against the concrete, erasing the design and turning it into a mangled lump of old bronze. When I got home, I'd put it with the others we'd found and destroyed.

"You notice?" Cormac said, gazing around, squinting into the damp air and streetlights.

"Notice what?"

"They didn't bring any werewolves with them."

We'd only faced vampires and human mercenaries. Caleb's pack and mine had been the only lycanthropes here. Jan at least should have been able to call on an army, like he had at Hyde Park.

"Maybe they didn't think they'd need them," I said.

"Or maybe your plan worked." His smile was thin, amused.

"You mean I actually might have incited a werewolf rebellion? What're the odds?" I wanted to laugh.

He just shook his head, walking away, toward Caleb's car.

It was all over but the shouting, as they say. Caleb and Ned argued about cleanup—they both had ideas of what should be done with the bodies, any CCTV footage that had recorded us, and how we should otherwise make the scene look like we'd never been here. Ben kept wanting to call the cops because he assumed they'd show up eventually. Then Ned announced that he'd already called the cops—and told them to stay away. Because apparently he could just do that.

This wasn't my territory. I left the mess to them.

Caleb drove us back into town. Jill and Warrick were in another car, with Michael's body.

"I'm sorry. About Michael," I said. "It was a high price to pay."

After a moment, Caleb said, "Thanks."

Cormac had the front passenger seat. Hunched over, tense and quiet, Tyler was in the back with Ben and me. He was still recovering from post-traumatic stress from his time in Afghanistan. I couldn't tell if he was about to relapse, and if we needed to get him someplace safe.

He turned to me. "Can I use your phone to call the States?"

"Yeah, of course." I handed it over.

He dialed and pulled at his lip waiting for an answer. When it came—a woman's straightforward hello—Tyler transformed. His expression brightened, the tension left his shoulders. If he'd had his tail, it would have been wagging.

"Hey. Susan. I didn't wake you up, did I? I don't even know what time it is there. No . . . no, I'm okay. I just wanted to hear your voice." The woman's response sounded pleased, and she chatted happily at him. Tyler was in bliss.

That . . . that was *awesome*.

Chapter 23

WE CALLED Shumacher to let her know everything was all right and delivered Tyler safely to the hotel for a hot shower and sleep. Then Caleb dropped us off at Ned's for showers and sleep of our own. When I really looked at the grizzled werewolf, he seemed the most tired of any of us. His face sagged, and his shoulders were rigid with the effort of keeping them straight.

"Get some sleep," I told him before shutting the car door.

"You giving me orders now?" he grumbled, and I smiled and let him go.

Emma waited in the parlor for us, even had hot tea and food ready. She didn't ask what had happened—Ned had probably called her already.

The tea felt amazing. Like a warm blanket on the inside. Emma watched us, wringing her hands.

"You know that Flemming's dead?" I said. She was another of his victims, albeit indirectly.

"Alette will be glad to hear that," she said, flattening her hands to smooth out her skirt. "It feels like the end of an era."

"Maybe just the end of a chapter," I said. "There always seem to be more jerks to take the place of people like that." Not to mention Mercedes and Roman were still on the loose. This seemed a strangely muted victory.

I STILL had that speech. That I hadn't written. My worry about it seemed so petty. How many people had died in the battles we'd fought over the last two days? How many more would die?

What had I really thought this conference would accomplish?

Ben waited with me at the front of the auditorium, clinging to the side wall, looking over the crowd that filled the seats. Full house. And everyone was staring at *me,* which made Wolf want to growl. I had tried to dress nicely without being too formal. I wanted my outfit to say "hip talk-radio host." I don't know if my jeans, gray jacket, and red silk T-shirt managed it. I mostly felt like I was trying too hard. I'd scratched some notes and held the sheets of paper in front of me, for all the good it would do.

"Have you decided what you're going to say?" Ben asked. He stood at my shoulder, looking out like a bodyguard.

"Well, sort of. I know what I want to say. I just don't know if I should."

He took my hands, folding both of them inside his,

and kissed my forehead. I leaned forward until I rested against his chest, my head nestled on his shoulder, my body pressed against his. He wrapped his arms around me.

"I've never known you to hesitate about saying anything, whether you should or not."

I could have just stayed there, wrapped up in him, filling my nose with his scent, skin, and sweat, a touch of aftershave, the hint of fur under the skin. He was civilized and wild at once, an anchor in a rolling sea.

"You'll be here when I'm finished? Right here?"

"Are you okay?" He pulled away and touched my face, brushing light fingers along my jawline.

I nodded, but my lips were pursed.

"I won't move an inch," he said.

"Okay. Thanks."

The rumble of a hundred murmured conversations carried over the auditorium. The crowd waited. I squeezed his hand, letting it go only after I'd turned away.

Nell Riddy, the conference director, waited at the edge of the stage with us. "If you're ready, Ms. Norville, I'll introduce you."

"Yes, that's fine. I'm ready." I folded my pages to keep from crumpling them. I was increasingly coming to believe that preparation was impossible—only agility, so that one might hope to remain upright while scrambling.

Standing at the podium now, Riddy beamed while she talked about me in hyperbolic terms, describing me as a "pioneer for paranatural rights and recognition," and "a thoughtful commentator on the shape of new identities." I wanted to push her aside and yell, *you know I've been faking it, don't you?*

"Now, may I present this afternoon's keynote speaker, Kitty Norville!" She gestured toward me, smiling.

A waterfall roar of applause followed, and I felt detached from it. That couldn't be for me—the noise was a polite reflexive response, a bit of punctuation between one sentence and the next. I ought to be enjoying this—I was rarely on stage to enjoy my notoriety firsthand. Instead, I felt like I was floating toward the podium, drifting on air made of molasses.

At the podium, I gripped its edges before gazing out over the auditorium. A thousand people turned toward me, and many of those stares were challenging. Wolf rose up, trying to match all those challenges in return. We were cornered, we could fight, we could run—but Wolf wasn't in charge here. We would stay.

The podium had a microphone. A slender flimsy thing, it didn't look like *my* microphone, my familiar antiquated lump at KNOB. But it was a microphone, and I knew what to do with it. This was just like the show, and I could handle it. I set my pages on the podium's slanted surface and let myself smile.

"Thank you," I said, and the applause faded. "I very much appreciate the honor of being asked to speak to you all. I hope I can live up to your expectations." That got a few chuckles.

I could still change my mind. I could keep it light,

tell my story, be rousing and inspirational. That was what they'd come to hear, after all. I took a breath to settle myself, and imagined I was in the KNOB studio.

"I think I've been lucky, which may come as a surprise to a lot of you. After all, I'm living with a chronic, life-altering disease, which I contracted in a violent attack. But I've had the most interesting conversations since then, and I can't help but wonder if that isn't what it's all about.

"I've met so many people, so many different kinds of people. Even just this week I've met so many people, as if this conference is a microcosm of my life. Or this conference has brought these disparate parts of my life together. I've made friends, learned a little history. I've discovered family I didn't know I had. I've learned a lot.

"Over the last few years, I've met people infected with vampirism who've been alive for hundreds of years, who can tell me stories about Shakespeare and Coronado. I've met people who were only infected with vampirism in the last year, and learned about how they're dealing with it. I've met all flavor of lycanthropes, and learned about how they're different from me, and how we're the same. I've learned that some of those fairy stories I grew up with really did happen. I've met djinn and wizards, medicine women and skinwalkers, scientists and philosophers. I've met the ghost of a woman who was wrongfully executed for murder a hundred years ago, and I've met her descendents. A lot of these people I'm honored to call my friends. Because of that, I don't just believe we can all coexist, I *know* we can. Which is why seeing the protests outside the hotel this week has been so difficult. Because it makes me worry.

"I try to resolve conflicts by talking. I've built my career on it. Actually, I try to avoid conflicts entirely by talking. Usually it even works. But I don't know if it's going to be enough.

"History is filled with groups of people slaughtering each other over their perceived differences. For me to make a list of such atrocities would belabor the point, and be woefully incomplete. I'd end up leaving out someone who doesn't deserve to be ignored.

"It usually seems like the first step on that path happens when one group defines another as not like them—not human. That opens a floodgate. I worry that we're seeing a new floodgate, and that we're watching it open, just a crack. Just a little trickle of excess water is coming through—nothing to get too worried about, right? But I worry. When someone out there says that I'm not really human—what are they giving themselves permission to do to me?"

How much could I get away with saying? What did I have to say so that people would take me seriously, and not write me off as crazy? I didn't know. But I had to say something; I would never get another chance to declare.

"So yes, I have a lot of stories, I've met a lot of people. Some of them are my friends, some aren't. Some think I'm human, some think I'm not. As long as I can keep talking about it, I feel like I have a little control over my destiny. There are, of course, people who want to take that control away. From all of us.

"Of all the stories I could tell, the one I really want to talk about features a man named Roman. I met Roman about three years ago, back home in Colorado. He's a vampire, about two thousand years old, which is astonishing, I know. One of the things I've learned is that the old ones get that way by keeping quiet, staying hidden. Working from the shadows. Roman was originally called Gaius Albinus and was a centurion in the Roman military. These days, he calls himself Dux Bellorum. It means leader of wars. Just to make clear, Gaius Albinus is not my friend. He's one of the people who would create divisions, who would separate us into factions and then pit us against each other. Who has decided that since we are different, we don't deserve the same access to freedom, to respect. Dr. Paul Flemming, and those who adhere to his philosophies, is another one of these people." I felt weird, speaking ill of the dead, but if I was going to name names, I couldn't stop now. People had to know.

"I think we're going to see more of this rather than less. I think we have more violence ahead of us. Maybe even a war. But I think we can do something about it. Moving forward, each of us—all of us— may have to choose sides in a conflict we don't even know is happening, and we may have to fight for that choice against forces we can't even see.

"As always, I turn to conversation as a solution. I

ask you to stay in touch with each other. Talk to each other, tell each other your problems, get help. Isolation is dangerous, because when we're isolated our enemies take advantage of us, make us afraid, and use that fear. They will divide us and label us. Together, though—together, we're a fortress. Communication— the basic act of talking—has always been my most powerful weapon, and I believe it can save us. Thank you." I turned a weak and weary smile to the audience.

The applause was polite at best. The faces looking back at me showed confusion in pursed lips and furrowed brows, and even smirks. Derisive frowns. Some heads shook in what seemed to be disgust. Half the crowd was already out of their seats and filing out of the auditorium, and the conversation grew loud.

That was all okay. I wasn't here to make friends or win any popularity contests. I delivered my warning. I'd accomplished my goal. And now I wanted to go home. I strode back to the edge of the auditorium, and to Ben, who was right where he said he'd be.

Riddy was waiting there as well. She was one of the confused ones; her smile had turned stiff. Still, she offered her hand to shake, which I did, and thanked me. "I must admit, Ms. Norville, it wasn't quite what I was expecting."

"Yeah, I had a feeling," I said, apologetic.

"But it's an excellent message. That was meant to be the whole purpose of the conference—fostering communication. I do hope that's what people take away from all this."

I had to smile at her optimism. "I'm very glad I could be a part of it all."

She thanked me again and excused herself, leaving Ben and me together, watching the auditorium empty out. Part of my hesitation came from not knowing how he would react to my rant. I hadn't consulted him, and maybe I should have. He might have talked me out of it—and that was probably why I hadn't talked to him first. But after all this, if he was angry at me, too, I wasn't sure I could bear it.

His smile was crooked, but it was there. His gaze was steady, and his hands were in his pockets, casual. He seemed amused. I just stood there.

"I love you," he said.

It all came down to that, and I was happy.

"Really?" I said. He opened his arms and gathered me close. We stood like that, holding each other, for what seemed a long time.

Reporters found me in the lobby. I knew there'd be questions. I'd be answering questions for a long time. If I gave them a few sound bites, maybe they'd leave me alone.

"When you say war, do you mean that literally? Or is it some kind of culture war?" Of course that was the word the press would latch onto. The guy was an American with press credentials from one of the big science magazines.

"Um, yes?" I said. "Both? I can handle a culture war. But I'm pretty sure this is bigger than that."

"But you don't know?"

"I know there's something out there, and it's not pretty."

The guy sounded frustrated. "If you don't know what's going on why make a big stink about it? You trying to start a panic?"

"It wouldn't do any good to keep it to myself," I said.

"But you have to admit the possibility that you may be deluded," said another reporter, this one British.

Yes. I supposed I did.

"I think we're done here," Ben said, and shouldered his way between them and me, guiding me to the side hallway. A few of them followed, still calling out questions, until Ben threw a glare over his shoulder. I wished I could have seen it, because it stopped them.

We reached the shelter of the relatively quiet hallway, where Shumacher and Tyler were waiting.

I winced. "I suppose you saw the speech."

Shumacher's lips pressed into a thin, anxious line. "I'd say you were scare mongering if not for what happened to Sergeant Tyler yesterday. Flemming's vanished again."

"Yes," I said flatly.

Tyler had recovered admirably. His gaze was steady, determined, and his body was a wall, standing firm. A well-muscled, intimidating wall. "If you need me, for anything at all, call me."

And he would come running. I could count on him. "Thank you."

"You've rescued me twice now. I owe you."

"You don't owe me," I said, shaking my head. "We help each other, that's what friends do."

"I owe you."

"Don't argue," Ben said near my ear. Right.

"You guys off tomorrow?" I asked.

"Yeah. It'll be really nice to get back home." His sigh was heartfelt.

I smiled. "Say hi to Susan for me."

He ducked his gaze, but not before I caught the gleam in his eyes.

AFTER DARK, we returned to the house in Mayfair, where Cormac was waiting for us. In any other context, we'd all have a lovely farewell dinner with our hosts. In this case, however, we'd made sure to eat before the gathering.

Marid stood at the front gate, and we lingered. The old vampire leaned on his cane, gazing upward, as if he could see stars.

"When are you heading back home?" I asked, drawing his attention from the sky. "Where is home, by the way?"

He shrugged. "I'm like Mercedes, I don't have a city of my own. I'm a Master by dint of age, nothing more," he said. "I'm thinking of moving on, anyway. It's time to wander a bit."

"Oh?"

He narrowed his gaze. "Perhaps look for Roman while I'm at it."

"Ah." I nodded thoughtfully.

"You did it," he said, strolling along the narrow courtyard without needing the cane. "I told Ned you would. He wasn't sure. He said you'd be too worried about protecting your loved ones. He was sure you'd play it safe in the end, rather than expose us all. I told him you're a crusader. I was right."

Ben and I faced him, our arms touching. There was only one of him, and we were strong.

"People need to know," I said. "That's all. Roman can't work in secret if everyone knows."

"But have you warned everyone about the coming war—or dragged them into it when they might have been safe?"

"They wouldn't have been safe," I said. "Not in the long run."

"How like a vampire, to speak of the long run."

"I can't tell—are you happy about what I said, or not? Is Ned?"

"Oh, Ned and Antony both approve. They like you very much. They like the idea of a Regina Luporum. They cheered when they watched the video of your speech."

"Regina Luporum—I still don't even know what that means," I said.

He chuckled. "It's not anything official, it doesn't come with a crown or any real power or territory. It's more . . . an idea. Rex Luporum, Regina Luporum. That there exist wolves who will stand up to vampires, that will choose solidarity over warfare. Do you know the story of Romulus and Remus?"

"The founders of Rome who were raised by . . . a wolf . . ." I stared.

"Many of the old stories are simply metaphors."

"You're saying that a *werewolf* helped found Rome? And that she had *children*?" That spark of hope hadn't quite died out, apparently.

"Werewolves can't have children, Kitty," he said. "It's a *metaphor*."

"So Regina Luporum is a label you made up. It doesn't mean anything."

"It means whatever you want it to."

He didn't show any sign of retreating back inside, so I stayed with him. "Did you know her? The wolf of the Rome story?"

"Yes," he said.

I waited for another long pause. "And . . . ?"

"She'd have liked you, I think."

"And . . . ?" He didn't offer anything else. I sighed. "So what about you—did you like the speech?"

"Honestly, Kitty, one way or another it doesn't matter. Whatever happens, happens. I know how to go to cover if I need to."

You didn't get to be twenty-eight hundred years old by joining crusades, I supposed. "Then we won't be able to depend on you when the time comes?"

"Perhaps when the time comes, I'll call on *you*," he said, smiling a sphinx's smile. "Shall we go in?"

Ned and Emma had arranged a pleasant gathering in the parlor, and I again flashed on those BBC costume dramas. Emma and I ought to be wearing empire-waist gowns, the men should have had cravats. Ned was the only one wearing a cravat tonight. The three of us who lived and breathed had tea and a decadent selection of pastries. The vampires watched us indulgently.

Ned delivered a report, condensed from information gathered by the police, the American authorities, and British intelligence. This had gone quite high up, apparently. They theorized that Flemming learned about Sergeant Tyler's unit of werewolves in Afghanistan. The unit had originally been led by one of Flemming's own interview subjects, the werewolf Special Forces captain who had turned the others. When the opportunity came to get his hands on the sole surviving member of that unit, he couldn't resist. He'd never really been one for conventional methods—or civil liberties, for that matter.

He'd hired himself out as a paranormal security consultant, and a third party—an as-yet unidentified third party—had agreed to fund the "acquisition" of a real-live Special Forces werewolf. The project had two purposes: recruit Tyler himself, and use him to train up a new unit of paranormal soldiers. They had felt confident Tyler *could* be recruited, or suborned, which just went to show how bad their information was.

The fact that Flemming had been killed in the course of Tyler's escape was known, but suppressed. As was the fact that Tyler had help. Ned's people, Caleb's, and mine were all left out of it. Apparently, we had Ned's influence to thank for this.

Ned had fed them all the information he could about Roman, but the mastermind remained invisible.

"Is Tyler going to have to watch his back for the rest of his life?" I asked.

"Probably," Ned said. "But he'll have help, now that his own government is aware of the issue. Your Dr. Shumacher is on the need-to-know list for the report. Don't look so distraught. It's like you said this afternoon: knowledge is power. Our enemies have blown their cover. They won't find it so easy to hide anymore."

Conversation turned casual after that. As casual as it could with Cormac sitting near the doorway, his hand occasionally touching the stake he kept in an inside jacket pocket. He never took off the leather jacket. The vampires didn't seem offended. Antony asked how I got into the talk-radio business, then how I met Cormac, and so on. I poked them with a few questions of my own—where they'd come from, who they'd known, interesting and harmless historical anecdotes. Fascinating, to hear them talk about London's Great Fire like it happened a year ago.

We relaxed. This almost felt normal. Except that out of the seven of us only three had heartbeats.

Antony and Marid excused themselves to retreat to their lairs, Antony to Barcelona and Marid to . . . wherever. Antony at least offered us an invitation to come visit.

I should have been comatose with exhaustion, but I kept wanting to draw out the evening. I only had another hour or two to spend with Emma and Ned until dawn took them away. Time enough to sleep later.

"I have a question for you," I asked, and Ned cocked his head, inquiring. "Why? You'd lived a long and successful life before you became a vampire. What happened? Did you choose it?"

His smile was wistful; his gaze looked back through time. "No, I did not. Do you know the story, that during a performance of *Faust* I managed to conjure a real demon? And because of that I quit acting, left the stage forever?"

"I think I read about that one," I said.

"It was true, in a manner of speaking. Though it wasn't a demon I conjured but a vampire. He became a bit of a fan, you could say. I was on my deathbed. You're right, I had lived a long and fruitful life. I felt I'd atoned for my sins with monumental acts of charity—a school, a hospital. I was ready to slip from this world. But he thought the world should not have to lose me.

"It was a strange thing. I suppose I could have ended my existence anytime I chose after that. Emma's told me about her first days after being turned, and I felt much the same way. But even in such a state, suicide is not instinctive. Then there was the school, the chance to see it continue. It's *still* here. Isn't that amazing? Did you know there are streets named after me? They're still putting up signs and statues to me in Dulwich? How many people get to see their legacy bear such fruit? I've been privileged to witness it. So you see, I found reasons to go on, as most of us do. I had a chance to look after my city. I took it. And here I am."

"You should write a book," I said. "Memoirs covering four hundred years. That would be awesome."

He seemed to consider, this new thought lighting his eyes. "Perhaps I will."

WE HAD one last adventure before leaving the U.K. As promised, Caleb and part of his pack took us running in British wilderness, in the Dartmoor region in Britain's southwest peninsula. "*Hound of the Baskervilles* territory," he told us, winking.

The land was rugged, windswept, marshy, desolate. Rolling hills covered with grass and scrub, outcrops of weathered gray stone, a blustery sky overhead. It was beautiful, perfect for running, as Caleb had promised. We Changed, stretched our four legs, and ran for hours, pounding out the stress of the week. I remembered little about that time but the cleansing wind rippling through my fur.

Caleb's pack took us in as respected guests, but Ben and I kept apart. This wasn't home. Even the rabbits we caught tasted different. We woke up restless in the shelter of rocks that weren't Rocky Mountain granite.

We agreed: it was time to go home.

Epilogue

IN AN ideal world, everyone who heard the speech would take me seriously, the UN would set up a supernatural task force to promote equality and understanding, and forces around the world would unite to locate and oppose Roman. It would be a new golden age. What would probably happen—everyone would ignore me, and I'd go back to being a cult talk-radio host. But then there was the worst that could happen. Torches and pitchforks, I joked with Ben. The wrong kind of people would take my speech seriously.

I hadn't been home a week when police in Boston caught an arsonist who had burned down an apartment building because he believed vampires were living in the basement. He declared to the judge during his arraignment that he was justified because a war was coming, and he had to destroy them before they came after him. Investigators didn't find any evidence of vampires in the wreckage—not that they would have. But a young couple whom neighbors described as goth were killed in the fire. Police theorized that the crazed young man had seen them, constantly dressed in black, and made a misguided assumption.

Commentators discussed how "polarizing influences" could only make this kind of tragedy more common. They didn't mention me by name, but they might as well have.

I SAT in the KNOB conference room with Ozzie and Matt. They'd been my producer and sound engineer from the beginning. We'd had dozens of meetings in this room, with its timeworn walls and scuffed carpet, cheap laminate tables and stained whiteboard. I remembered sitting in on programming meetings back when I was a late-night variety DJ and not a syndicated talk-show host, before anyone knew I was a werewolf. Before any of this. The smell of a decade's worth of spilled coffee tinged the air. It smelled safe to me. This room should have been safe, but Ozzie was regarding me with such a look of disappointment, and Matt wouldn't look at me at all.

"We've only had twenty outright cancellations," Ozzie said, looking more harried and middle-aged than usual. *Only*. As if that wasn't an actual, measurable percentage of our market. "We'll probably have more, depending on how you follow up. Do you know how you're going to follow up?"

"I'm not going to apologize, if that's what you're asking."

"I'm not looking for an apology, I'm looking for an explanation," he said.

"I told the truth."

He began pacing, gesturing broadly, lecturing in a tone of frustration. "You're supposed to be the one calling bullshit on the conspiracy theories, and here you are, drinking the Kool-Aid—"

"I wouldn't have said it if I didn't believe it."

Ozzie put his hands on his hips and sighed. Neither one of them would look at me now. I stared at Matt, trying to get him to glance up. He'd always been on my side. He'd seen some of this firsthand. I thought he would trust me.

They didn't believe me. My Wolf side bristled, crouching in a figurative corner, teeth bared in challenge, growling. My body tensed, my gaze narrowed. They couldn't read the signs.

I didn't belong here.

Ozzie continued, oblivious. "Kitty. This show is your baby. You made it what it is, no one's going to argue about that. No one else could have done what you've done with it. I've never told you what to do, what to talk about, how to run things. I've never suggested an agenda. But I'm telling you now—you have to backpedal. Get back to basics. Bring on some cream puff interviews. Because if you keep on, if you turn *The Midnight Hour* into a paranoid soapbox—no one will listen to you." No one but the real crazies, he meant.

"It's not paranoid—" I stopped. I'd been about to say, *if they're really out to get you.* I thought I knew what this looked like from the outside—crazy, ranty, unbalanced. I thought if I could just convince them, if I could prove to them that I wasn't crazy . . . Maybe I didn't know what it looked like. Maybe I really had turned a corner. How would I ever know?

"I don't know what I'm going to do," I said finally. "I have to think about it."

"Take a couple of weeks off if you need to," Ozzie said. "We can always rerun old episodes."

"*That* won't look bad," I muttered.

"Then come up with something," he said. "Come back Friday and *do* something about it." He marched out of the room, his lips pursed with pity and disappointment.

I waited for Matt to do the same. He was my age, stout, cheerful, with dark hair and faded T-shirt and jeans. He leaned back in his chair, arms crossed, and finally regarded me like he was listening to a new album and trying to decide if he hated it.

"Well?" I finally asked because I couldn't stand it anymore.

He ducked his gaze, hiding a smile. "Kitty. I'm with you. I've been with you since you sat in that studio"—he pointed down the hall—"and said you were a werewolf. I can't say I understand any of this. I can't say I ever did. But I'm not going to quit on you now."

If he had . . . I don't know what I would have done. Found someone to replace him, I supposed, but it wouldn't have been the same.

"Thank you," I said, my voice cracking.

"You're welcome."

* * *

THURSDAY NIGHT, I was at New Moon. Cormac had checked in with his parole officer—no harm done there—and was back at his warehouse job, playing the good citizen. He was getting pretty good at it. Ben had had a client call him from the county jail. The client wouldn't talk over the phone about why he'd been arrested, so with a long-suffering roll of his eyes, Ben had run to the rescue. Life was getting back to normal.

Shaun was managing the restaurant tonight. He'd been hovering, crestfallen when I snapped at him to leave me alone. I was reading a popular history of London I'd picked up at the airport on the way home, and had a pen and notepad to make notes. I was trying to think of some innocuous anecdote to focus the show on, but I found myself wanting to talk about Ned, the convocation of vampires, Flemming, what had happened to Tyler, and every encounter I'd had with Roman and Mercedes. Maybe I could come up with a compromise.

The e-mail comments I'd gotten through my Web site—not to mention blog posts, forum comments, op-ed pieces, essays, and rants—gave me an idea of what to expect when I opened the line for calls next time. Half the commentary was some form of, "Are you crazy?" Had I finally gone around the bend? Was I even really a werewolf or was this all an elaborate hoax? I hadn't heard that one since my Senate testimony. I expected all of that. The problem was the other half of the comments, which assured me that I was exactly right, there was a mysterious global conspiracy, and here was the lengthy detailed explanation. My favorite so far described the baby-eating lizard aliens who made their home in a tunnel system deep below Denver International Airport. Awesome.

When I said, "But I'm right, my conspiracy is *real*," I sounded just like the baby-eating lizard alien people.

Ben and I had started looking at houses in the western foothills. He was right, it was probably time. The condo felt too temporary for our increasingly settled lives. If I wanted to start a family like I kept talking about, more space would be useful. The trouble was, lost market share meant lost income. Even if I could put a book proposal together and sell it tomorrow, I couldn't count on seeing the money for months. Ben was confident we could scrape together enough for bigger mortgage payments. I wasn't so sure. I seemed to have lost my optimism somewhere along the way.

When my phone rang, the sound startled me. I'd been lost in my own world, and I hadn't expected anyone to reach into that world to grab hold and yank me out.

Caller ID said Rick, which was a relief. He couldn't possibly be disappointed in me. "Hello?"

"Kitty. Do you have time this evening to stop by Obsidian? I'd like to show you something."

"Is anything wrong?"

"No. At least not more so than usual." The distinction didn't seem to bother him; he sounded as easy-going as he always did.

"Yeah. I can be there in an hour or so."

When I arrived at Obsidian, the art gallery he owned, I went to the basement stairs. Rick was waiting at the door for me, so I didn't even have to argue with any flunkies about letting me in. He and his Family kept a lair here, an office and apartments, though I'd never seen any part of it other than the main hallway and the office and living room in back. Just like Rick had never seen where the pack spent full moon nights. We had our separate realms. It was a wonder any of us ever worked together.

Rick politely ushered me into the wide living room, which had sofas and a coffee table on one end and a desk and shelves on the other. The place was simple, functional, livable.

"Have a seat," he said, indicating the comfortable chair on the other side of the desk.

"What's this about?"

I resisted looking over my shoulder for the practical joke. He opened a drawer and produced a padded shipping envelope, already opened. I didn't see the return address or stamps, but it looked battered, as if it had traveled some great distance. Turning it upside down, he shook, and a packet fell onto his desk. Thick, heavy, made of some expensive, cream-colored paper, it looked like a wedding invitation, or a medieval deed.

His smile was cryptic. Mischievous, even. He turned it right side up, showing me the wax seal, the thick red blob imprinted with an ornate crest. Medieval deed it was, then.

The seal had already been cracked. I unfolded the thick paper to reveal writing, ornate and curling, in dark ink that seemed to glow against the rich paper. I could make out letters, put some of them together into words, but the language was Latin, which I recognized but couldn't read.

"What's it say?" I asked Rick.

"It's from Nasser, who is the Master of Tripoli. He's requesting a meeting to discuss ways in which we might oppose Dux Bellorum and . . ." He picked up the page again and read a phrase. ". . . *terminamus ludum longum.*"

"Which means . . ."

" 'We end the Long Game.' Once and for all. End it without finishing it. He saw a video of your speech in London and wants to meet you. He didn't know there was anyone else in the world opposing Roman, and now he does. Should I invite him to visit?"

Stunned, I turned the words over in my mind, trying to parse what they meant. Someone had heard me. A knot of hope settled in my chest. *Terminamus . . .* had a nice ring to it.

"Then it worked," I said softly. "The speech—it wasn't for nothing."

"Oh, no," Rick said, and the smile turned wide and pleased. "I think it worked very well. I think it did exactly what it was supposed to. Assuming you meant it as a call to arms."

I leaned forward, elbows on the desk, and covered my face with my hands. It was like I'd been holding my breath since London, and the releasing sigh reached every nerve. I couldn't even move.

"Kitty?" Rick prompted.

"I just keep telling myself it's going to be all right."

He cocked his head, a bemused furrow marking his brow. "I think it will. Eventually."

"You've been saying that for five hundred years, haven't you?"

He just smiled.

"GOOD EVENING, and once again you're listening to *The Midnight Hour,* talk radio with teeth. We've been talking about conspiracy theories. Especially supernatural conspiracy theories. There are an awful lot of them out there, and I've got some of my own as most of you well know."

In the end, my solution was to not really do anything at all. Run the show like I always did, speaking with the same easy tone I always used. Keep it chatty, keep it light. I didn't have to defend myself. I didn't need to convince anyone or change any minds. I just needed to be myself, and keep being myself, like I always had. Anyone who got belligerent or confronted me—well, I'd do the same thing I always did. I'd just talk and see what happened.

My next caller was male with a drawling, pompous

voice. Determined to put li'l ol' me in my place. "The problem with these so-called theories—every last one of them—is that they attribute vast unlikely powers of organization and influence to groups that in the real world can't balance their own budgets." The pointed *obviously* was unspoken.

He couldn't have fed me a better line if I'd scripted it. "How about this: that apparent inability to balance a budget? It's a front to make you believe there couldn't really be a conspiracy."

"That's ridiculous!"

"That's what you're supposed to think!" I fired back, getting into the spirit of the viewpoint I was channeling. "Therefore you'll never even consider the Byzantine network of control and oppression hidden behind the façade of incompetence!" I made my voice calm again. "You see how this works, now?"

"You're crazy, you know that?"

I sighed. "That might mean something if you weren't the"—I checked the sheet of scratch paper because yes, I'd been keeping track with hatch marks—"twelfth person to say that tonight."

I hung up on him before he could hang up on me. "There's a paradox inherent in the very idea of a conspiracy theory. For example, if an alien civilization has the technology to travel the vast distances to bring actual craft here to Earth, don't you think they'd also have the technology to keep out of sight if they didn't want to be seen? And the technology to examine a person's insides without probing? I mean, *we* have that technology right now! The second paradox: if it's a truly competent, effective conspiracy, none of us will ever know about it. I humbly submit that a vampire who's been around for two thousand years will be very good at covering his tracks. And yes, I'm fully aware that I can't prove any of this.

"So what's the solution? What do you do when your life seems to be under the power of some sinister unnamed force? I've got Parnell from San Diego on the line. Hello."

"Hi, um, yeah. Thanks for taking my call. I wanted to ask you about this documentary I saw awhile back, about how the British royal family are all werewolves?"

I regarded the microphone. "Yeah. I saw that one. You know it wasn't a documentary, right? It was a horror movie. Fiction. Not real."

"Oh. Are you sure? It looked just like one of those dramatic reenactment things, you know like they do?" The guy sounded genuinely confused, which kind of confused me. I didn't think it was this hard.

"I'm pretty sure it was a movie." If only I could be this sure about *everything*.

"You don't think it's based a little bit on a true story? You were just in London and all, I thought maybe you'd be able to tell."

"If the British royal family are werewolves? I never got anywhere near them. The queen doesn't live at the airport shaking the hands of everyone who flies into the country."

"Oh. Well, okay. I guess."

"Right," I said, sighing. "Next call, please. You're on the air."

"Hi, Kitty, I'm such a big fan, it's so good to talk to you." She was a woman, her voice clear and straightforward. She sounded sensible, at least. One could hope.

"What's on your mind?"

"Well, I know you've been getting a lot of crap lately about some of the things you've been saying, that people say you're stirring up trouble and all. And, well . . . I live in Denver and I've been listening to you from the beginning. Whatever happens, I hope you don't stop doing what you've always done."

I leaned on the desk, feeling suddenly tired. "I've been a little distracted," I said. "Just what is it I've always done? What do you think I've always done?"

"You help people. That's why you started, right? To help people. Please don't forget about that."

I felt like I'd been punched. I wanted to cry—and I wanted to give her a hug. I didn't know what was going to happen. Not with Roman, the show, a new house, a new book, any of it. But the only way to find out was to keep moving forward.

"I'll do my best," I said finally.

"Thank you," she said, sincerely, emotionally.

"No," I said softly. "Thank you."

Acknowledgments

Thanks on this one go to Mom, Dad, Daniel, Derek, Yann, Elaine, Emily, Trevor, Damian, Zeke, Max, Yaz, Jeanne-Marie, Jim, Ty, Jayné, David, Stacy, Cassie, Ashley, Carolyn, and Lora. That's not everyone who deserves thanks, I'm sure. But their help was especially useful during the time I was writing this particular book. So, thanks.

Love 😊 Funny and ♥ Romantic novels?
Be bitten by a vampire

Merit thought graduate school sucked – that is, until she met some real bloodsuckers. After being attacked by a rogue vampire Merit is rescued by Ethan 'Lord o' the Manor' Sullivan who decides the best way to save her life was to take it. Now she's traded her thesis for surviving the Chicago nightlife as she navigates feuding vampire houses and the impossibly charming Ethan.

Enjoyed Some Girls Bite?
Then sink your teeth into Merit's next adventure: Friday Night Bites